BREAKER

— OF —

MOUNTAINS

AMELIA COLE

ALSO BY AMELIA COLE

Dance of Inanna Vela Series Prequel Ebook (available for free download at ameliacolebooks.com)

Bridge of Eternity Vela Series Book One

Breaker of Mountains Vela Series Book Two

Vela Book 3 TBA 2024

For Content Warnings, please see my website at www.ameliacolebooks.com

For my family, both in blood and in spirit

The destructive mace set fire to the mountains.

The murderous weapon smashed skulls with its painful teeth.

The club which tears out entrails gnashed its teeth.

—Lugal-E Ninurta, The Exploits of Ninurta, 3000 BCE

CHAPTER

ONE

The lavender bridesmaid dress cascaded like spilled paint at my feet as my toes sank into the carpet.

"I swear to god, Elly," Jason said from where he reclined on the hotel bed, his hungry gaze sweeping over me. "You're going to be the death of me."

I responded with a playful smirk. "No one is twisting your arm to keep staring, you know."

He chuckled, his hands finding their place behind his head as he leaned against the headboard, making no effort to avert his eyes. Wearing only the black pants from his tux, the flush from our afternoon soiree still lingered on his face and muscled chest.

With a soft sigh, I retrieved my dress from the floor and slipped it over my shoulders, then turned to face him. "Zip me up, please?"

Jason's footsteps approached as he stood behind me. His hands glided over the tops of my shoulders, tracing a tantalizing path down my back, sending a shiver of goosebumps across my skin. Leaning in, his warm breath danced against my ear as he whispered, "Don't ever think I won't crave you. As long as I draw breath, your presence will always command me."

My breathing quickened at the desire coating his words as I turned to face him.

"We should go," I managed, suddenly feeling a rush of awkwardness after the intimate confession he'd just shared.

Drawing nearer, he pressed a gentle kiss to my lips. "We don't have to."

I shook my head. "We're already late for the reception, and I'm certain my mom is already orchestrating a search party with the hotel security to comb through every room until I'm found."

Amusement danced in Jason's eyes as he laughed. Over the past two months, we'd been mercilessly subjected to the pre-wedding planning chaos, and I was embarrassed by the number of tense family dinners and Zoom calls he'd been present for. That he hadn't boarded the first plane back to the Middle East when my mom had asked him to plan the bachelor party had spoken volumes about how strong his commitment was to our relationship this time around. Witnessing a supernatural event changed a person.

"Besides," I continued. "I promised Cara I'd take candid photos that the photographer might miss."

A tender touch of his thumb against my cheek sent a flurry of butterflies swirling in my belly. The temptation to change my mind, shed my dress, and playfully throw him back onto the bed was almost overpowering.

Almost.

"All right," he said. "Two hours of dancing and toasts. Then I'm not letting you leave this room until housekeeping knocks on the door."

A delicious shiver raced up my spine at his threat. Ever since he'd returned to his work at the agency, his desires had been insatiable, and his attention had been unwaveringly focused on me. To be honest, I had eagerly welcomed every moment of it. The wreckage of our past failed relationship seemed like a distant memory now.

He draped his tie around his neck, carefully knotting it in place. We'd taken advantage of the thirty minutes of free time between the ceremony and reception while Cara and Shawn had their first photos taken as husband and wife, and it proved to be a delightful means of passing the time.

After ensuring we were both neatly dressed and any traces of our intimate liaison erased with a fresh application of lip gloss, mascara, and smoothing of hair, we moved out into the hallway. As we strolled toward the elevator, Jason's fingers entwined with mine. A faint tingling sensation stirred in the remnants of the scar on my palm, a mere echo of the magic I'd once possessed. The moment the statue had shattered, the magic it had contained disappeared. Evidently, the Guardian's potency had been intertwined with the imminent risk of the bridge's activation.

I had no shame in admitting that I missed it, yearning for both the power and Enheduanna's nightly presence in my dreams. Scared and confused, she'd been a source of strength as I struggled to learn my purpose and how to control the ancient power that was both as dangerous as it was beautiful.

Upon our return from Iraq to the United States, I'd tried a few times to summon it. I'd experimented with lighting a piece of paper on fire or shattering a rock I'd collected by the harbor. Nothing. I was back to normal, at least as normal as someone like me could be.

Still, there were moments when I'd be on the fringes of waking up, and the memories of the times I'd used my power were so vivid, and I'd fully awaken with adrenaline coursing through me and my scalp tingling akin to brushing against a live wire.

Jason hit the button for the first floor, and we rode it down to the lobby. Noise emanated from the ballroom across from the conference center, and we stepped into the spacious room decorated with ribbons of lavender and cream. Dominating one wall was an arched arrangement of balloons forming the letters 'C' and 'S', positioned behind an elongated table meticulously set for the bridal party. The central chairs, intended for Cara and Shawn, remained unoccupied. Nearby, two groomsmen engaged in conversation beside their assigned seats while a noticeably bored bridesmaid occupied her own chair.

"I should go rescue her," I remarked.

Jason's gaze drifted to the bridal party table. "Oh, are you afraid you'll have to be another bridesmaid in six months? I can't deny I wouldn't mind seeing you in more of these dresses." He paused. "On *or* off."

I swatted him. "Go find a drink and a corner to lurk in."

"Corner?" Jason scoffed. "You're kidding. My bachelor party was so epic, I've had two more offers to host."

I grumbled. I'd heard all about the bachelor party. The retreat into the woods and the hike that had led to an oh-so-friendly nature club where clothing was not only optional but discouraged. Jason had returned three days later with a smug grin, smelling of campfire smoke and mosquito bites on areas of his body that shouldn't get mosquito bites.

I made my way over to the table where Kylie was seated.

"Hey," I said, positioning myself between her and Paul, Shawn's cousin, and Logan, his college roommate and a new coworker at the tech firm.

"You see Cara yet?" I asked.

Kylie shook her head. "They should be here anytime. I tried

to gather everyone to wait by the door, but that all kind of fell apart." She frowned, looking discouraged.

"I wouldn't worry about it. We got Cara down the aisle and a ring on her hand; the rest is just gravy."

A small smile formed on Kylie's face. "That's true." Her face shifted to the chair next to her. "Oh yeah, I brought your camera bag from the makeup prep room. You left in such a hurry when Jason said he needed your help with something."

A slight heat brushes the tops of my cheeks. Apparently, I hadn't made a stealthy getaway as I'd thought.

"Thanks for bringing it," I said, ignoring the blatant look on her face wanting more details. I'd abandoned my leather shoulder bag that I used for work trips for a more classy, white quilted one that could easily double for a purse. My therapist had told me the change was good and would help me move on from the trauma I'd experienced two months ago. There was no way I could tell her everything, but I told her enough, at least what Division 12 and the CIA would allow me to say, and she'd managed to help me forgive myself for Taamir's death, and I was sleeping better. How much was because of our one-hour sessions or Jason's warm body next to me at night was up for debate.

"He's great, you know," Kylie said, picking up a glass of water, which had one lonely chunk of ice left in it.

Her eyes moved to Jason standing by the buffet table, currently covered in hors d'oeuvres and the bridesmaid's bouquets in vases. The reusing of the custom bouquets had been my idea, a weak attempt to encourage her not to spend every cent on decorations that only needed to last for four hours, and no one would notice anyway. "They're here for you guys and the free drinks," Jason had so eloquently put it, taking my side.

Cara still had hesitated, but when Shawn had mentioned

that would leave more in the budget for their honeymoon, she'd finally caved.

"He is," I said, replying to her.

"You guys going to be setting a date soon?" Kylie asked.

I'd be lying if I hadn't at least thought about it. Things had been going so well that I hadn't dared jinx it. Jason had been working in New York at one of Division 12's main offices, and while he assured me he was happy running ops from the desk side, I knew he missed the field.

I smiled, staring wistfully at Jason. "Sure, eventually? We're just in a really good place right now, and I kind of want to enjoy it."

"That's totally understandable. After everything you went through in Syria and Iraq, Cara was a mess when she heard you were in the hospital." She paused, setting her drink down. I could tell she was curious, wanting me to talk about what happened. I'd been fairly tight-lipped, not wanting my accident and event to steal the light from Cara's "most special day."

"Do you plan on going back? Working there again?" she asked.

"Of course," I said without hesitating. "I don't think I'll ever quit doing it, although I might look into going to somewhere a little less volatile for a while."

Kylie laughed a little nervously. "I could never do what you do. You are way braver than I am."

"Are you kidding?" I scoffed. "You manage to keep your sanity while dealing with 6th graders all day."

Kylie shook her head and started to say something about the summers off, and her parents' lakeside cabin was the only way she did when the murmuring in the room stopped.

Cara and Shawn, holding hands, entered, both beaming with joy. Cara had pinned up the back of her dress' train, and Shawn had taken off his jacket. The banquet room roared with applause and congratulations as the happy new couple made their way slowly to the bridal party table.

Kylie and I hurried to their side, helping Cara navigate the mass of people, each one wanting to wish her a personal congratulations, take a picture, or just hug as if wanting a piece of the happiness to rub off on them. It was Cara's moment in the sun, and she was eating it up. Shawn would lean over and kiss her every few seconds, and the crowd would go wild again with oohing and awing and take photos with their phones.

Finally, we reached the table and sat in the center, with bridesmaids on Cara's side and groomsmen on the other. A DJ announced that food would be brought out soon and switched the mellow instrumental background music to modern pop songs everyone knew the words to.

Not part of the bridal party, Jason assumed a chair at a table closest to us and made it nearly impossible for me to focus on any other conversation with the constant lustful looks he kept giving me.

Plates were brought out to serve the bridal party table first before the servers fanned out to the other tables. Champagne was poured, toasts were given, and before I knew it, I was tearing up over Shawn's anecdote about how he and Cara first met at a local brewery's trivia night and had been playfully competitive. I'd heard the story from Cara's side, but hearing it from Shawn was so much more real, and hearing the genuine love in his voice combined with the three glasses of delicious champagne tipped me over. Then it was my turn, and I was grateful I didn't have to follow the man of honor, who I knew to be an outrageously funny storyteller. I took the microphone from Shawn and got out of my chair. The room was silent except for an occasional clink of silverware or chair shift.

I cleared my throat and read the script I'd written and re-written on my phone's notes app. I'd planned on rehearsing it one more time with Jason in the hotel room before this, but that obviously hadn't happened. "Cara, my little sister," I started. "You have always been the cooler one. You are way more athletic, pick out the best clothes, and can manage a cleaner cat eyeliner than I ever could."

Cara dabbed at the corner of her eye and stared up at me with a soft smile on her face. My chest warmed at the adoration on her face. I loved my sister dearly even if we couldn't be more opposite. "I feel like sometimes I'm the younger sister, looking up to you when you make all the right choices. Especially your choice in picking an amazing guy like Shawn." I turned to look at him. "I'm so happy to be gaining a brother like you. You two deserve each other, and I wish all the happiness in the world for you both." I sniffed, emotion tightening my throat.

"Congratulations," I said and passed the microphone to Logan.

Jason flashed me a warm smile and a dorky thumbs-up as I soothed the ache in my throat with a sip of champagne and was relieved the speech was over and I hadn't made a total fool of myself by bursting into tears.

"All right, all right," Logan shouted, giving a pretty spot-on Matthew McConaughey impression and startling an elderly couple with the unfortunate luck of being seated close to us. "Cara and my boy Shawnathon. I couldn't be happier for you two crazy kids. When my dude here said he was going to propose to you, I said, man," he said, pointing at a thoroughly embarrassed Shawn, "you are the luckiest son of a bitch in the world."

The DJ switched out the music to dance music and announced the cake would be cut soon.

Mom came and waltzed me around the room, introducing me as her "other daughter" and the "one who went to Columbia for a wasted journalism degree." Never missing an opportunity to subtly hint that I was the lesser of her two children. The one with so much wasted potential. The one that would never settle down, never get a real job, never give her grandkids.

I bit my tongue, smiling and nodding to the distant cousins and country club friends she and Charles, Cara's dad and my stepdad, had made since joining two years ago. Mom hated golf, but she loved the gossip and luncheons.

Jason stood silently by my side the whole time, shadowing me, and I couldn't shake the protective aura he projected. I hadn't gotten used to his constant presence quite yet, and while I loved him being around, it sometimes felt like he thought I was some fragile heirloom that would spontaneously break if he wasn't close by to catch it.

I flexed my hands. I wondered if he'd still treat me the same if I still wielded the power I once had. With it, I had proved more than capable of protecting myself. But now it was gone, and I wasn't one to wallow in self-pity. I still missed the security it had given me. The edge to keep me safe should the circumstances arise, with or without Jason nearby. That was something my therapist should be unpacking, but mentioning that I had once had magical powers didn't seem like the best way to prove to someone you were mentally healthy.

The DJ called out for Mr. and Mrs. Allen to take their first dance. Taylor Swift's acoustic version of Love Story strummed through the sound system. Shawn swept Cara up in his arms and carried her to the center of the floor. The song she'd stressed over for months played, and they nuzzled each other, swaying to the rhythm.

The photographer snapped a series of pictures, and I took a few of them from different angles, trying to capture their adoring smiles and the faces of the guests. Soon after, the DJ invited others to join them, and I yelped as Jason's arms embraced me from behind. "care to dance," he breathed into my ear. I clipped the lens cover back on my camera. "I don't know. My dance card is pretty full."

Jason spun me around to face him, a playful smirk on his lips. "In that case, I might just whisk you away from here before they get a chance to steal you from me."

I chuckled. "Fine. I'll try and squeeze in one dance. Let me put my camera away first."

Jason released me, and I weaved through the sea of guests, all trying to crowd onto the dance floor as the song changed to a faster, upbeat one that drew in everyone, including the little kids.

At the table, I found Logan and Kylie deep in discussion about the pros vs. cons of home-brewing Kombucha. I paused behind Logan and gave her a 'Do I need to save you?' look, to which she replied with a quick, reassuring smile that she was fine.

My bag was where I'd left it on the back of my chair, and I tucked my camera gently inside it. Once secured, I looked up, scanning the faces for Jason. The DJ's laser and strobe lights bounced over the swaying bodies and made it impossible to see anyone in detail. Finally, I spotted him in the far corner where mom had encouraged Cara to seat the most outspoken of the relatives so their loud voices and often strong opinions wouldn't interfere with the rest of the group.

Jason stood next to a man in a green t-shirt and khakis, and the look of someone who would just as likely kill you as save you. My stomach twisted. Dammit, I'd bet all of Cara's wedding presents the guy Jason was talking to was a Division 12 agent, and what they were discussing was anything but the happy nuptials.

TWO

I frowned at the sight of Jason talking with the Division 12 agent. The song changed again, and Logan and a giggling Kylie sprinted to the dance floor where dozens of guests were doing the Cupid Shuffle.

The DJ remixed it so it went back and forth, blending with another popular song, and the guests were having a blast.

I started to where Jason was standing but then hesitated. What if it was a secret Division 12 conversation, and he didn't want me there? Surely, they knew he was on vacation and had put in for the time off, so whatever reason they were here had to be urgent. I pursed my lips and sidestepped to the drinks table. I ordered a rum and coke, my eyes passing over the three cases of empty wine the wedding attendees had drank.

Keeping to the shadows to avoid drawing Jason's attention, I swiped on my phone's news app and briefly scanned for any national or international emergencies that might have occurred in the last three hours. Anything that might be the reason the agent was here talking to Jason. No assassination attempts, no missing diplomats, no stolen weapons or drug seizures, nothing unless Division 12 had decided to start tracking the marriages of a certain celebrity couple that I, too, was equally shocked were splitting after thirteen years.

Jason's eyes drifted toward me, and I smiled, held up my phone, and directed it toward the dance floor, pretending I was taking a video. Jason's face gave nothing away, although there was a slight pinch between his eyebrows.

I swiped another glass of champagne from a server and then found a table to perch it on while capturing candids with my camera. Four songs, an impromptu karaoke session from the groomsmen, and a conga line later, it had been well over twenty minutes since I'd seen him last. I checked my phone. I'd been tagged five times on socials from family and guests, but nothing from Jason.

I couldn't ignore the subconscious fear that he had done it again. He had left without a goodbye and without any warning. I wandered into the lobby, passing by the bar and lounge, thinking maybe they had gone that way. My head was swimmy from the champagne, and I worked my tongue along the backs of my molars, trying to do a quick job of sobering up.

Jason had more than apologized for what he'd done. Saving my life on at least two occasions had spoken volumes, although he'd proceeded to lavish me with flowers, fancy dinners, and spa days. It had actually been hilarious to see him acting all cute-like, as though he'd found a how-to guide on being an amazing boyfriend and followed it to the letter. While the ground wasn't completely solid, I felt more trust in the foundation of our relationship than I had ever before. And until he did something to prove me wrong, I needed to trust that he wouldn't repeat the same mistake twice. This was stupid. Was I really out here searching for Jason, or was I avoiding the happy people at the wedding? A knot formed in my throat. God, my therapist would've loved to unpack that little statement.

I sighed and adjusted the shoulder straps on my dress.

Making my way back to the banquet room when the agent who had been speaking with Jason appeared in front of me, blocking my entrance. He was older than I'd originally thought, with streaks of silver above his ears and creases so deep in his forehead I wondered if he ever relaxed.

I cleared my throat. "If you're looking for Jason, I don't know where he is."

The man's eyes narrowed. My knowledge of him being an agent concerned him. The agent's disguise of 'just another wedding guest' was good. I had to give him that. What with the no-brand name mint-green collared shirt that looked straight off the rack from any department store, khaki pants that still had the creases in them, and plain brown dress shoes with worn soles. But it was the intense look he had that Jason shared. The watching of the corners, the assessing the exits, like a rat in a nest of vipers, always on edge, always ready for an attack. It was subtle, but it was there.

"I already spoke with Jason," he said. "Please come with me somewhere more private so we can talk."

I blinked in surprise. "Me?"

"Yes," he said and reached out as if wanting to grab my arm.

I pulled it from his reach. "No," I said hesitantly. "I have breakfast with my family tomorrow, but can—"

Agent Rodriguez was already shaking his head before I could finish. "I'm afraid this matter is urgent. I need you to come with me immediately."

"What? No. Are you insane? If you weren't aware, I'm at my sister's wedding. I can't leave right now."

Our heated conversation drew a few curious looks, and I lowered my voice, glaring at him. "Look, I'm not going anywhere with you until you tell me *what* is going on."

The man's chin tilted slightly, annoyance flickering in his eyes. "Fine. It's about the statue of Inanna."

My heart shuddered in my chest at the unexpected response. I'd assumed I'd closed the door on that part of my life. Moved back to New York and started fresh with Jason.

While I'd never forget the equally terrifying and fantastical things I'd experienced, I *could* put them behind me. With my ability to manipulate matter, I had been a person with a different life and a different future. One that I would never get to live. With time, I knew I'd grow to accept this. Well, time, therapy, and someone like Jason who'd seen it all too and let me cry when I needed to, vent when my tears had dried up and made me laugh when I didn't know what to do.

It had been as though I'd borrowed someone else's life for a specific purpose. I'd fulfilled my duty as Guardian and stopped a worldwide disaster from occurring. All for the steep cost of losing my magic and my connection to the high priestess, Enheduanna. She'd been my guide, my tether to the world where gods and magic existed. My link to an ability, I now understood, was more powerful than anything I could've imagined. "The statue? Last I checked, it was nothing more than broken bits of bronze and stone."

The man pursed his lips. "It is in fragments, yes. However, something," the man hesitated, his eyes scanning the space behind me. "Something has happened." He paused. "*Is* happening with it."

"What do you mean, 'something has happened?'" My patience for this conversation was waning. All the subversive talk was only making me more frustrated and confused, especially when Loveshack was blaring from the reception, and it was *the* one song I'd been looking forward to dancing to.

I crossed my arms over my chest. "Fine. Agent..."

"Rodriguez," he said, finishing for me. "Agent Manuel Rodriguez."

"Awesome. Well, Agent Rodriguez, I need ten minutes to

prove to my family that I'm the selfish, inconsiderate person they think I am."

Agent Rodriquez looked like he was about to argue, then changed his mind, instead handing me a room key. "Ten minutes. Room 344."

I found Cara and Shawn at the table, taking a selfie with the rest of the bridal party crouched behind them. The selfie *I* should have been in. My stomach sank.

"Cara," I said, my stomach twisting into knots from the guilt. She lowered the phone, still smiling, and looked at me. "I'm so sorry," I shouted over the music. "But something has come up, and I have to take off."

The smile melted from her face, and she raised her eyebrows in alarm as panic reflected in her dark green eyes. "Wait, what? Are you serious?" she leaned over the table. "Are you okay? Should I get mom?"

I shook my head. "No, no, everything is fine. It's just, you know, it's just Division wants to follow up on everything that happened last April in Iraq."

She blinked, and her mouth gaped. "They need you, like *right* now?"

I frowned. I was breaking my baby sister's heart, and I doubted if I'd ever be able to make this right. "Yes, now. I'm really sorry. I don't have a choice."

"Will you be back soon?"

I shrugged. "I'm not sure. I hope so. They never tell me these things."

"But we haven't cut the cake yet," she said, sadness tracing the edges of her voice. "And I need you to help me with the bouquet toss, and then there's the family dance, and I wanted more pictures..."

"I know," I said, not letting her finish. I sniffed, tears burning at the corners of my eyes. "Look, I promise I'll try and be back as soon as possible." Before she could respond, I hugged her and then turned, fleeing the room, not bearing to look at the hurt in her eyes anymore.

As I rode the elevator up to the third floor, I tried to clear my head, pushing away the dark thoughts of guilt that clung to me. I slipped the key card over the lock in front of room 344 and stepped inside, still wearing my bridesmaid dress.

Jason and Agent Rodriguez were staring at a pair of laptops on a table. They both looked up, and when Jason's eyes met mine, his face softened, although anxiety marked the corners of his eyes.

"I've got a secure line set up," Agent Rodriguez said, interrupting us.

"Elly," he said, leading me to the table. "You need to see this."

I nodded, wiped a stray tear that had clung to my cheek, and followed him, still not sure what 'this' was. After I'd severed the connection to the Bridge, Derek had fallen off the altar and the statue, which had been in his backpack and broken. Any connection I had to Enheduanna and the use of my magic had gone with it. Division 12 had taken the statue not just to keep it safe but also to examine if there was any residual information they could get from it. I'd assumed it was worthless, nothing more than broken shards of four-thousand-year-old bronze. Apparently, I'd been wrong.

In the hotel room, two laptops were open, their monitors glowing in the lamplight. A camera had been mounted on a tripod and was set up facing a chair.

Jason took my hand and pulled me to face him. "Listen. They just want to talk to you, okay? You don't have to say anything you don't want to, and if at any time you want to leave, I'll make sure you can."

Jason slid a chair over, and I sat, facing the laptops. Agent

Rodriguez clicked to open a window showing a video feed. Another man, close to my age, with pale grayish-blue eyes and shoulder-length hair, sat staring at the webcam. He sat in a darkened room, his face illuminated by his computer, although I did see long rectangular tables and other computers behind him.

"Hi," he said, waving. He chewed on his left thumbnail, his eyes darting from the screen to something I couldn't see in front of him.

"Hi," I replied. "Jason said you had something to tell me? Something with the statue?"

The man's head bobbed. "Uh yeah. I'm Eddie, Eddie Steinberg. I'm in Division 12's analyst department, and, well, I'm not an official agent yet, but in two years, I hope to—"

"Eddie," Jason said, leaning forward and resting a hand on the table next to me. "Just tell her what you told me."

"Right," he said, stammering, and a second window appeared on the monitor next to the video. The broken pieces of the statue were neatly situated in a plastic box lined with gray foam. Inanna's face was partially visible, as well as her broken arm and hand. The map to Ur was missing, and I assumed it was the base was the brown dust in the small glass jar nestled in the foam. "So, we first analyzed the material, checking for any radioactive contaminants that would affect the other artifacts we have stored in the warehouse. It came back as seventy-two percent copper, twelve percent tin, and another eighteen percent metalloid arsenic."

Arsenic. Well, that certainly wasn't good. It's not like I hadn't packed it around in my bag or had my hands all over it. But honestly, I wasn't all that surprised I'd been exposed to something toxic. While I knew Enheduanna's trapped soul was the true cause behind my incredibly vivid and spontaneous visions of ancient rituals and gruesome battles, arsenic definitely could have contributed to them.

"Anyway," Eddie continued. "Those materials we all expected for something created by the Akkadians and Sumerians thousands of years ago, so no surprises there. However." He paused, and the video changed from the broken statue to a chart with a line graph. "We examined it closer under an electron microscope since we wanted to see if there was any way to know which region the copper was mined from, and this..." he paused again, sounding a little breathless. "This we never could've expected."

I stared at the chart, seeing the line trace up and down like a heartbeat on a hospital monitor, cresting up before plummeting over and over again. "I don't understand," I said. "What am I looking at?"

Eddie chuckled dryly, sounding more than a little giddy. "When you use an electroscope, the instrument detects vibrations, different frequencies that certain chemicals or materials give off, allowing you to isolate the molecules and read their unique signature. Say, like with the copper used to make the bronze, that specific copper came from a mountain north of what is now Iran since we can trace it to other artifacts made in the same time period."

"Okay..." I said, with the growing worry that I'd piss off my mom and let Cara down for no reason. "And how is that a big deal?"

He shook his head. "No, no, that's not important. We already know all of that. What is important is the one frequency we *couldn't* identify. A wavelength that doesn't match any materials in our databases. A truly unique signature."

"So, are you saying it's a new type of material? How is that possible?"

Eddie clapped his hands together. "That's just it. It isn't!"

I bit my lip, looking over at Jason, who had seated himself on the edge of the bed. He caught me looking and pointed at the screen. "Just wait, trust me."

I sighed, twisting my mouth in annoyance, as I returned my gaze to the video feed. "Fine. You found a new material, a new element. I guess congratulations. There has to be an award for that, maybe Harvard or the Nobel Peace Prize? I still am at a loss as to why you needed to tell me."

Eddie frowned as if disappointed that he had to explain it further for an idiot like me. "It's not just the material. It's the signature itself. Look." The screen changed again, and this time, there were two lines on the bar graph, one red, one blue, and they nearly synced in perfect rhythm as they bounced up and down on the screen. "Every star in the universe gives off a unique wavelength, makes their own sound."

"You mean like pulsars?" I said, proud that I'd taken the astronomy elective my sophomore year of college.

Eddie bobbed his head eagerly. "Yes, pulsars are just one kind of star, though. They're the loudest, so scientists study them the most; however, every star gives off a low-level sound, an echo as the light pings off of it, and only recently have we had telescopes sensitive enough to detect it."

I watched the lines snake across the screen, and my own pulse vibrated in my ears, my thoughts leaping ahead to what he was getting at.

"The frequency coming from the statue is an identical match to one star in the entire universe. A pulsar star in the Vela constellation."

CHAPTER

THREE

The air whooshed from my lungs as lightheadedness overtook me. How could an inanimate object, a metal statue that a sculptor had carved four thousand years ago, give off the vibration of a star? There had to be about a thousand laws of physics. Of course, how could a bridge made of starlight appear in an underground city that wasn't supposed to exist? While that, too, would've broken all the laws of science, it had happened. I had been there, witnessed it, felt the weight of the bridge, the power from some other world. I shook my head, clearing my thoughts, as I remembered all the non-normal things that I once could do. Turn stone to ash.

Incinerate wood, paper...people.

A rise of bile coated my throat. I had used that power, that magic, to hurt people, kill people. It had been too strong for me to control. Perhaps that was why Enheduanna and the goddess Inanna had taken it from me. Perhaps it wasn't because the stone had broken but because I had proved not to be worthy to wield it beyond my singular duty. The ability had been a loan, nothing more, and to think I'd have it permanently had been ignorant on my part.

Agent Rodriguez cleared his throat. "Division 12 has given me full authorization to pursue this. They're afraid knowledge of it is going to leak out of the agency, and the NSA or CIA will get wind of it, have a judge issue a court order to invade the agency, and confiscate it."

"Eddie, what all do you need from us?" Jason said, readying his phone to place a call.

A choked laugh came from Eddie via the laptop's speakers. "Another microscope would be nice; the one we have is old, and the software is outdated. We don't use them much here, and I know they're expensive…"

"Fine, consider it done," Jason said. "What else?"

Eddie wiped his lips. "Uh, constellation charts from the past hundred years and any records of vibrations coming from the Vela constellations. I can use the data to make a better analysis, maybe find any deviations in the patterns." He looked up from where he'd been staring at the floor, and our eyes met.

"You," he stammered. "You are the one that found it, right? The statue? You're the one who found the map on the base?"

I nodded, recalling the bleak memory of standing in the ruins of what had been my apartment belonging to my driver, Taamir, and discovering the map of ancient roads leading to Ur. I'd had time to ponder that moment, replay it over and over again, and with a sinking feeling, concluded that if I'd been given more time with the statue, I might have unlocked more secrets.

It appeared I had been right.

"The vibrations are too scattered, too random for the computer to detect any sort of patterns. It's like someone dropped a hundred stones into a pond, and the waves are crashing into each other, so it's hard to pinpoint the origin." Eddie paused, frowning. "The head scratcher here is that there isn't a stone. It's like the vibrations are coming from echoes and making phantom waves, which makes them even harder to assess since the wavelengths are so short. So weak, in fact, I'm surprised the machine even detected it." He switched from chewing on his right thumb to his right index finger. "What we need is a way to amplify the vibrations." His gray eyes, hooded under unfairly long lashes for a guy, landed on me. "You had a connection with it before. Do you think you might be able to help us?"

My tongue pressed against the roof of my mouth. He still believed that I had an influence over the statue even though it was shattered. Obviously, he was smart and highly qualified, or Division wouldn't have ever hired him, and I knew the agency wouldn't have assigned them to this without giving him all of the information, the hours-long interviews they'd had with us after the temple had collapsed, and we'd managed our way out of the underground city of Ur and back into the desert. I'd told them everything. I'd been impressed with the interviewer's impassive faces despite the fact that they were writing notes about visions of priestesses and ancient battles and solid stone doors exploding with the touch of my hand. They'd merely nodded, jotted it down, then asked for me to continue. I'd questioned Jason about it later, and he'd told me they knew secrets that would destroy the world. It was part of their leverage, their way of making sure clients who took contracts with them paid. Although I believed that bit to be true, I still doubted they'd had someone claim they had possessed magic powers.

"You don't have to do this," Jason said when I hadn't answered right away. He nudged my shoulder, his blue eyes boring into mine. "I know how much you've worked to try and put this all behind you. I see you struggling, Elly. So, if you want to stay, that's fine. I'm willing to go if you'd like and can report back anything more they find."

Report back.

I silently groaned. An hour in the presence of another agent and like the flipping of a switch, relaxed civilian Jason had shifted into serious, accomplish the mission, Agent Price, Jason. I shook my head, a decision already made despite the pang of guilt in my belly. "No. I can do it. I'll go." I lifted my chin and drew in a confident breath. "If he thinks I could be the amplifier or whatever, then I have to at least try."

Jason's jaw shifted, but he didn't argue. "All right."

Agent Rodriguez held his phone to his ear and said, "I'll arrange a car to take us to the airport and transportation there and back."

"I'll pack my things," I said, standing.

"And I'll make sure the lab is set up when you get here," Eddie called from the laptop, as if not wanting to be excluded from the conversation.

"Thanks, Eddie. We'll be in touch soon," Jason said, closing the video feed and shutting the laptop's lid.

Agent Rodriguez conversed on the phone about plane tickets and security measures and sat at the desk, drafting an email on the laptop.

As I moved to the door, Jason's hand caught my elbow and tugged me to him. "Elly, it's me. Be honest. Are you sure—"

"Yes," I said, cutting him off. "Seriously, I'm sure." Worry creased the corners of his eyes as they searched mine. What was he so scared about? That I'd see the statue and have a mental breakdown? Sure, it sucked that it was broken, and the door to whatever my life could have been was sealed shut, but I had it handled. I'd spent three months going to therapy, doing self-care, and spending every ounce of energy I could push from my mind. It was just broken bits of stone, so why was he looking at me like I was about to evaporate?

"I'm fine, Jason. Really," I said and kissed him lightly on his cleanly shaven cheek. He'd tagged along with the other groomsmen to a barber before the wedding and in my opinion, it had been money well spent.

His eyes softened. "I'll walk you to your room."

I shook my head. The thought of stealing a few more minutes of alone time with him induced a flutter in my belly, but as nice as that idea sounded in my mind, time was of the essence. Dragging out my departure any longer would only make it worse. Already, the claws of guilt that I was leaving, abandoning my sister on her wedding day, were sinking deeper with every passing second.

"Don't worry about it. I can pack by myself. Stay in case Agent Rodriguez needs anything." I started again to the door.

"Fifteen minutes," Jason called behind me. "We'll have a car out front."

I gave him a thumbs-up and stepped into the hallway.

I hurried to my hotel room on the second floor, the level closest to the banquet hall that had been booked in advance for the bridal party. Inside, I quickly changed out of my bridesmaid dress. I tugged on a pair of jeans, a white t-shirt, and a denim jacket Cara had gifted me as a bridal party gift, with sparkled stenciling on the back of my name like we'd been part of some motorcycle club. I found my discarded socks and black Converse tennis shoes under the bed. I hung up my dress in the garment bag and then flitted around the room, collecting my clothes, shoes, camera accessories, and a t-shirt on the opposite side of the bed that Jason must've left from the night before. I flipped open my suitcase on the bed and began rolling up my clothes and repacking.

I went to the bathroom to gather my toothbrush, makeup bag, and toiletries when I heard the beep from the hotel room door open.

"Really, Jason," I called from the bathroom. "You couldn't give me the full fifteen? I'm almost finished packing."

"Packing for what?" my mom said.

The world tilted under my feet, and I gripped the edge of the sink to steady myself. Fuck. I'd hoped I'd be able to slip out of here without her noticing. Obviously not.

Clenching my teeth, I stepped out of the bathroom, holding my toiletry bag against my chest like some sort of shield.

My mom stood in the center of the hotel room, next to the bed, in her dark purple evening gown and a disapproving frown on her face. "Cara told me you were leaving. I told her she was wrong."

Her hazel eyes, so like mine, were steeped with rage. "Once you leave," she said, her voice full of venom. "Don't plan on coming back. You've made it abundantly clear what is important to you. I've had it with your reckless impulsivity."

"You think I *want* to leave?" I argued.

"That's not the point," she said. "You are, which means you are disappointing all of us. This family, your sister," she stuttered. "All you had to do was show up. Think about this family for once in your life." Her words stung as if I'd been blasted by a sandstorm. I'd hoped the past month of cake tasting, brunches, and dress fittings had more than made up for me being out of the country for a year. Obviously, they hadn't.

"If your father were here..." she continued.

"Don't," I said, my voice low, a warning.

Her left eye twitched, and she hesitated, rethinking her tactic. Mom never talked about my father or his death when I was twelve when his fighter jet crashed somewhere in Russia. Only on certain occasions when she was determined to land a low blow. Occasions like today.

"My Dad would've done the same thing if it meant that he was protecting our family."

"Oh, so is that what you're doing? Protecting us? From what, Eleanora?" she tossed her hands as if monsters were supposed to miraculously appear around us. "Cause all I've seen are you sticking your nose into someone else's business, pissing off the son of a billionaire, and then gallivanting around with that boyfriend of yours that looks like he's always got a finger on the trigger of the gun he carries."

She paused, her eyebrow inching slightly higher. "Yes, I know he has a gun. I'm not an idiot."

"He has a dangerous job," I said defensively.

"I'm sure he does. Just like you, skulking around bombed-out cities, playing like some sort of spy with your camera while bullets whiz inches away from your head."

My temper spilled over. "I don't have time for this." I pulled against her, starting for the doorway.

"If you leave now. You won't be welcome back."

My footsteps hesitated at the threshold, and I squeezed my eyes shut. A single hot tear spilled down my cheek, and I angrily wiped it away. I knew this day would come; I just never expected it to be today, at Cara's wedding. "You might not understand it now," I said, turning a hard gaze on her. "But what I do helps people. Which is more than you can say."

Without waiting for her response, I briskly exited the room, my heart pounding as I hurried to the bank of elevators. My throat clenched, and I struggled to keep my breathing steady as I wheeled my suitcase into the elevator. I knew what I was doing was right. If Division 12 really had found something about the statue, then that meant the Bridge could be under threat again. My assumption of a secure world was crumbling, thrusting me back into a realm of purpose and responsibility. A mission awaited me, a renewed sense of duty. Yet, beneath the certainty, a tantalizing possibility lingered – a chance to reclaim what I had lost, to reignite the dormant embers of my magic, my power.

Maybe, just maybe, my mom had been right.

Maybe I was being selfish.

FOUR

On the elevator ride down, a quiet voice whispered in my ear. Was I doing this to protect the Bridge and my family, or was I doing it because there was a chance I'd get my powers back? Having access to my magic again would mean that I could show my family that I wasn't crazy and the good I was doing was worth the sacrifices. My photos appearing on the TV news channels, in magazine articles, or displayed alongside newspaper articles hadn't been enough to prove to her that what I was doing mattered, but having actual magic now might change her opinion. She'd thought it was a waste of a journalism degree and that I was on some sort of mission to lead myself to an early grave doing what I did. But that wasn't it at all. I loved my life and the power I had when I wielded my camera. Even without the magic, I was still capable of doing some good in the world. Just not quite as much as before.

A black SUV was waiting for me in front of the hotel. Agent Rodriguez was in the driver's seat and motioned for me to sit in the back.

Jason was already seated in the opposite seat, and he smiled as I entered.

"How are you doing?" he asked.

I shrugged, feeling almost numb from the stressful conversation I'd just had. "Fine, feeling like a total asshole, but you know."

Jason slid his hand into mine and gave it a light squeeze. "This feels like shit right now, but sometimes we are assholes to the people we love for the right reasons."

I bit my lip, looking over at him. My nerves were fried, and I had to fight the urge to replay the memory of him leaving me last summer for what he'd insisted and later had proved had been for the 'right reasons.'

"I know," I said. "Still, I don't know if Cara will ever forgive me." I left out the bit about my mom's ultimatum.

"She's your sister, Elly," Jason continued. "She'll drink champagne, dance to Uptown Funk, and then she and Shawn will fly off to France, where they'll get busy making babies."

I wrinkled my nose, still envisioning an eight-year-old Cara with missing front teeth and freckles. I sighed. "I hope so."

"Well, then," Agent Rodriguez continued, "you might be able to see something I'm missing. It'd be great to have an extra set of experienced eyes on this." He turned away again, looking to where Jason was feverishly typing on his phone. "Another assistant, maybe one with an archaeological background, would be nice. They could examine the fragments themselves and compare them to others of similar structure and design."

Jason looked at me. "I might know someone," he said, giving me a private smile. I knew exactly who he was talking about. There was one person who was not just extremely knowledgeable about Sumerian history but was equally as trustworthy.

"You're thinking of calling Kat?" I asked.

Jason shrugged. "Why not?"

My lips formed a thin line. "Are you sure you want to drag her back into all of this? I mean, involving her with the agency?"

Jason's mouth twisted, and he arched an eyebrow. "No, of course, I don't. But it'd be stupid of us to think if we put out a call to universities and museum research departments around the world looking for a Mesopotamian historian and not have Kat catch on. She has connections everywhere, Elly, and she is far from dumb. As soon as anything is mentioned about the Vela constellations and Sumeria, my phone will be ringing."

I chuckled at the tenseness in his voice. "You're scared of her."

"Damn right, I am," he said firmly. "If I got on her bad side, I couldn't fathom the consequences. She's one of the biggest tactical advantages I have over there, and if she decided to withdraw her influence, I'd lose valuable assets and connections. I might as well kiss ever working in the Middle East again goodbye." He paused, lowering his voice so only I could hear. "Oh, and any holiday dinners with the family would be even more awkward."

I folded my arms and leaned back in the chair. Kat had been invaluable when we'd been trying to learn more about the statue, who was after it, and the why. If we lost out on her wealth of knowledge just because we were afraid of getting her involved... "Fine," I said. "But the second we get wind of anything dangerous or Division 12 tries to pull a fast one, I want her cut loose."

This time, Jason raised both his eyebrows, surprised by my conviction. The lamplight danced in his blue eyes, summoning forth the look he'd given me earlier when he'd whisked me away to the hotel room after the ceremony. "All right, agreed."

～

WHEN THE PLANE touched down at the private airstrip, a black SUV with tinted windows was waiting for us. Jason helped me with my bag. I'd packed only two changes of clothes and bare essentials since I hadn't planned on staying at the hotel after the wedding for more than a weekend. I hoped that this trip wouldn't require more than an overnight stay and that my relationship with my mom and Cara could be salvaged the sooner I finished here and the sooner I got back. I'd sustained a steady buzz on the rum and cokes the private plane attendants gave me for the four-hour flight, yet still, the alcohol had done little to ease the guilty pang between my shoulder blades. Jason was sympathetic and instinctual, which gave me space to process the choice I'd made.

While he understood the gravity of my decision to leave Cara's wedding early, I don't think he comprehended the long-lasting effects of letting someone you care about down. He was a good man, but taking on mission after mission where you never knew if you'd come back takes a toll on a person's conscience. Empathy had no place in undercover operations.

His ability to repress emotions and wall himself off had been his key to surviving situations that would've left most people needing therapy and running from their shadows.

For the majority of the flight, Agent Rodriguez had been on video calls related to coordinating the items and resources Eddie had asked about. Jason had either dozed, looking the epitome of relaxed, or answered Agent Rodriguez's questions regarding timelines of the events in Iraq, what other agents were involved, and what sort of risks were involved.

I could see the muscles in Jason's neck tense at the word 'risk' and knew he was thinking about me and the powers that I had had. The powers that had caused men to burn and stone to melt.

I flexed my hand at the phantom echo of magic.

Once seated in the SUV, the driver drove through a chain link gate guarded by airport security personnel wielding hip side holsters and grim faces. I knew headquarters was in New York; however, the palm trees and patches of sand dunes along the roadway were a dead giveaway. This was definitely *not* New York.

We drove along a winding road, passing fields of citrus trees and cypress trees bordering the edges of glistening ponds and streams. The SUV finally turned off on one such driveway, and soon, the road behind us vanished. The car bumped along the gravel road until the trees cleared, revealing a relatively small stone building. Growing up in a small town outside Sacramento, we'd had school dances hosted at a local Grange building that was part-time church, part-time bar, and this structure with fading white paint and cinder block foundation was in worse repair than that.

We pulled up to the front of the building, where a man and woman wearing navy blue suits stepped forward. Getting out of the car, Rodriguez swiftly switched positions with one of the guards. Jason grabbed both our backpacks, and I followed his example, climbing out of the truck. The humid air embraced me, and tiny droplets of moisture clung to my face and neck.

Jason handed both bags to the other guard. "Take these to level ten, room 883." The guard nodded and waved over another similarly dressed security guard whom I had been nearly invisible from where they'd been lurking in the shadows beside one of the stone columns supporting the covered entry to the building.

We passed through a single steel door, reminding me of the freezer storage closet I'd used when I'd had a summer job in high school at a local cafe. The walls contained no windows, no flower-filled pots, and most definitely no signs indicating what it was. It was as if the construction had finished part-way through, leaving a shell of a building, just the basics; however, once we were inside, that all changed.

The floor was a dark gray industrial-style carpet that ran the length of a dizzyingly long hallway. Jason led the way, his chin tilting up in a way that only came from the confidence of being here many times. While this wasn't his main office, I knew he'd been to others when specific equipment or teams were needed.

We passed no one in the halls, and I almost believed we were the only ones here until I heard an automated voice announcement come over an intercom system asking for Sierra's team to report to the helipad for delivery. I smirked, only able to imagine a delivery of what or whom they were referring to.

The hallway ended at a wall containing four elevators, all with black doors, gleaming with such a polished surface I could see my reflection on them. I felt a sense of deja vu from when I'd seen the black stone altar in the temple in Ur. It was a thousand broken shards now, just like the Inanna statue.

Jason's eyes glided over me as if reading the direction my thoughts had gone, and placed a hand on the small of my back.

"Stay close," he said. "This place is a maze, and I'd hate to lose you."

My cheeks warmed, recognizing the double meanings of his words. "So, what are we talking about? The building aboveground is only a fraction of the building. The rest is all underground?"

Jason thumbed the call button to the elevator to our right. "Something like that," he said, smirking.

I laughed dryly. "Are they all like this, then? Big concrete icebergs?"

The elevator doors slid open, notably without the usual ding that I'd come to expect, and Jason guided me in. The doors slid closed, and Jason folded his hands in front of him, staring straight ahead. "Some are. This one, in particular, is more for research and has specialty facilities."

"Like Eddie's lab?"

"Yes." Jason laughed. "Although, I'm sure Eddie would get a kick out of you calling it that; it's really known as the UAI: Unidentified Artifacts Investigations."

A whole lab dedicated to unidentified artifacts. Now, why wasn't I surprised? Division 12 was connected to the CIA with even more liberties and money. Of course, they'd have an entire investigations department for strange items. Hell, they probably sold off the technology once they'd determined they couldn't use it for themselves.

As we descended, the elevator suddenly jerked to a stop. I expected the doors to open, assuming someone else had pushed the call button on a lower level, but they remained firmly shut.

Jason tapped on the button to the eighth floor again as if the elevator's brain had forgotten what it was supposed to be doing.

His thumb jabbed the emergency release button, and he cursed.

"What is it?" I asked. "Is it broken?"

The doors didn't respond.

Jason took out his phone, then cursed again, obviously discovering there was no service down in the subterranean levels.

"What do we do?" I said, my voice laced with the first tell-tale whine of panic.

"Just keep calm," he said, and his tone was, in fact, that of a cool-headed person. "The electrical in this building is old, so they had to retrofit a lot when Division moved in ten years ago. There are always annoying glitches like this in the wiring. There are multiple backup generators on every level that switch on when there is a problem in the grid. I'm sure the doors will open any minute."

However, as the seconds ticked by, the elevator remained stationary and us suspended by cables that were being held fast by an emergency mechanism and an unfathomable distance from the bottom.

Even if Jason didn't want to admit it, we were trapped, and I fought against the desire to hold my breath. How much oxygen was in here? Cause that was the real dilemma, wasn't it? If the power was out as Jason suspected, the air conditioning had turned off as well, and the circulation of fresh air too.

Emergency lights flickered sporadically, casting an eerie glow that only proved to intensify the sense of fear. Sweat beaded along my brow as I felt around for something – anything – that might help me escape. The surrounding silence was almost deafening, punctuated only by our own ragged breathing. My heart raced faster with every passing second as broken images flashed before me like lightning; what would happen if we were stuck here forever? Could that happen? My thoughts whirred, traitorously summoning any and all movies, TV shows or books where people had died while trapped inside an elevator.

"Dammit," Jason's voice emerged from the darkness, filled with frustration more than the fear that gripped me.

The sound of his jacket rustling reached my ears, and a moment later, his hand found its place in mine.

"So, is *this* a normal glitch?" I whispered.

His reply was swift and certain. "No."

He released my hand, and my breath hitched in my throat. I imagined Jason's hands fumbling along the walls as he murmured to himself. "Maybe I can pry the doors open or something." I heard a loud bang as he smacked the metal doors. He let out a frustrated groan. "There has to be an emergency call button somewhere." Time slowed to a crawl, each passing second an eternity as thoughts of impending doom raced through my mind. My body tensed, and in the flickering light, the sensation of the air thickening around me, and I could almost feel the four steel walls gradually encroaching upon us.

Then, an abrupt jolt shook the elevator, accompanied by an ominous groan from somewhere above us. Jason's arms found me, snugging me to his chest, just as whatever emergency mechanism holding us failed, and we plunged uncontrollably downward, and a scream tore from my throat.

CHAPTER
FIVE

My arms shot out reflexively as if I could grab hold of something nearby, but I felt nothing but air.

Suddenly, the elevator jerked to a stop. The lights flickered on, and Jason's grip tightened around mine as relief flooded my body. We'd stopped. Somewhere, somehow, the emergency mechanism had kicked back on and stopped us from plunging to our deaths.

"It's okay, we're all right," he said.

I looked up at Jason, searching his eyes for assurance. His arms tightened around me as though he could protect me from the world's chaos with just his embrace. For a moment, time seemed to freeze, and I felt the weight of what we'd narrowly escaped. My heart hammered in my chest, reminding me that it still beat—that we were still alive. Jason's gaze was clouded with worry, his eyes asking questions that his lips didn't form.

I nodded, unable to make words form as adrenaline surged through my veins. Only when the doors to the elevator opened did I finally exhale and let the tension slowly drain from me.

Gray-tiled hallways curved out from the landing to our

right and left, with a ring of windows in the center revealing what I could easily assume was the agency's research lab. Overhead, lights still flickered and buzzed.

"The backup generator," Jason said, answering my unspoken question, still holding me. "It must've kicked on when the building lost power."

He settled a concerned look on mine. "It won't last long. Two hours, maybe three, so we must move and move fast."

I inhaled, using the fresh oxygen to steel my nerves. The truth was I didn't care what had happened, only that I would feel a hundred times better once I wasn't in the elevator anymore, and taking the stairs when given the option might be in my future, at least for a while.

Slowly, reluctantly, Jason released me as if he was unsure I could stand on my own.

We moved to exit the elevator, and never ever in a thousand years could I have anticipated the nightmarish sight awaiting us. Bodies lay strewn scattered throughout the corridors. Some were sprawled face down on the floor where they'd fallen. A pretty blonde was slumped over the body of her companion. A tray of lab equipment scattered before them. Shards of glass stuck out at jagged angles from the woman's arms, and blood dripped from the man's ear where a scalpel had caught the edge of his scalp. Jason thrust his arm protectively in front of me while the other hand reached for his gun.

"What the hell happened?" I whispered. "Are they...dead?"

Jason took two steps to the people closest to us and knelt. He placed a finger on their neck, checking for a pulse, and while the furrow between his eyebrows smoothed, the muscle in his jaw flexed. "They're alive. I can feel a pulse, and look, they're breathing."

I approached him, stepping softly, and yet my footsteps resounded loudly in the eerily silent space.

"They don't look like they've been shot, only that they fell?" I said. "Maybe they hit their heads at the same time and have concussions."

Jason carefully examined them, brushing the broken glass from the blonde's hair and gently pulling her to the side and off the man. My mind raced with all the possibilities that could've led to people passing out. Carbon monoxide was, first and foremost, a strong contender. We were underground, and the only source of airflow would come from ventilation ducks pumping fresh air from the surface. With the electrical system glitch that caused the elevator to stop, surely the vents had stopped as well. I sucked in a tentative breath. If bad air were the culprit, we were already fucked. A person couldn't taste or smell carbon monoxide, and you'd fall unconscious before your heart finally stopped. In all honesty, it wasn't the worst way to die.

But surely a place like this would have sensors for that sort of thing, and the odds of all the sensors failing were next to zero.

So, it's not carbon monoxide. Then what?

It was a Division 12 research laboratory, and although Jason had insisted it was only where they studied and stored the evidence for ongoing investigations, maybe they were working on something more dangerous than a Russian businessman's laptop or analyzing traffic camera footage outside an embassy.

My pulse quickened.

There was one other possibility, even as far-fetched as it seemed, I couldn't ignore. Derek Kane had been put on house arrest, but he was rich, ambitious, and well-connected. "What if this is Kane?" I asked. "What if he learned where this research facility is located and knew the statue was being kept here? What if he'd somehow planted a bomb or hacked the electrical grid to try and break in?"

Jason stood. "Unlikely. We have people watching Kane,

monitoring his phones, emails, everything, even what food he's having delivered."

"But not impossible?" I pressed.

Jason pulled back the slide of his gun, checking for the bullet in the chamber, before letting it click back into place. His eyes met mine. "I believe nothing is impossible anymore, Elly."

His words carried with them the weight of the memories of everything we'd shared. The impossibility that bronze statues could grant visions. Sand in caves could melt flesh like acid. That a fantastical and powerful magic that could manipulate Carbon atoms existed and that I'd once wielded it.

But there was more. The impossibility that the two of us, with our chaotic, often dangerous, career paths, could carve a way out for us to work. A relationship built from the ashes of mistakes and difficult choices that had grown into something longer, more enduring than before.

"However," Jason continued. "The lab techs screwing around with something else toxic or poisonous is a more likely scenario."

"If you think they accidentally released a biochemical weapon," I said, my voice nearing shrill as I pointed at the elevator behind us. "Then we were exposed the second we opened those doors."

The muscle in Jason's jaw shifted. "I know," he said, still gripping his gun. His blue eyes, which usually held a confident gaze, now shimmered with a subtle hint of uncertainty, like a deep ocean momentarily disturbed by an unseen ripple.

"It's Agent Price," he shouted, turning from me. "Is anyone hurt? Can anyone hear me?"

No response.

I held my breath, my eyes sweeping the rows of closed doors lining the hallway that formed a ring around a central laboratory. My mind spun a thousand horrific images as I imagined what lay beyond them.

Without speaking, Jason strode ahead, and I followed, even as my heartbeat thudded in my ears. Slowly, we opened each door, searching the interiors for anyone who was awake. Some were dark and empty, while in others, we found agent staff collapsed in their chairs and lying on the floor by their desks. Room by room, we moved, checking the people inside, and discovered the same thing. They were alive, just...unconscious, as if they'd simultaneously fallen asleep at the exact same moment while in the midst of going about their day.

In the farthest room, which was also spacious, we found a large man at a desk wearing a white lab coat and tie. His head was slumped on his chest as if he'd dozed off during a boring Zoom meeting. The nameplate on his door said he was Director of Research Thomas Nelson.

I pulled up my phone and saw the no-service indicator glaring back at me from the tiny screen.

"We're four stories underground with concrete walls," Jason commented. "Have to get topside to get any kind of signal." He jutted his chin at the laboratory surrounded by glass windows. "Long shot with the power outage, but the Internet might still be functioning, and I can try and reach someone that way."

Then he turned to me, his gaze gripping mine. Emotions swirled in his eyes, even behind the protective wall I recognized he wore when he was Agent Price instead of my Jason. A barrier that, subconsciously, I actively strove to tear down. We'd chosen each other, after everything. He didn't have anything to hide from me, and I had promised to do the same.

Finally, we stopped at the large pair of glass double doors leading into the main lab.

Jason reached to flip open the lid on the keypad, but I stopped him.

"Wait," I said. "What if the toxin came from the lab? Shouldn't we wait for the agency Hazmat team to get here or something?" While my question sounded logical, the truth was I didn't want to face what was in there. It'd been enough looking through all the offices, but those people hadn't been surrounded by often dangerous and sharp lab equipment.

Jason's face softened, sensing my undertone of worry. "There are emergency systems in place, alarms set to go off if they detect all manner of toxins. Carbon monoxide, anthrax, mustard gas. If someone so much as opens a rotten tuna sandwich down here, sirens will blast your eardrums."

I bit my lip, still not completely satisfied. "Is there a chance it was something that even the sensors couldn't have picked up?"

Jason shrugged. "Possibly. But then we're already dead, aren't we?"

I frowned at his matter-of-fact response, causing him to chuckle.

"Listen," he said, "whatever got these people down took them down fast. And you and I are still conscious, right? If there was a toxic chemical in the air, it must've either disappeared or been filtered out by the system when we were still in the elevator."

I folded my arms but had to admit he made a lot of good points. We'd been inside the elevator when this had happened. And even though the thought of it stalling and dropping was something I'd never care to experience again, us being trapped inside was the reason we hadn't been down here and been among the victims.

Jason typed in a long code on the keypad, and the door slid open.

The lab was filled with the hushed hum of machinery, and

the long table surfaces were a gleaming sea of chrome and glass. The air was heavy with the scent of chemicals, sterilant, and hot electrical equipment. Illuminated by blinking monitors and soft white light from above, everything in this place was pristine. Except for the bodies sprawled like rag dolls on the cold tile floor, some twitched involuntarily while others remained motionless where they'd fallen.

Jason walked through the lab, a mixture of horror and awe on his face. As he looked around, trying to decide what to do first, I noticed his gaze fall on something in the corner. Our eyes met, and he silently gestured to stay where I was.

One of the metal cabinet doors swung open, and Jason raised his gun, directing it at the cabinet, as a man in a white lab coat scurried down from where he'd been crammed inside.

My breath seized in my throat when I recognized the man as Eddie.

"Jesus Christ," Jason said, lowering his gun. "What the fuck."

Eddie smoothed his coat and looked at Jason first, then me. "You..." he stammered. "You're here, and okay?"

"Seems that way," I said. "Are you all right?"

Eddie nodded. "Yeah, I think so." He sat down the box he'd been holding onto a nearby table and patted his head and shoulders, then his legs like he'd somehow lost an entire limb and hadn't yet realized it. "Everything seems to be in order." He looked behind me, and his eyes darkened when they fell upon the unconscious bodies strewn about the lab.

"They're alive," I said quickly. "We checked. They're just unconscious."

Eddie's left eye twitched, and he wiped the corner of his mouth before leaning over the back of a nearby chair. His face paled.

"I had a feeling this might happen," he said, his voice low as if talking to himself.

Jason replaced his pistol in his holster. "What do you mean? What the hell happened?"

He adjusted his glasses— that now I was meeting him in person— realized were too small for his narrow face, and the sleeves of his lab coat fell above his wrists like Cara's shirts did when I'd borrowed them. He wasn't quite as tall as Jason's six-foot-four frame, but he was close. And with his broad shoulders and thick forearms, he'd be just as suited on the football field as in here, peering through a microscope.

Eddie sat the box next to a pair of computer monitors and lifted the lid. "I think I'm still conscious because of this."

He stepped back, letting Jason and I crowd closer to peer into the box. Inside, cushioned on padded foam, were the four broken fragments of what had once been a priceless bronze statue of Inanna. Under the harshness of artificial laboratory light, the shards of shattered stone and scraps of metal appeared as unremarkable clumps, devoid of a whisper of the profound magic that had once surged within the heart of the statue.

The oxygen left my lungs, and I found myself yearning to reach in and touch it, caressing the familiar curves of the goddess and the eight-pointed star she held.

"The statue protected me. Shielded me from whatever affected these people," Eddie said. "I'm certain of it."

"But how?" I asked, sensing the question weighing on Jason's mind, too.

"No idea." He glanced at his smart watch, which displayed time in binary code instead of numbers. "But we have twenty-two minutes to find out before the Director figures out the statue isn't in the vault in the basement like I'd put in the system, and she comes down here in person to find out why."

"Better hop to it then." Jason tugged off his jacket and hung it on the back of the chair. "Cause if the Director confiscates it, no one in this lifetime will ever get to lay eyes on it again."

45

SIX

Eddie slid into the rolling chair and wiggled the mouse to wake up the monitor. Jason had been right; the Internet was still working even though the lights and elevator were on the fritz.

He was even more twitchy in person than he was on the webcam, and his hair was overgrown, the brown tufts sticking out above his too-large ears.

Eddie cleared his throat. "So, what happened with the power outage and the elevator malfunction was an earthquake."

Jason and I looked at each other in disbelief. An earthquake? In Florida? Okay, sure, I wasn't a geologist, but I'd worked around enough natural disasters and seismically active areas to know while Florida had its own fair share of environmental catastrophes, earthquakes weren't one of them. In fact, one of the few tidbits of random information I'd retained from Jason and the trivia games he liked to play on long car rides was that Florida had no active fault zones.

"When the statue's vibrations started intensifying, I thought maybe it had been doing it the whole time and so pulled up seismic graph recordings for as far back as scientists have been recording them in an attempt to see if it had ever done so in the past when it was buried in Syria." Eddie smiled nervously and clicked open a window on the nearest monitor that showed a map of the world. Eddie tapped a finger on the monitor. "These are seismic disturbances from the past twenty-four hours. They're small but enough to trigger reading alerts."

I counted at least twenty pinpricks of red spread over the map as if the seven continents were an acne-riddled teenager who hadn't learned what salicylic acid was.

My eyes zeroed in on a red blob smack dab in the center of Florida.

"There. That's us," I said.

"Hmm," Eddie said, agreeing. "Approximately 37 minutes ago."

"So, you're telling me an earthquake made all these people go unconscious except you because of the statue?" My voice was harder than I intended, but my patience was waning. "That still doesn't explain why Jason and I are fine."

Eddie chewed his left pointer finger, and I could practically hear the gears turning inside his head. "You're right. None of it makes sense." His hazel eyes under thick brows were nearly level with mine even though he was sitting. "Unless you still have the powers or magic or whatever. The ones you said in your initial report summary after coming back from Syria?"

My throat tightened, and I rested a hand on the desk, feeling suddenly lightheaded. I shook my head as the thoughts flooded me, memories of being questioned by a rotating cast of Division agents over an exhausting two days. All asking to see the scar on my hand, asking me to explain what specifically my abilities could do, and then facing condescending looks when I was unable to demonstrate.

"I was one of the interviewers, you know," Eddie said, his voice gentler than before. "I believed you."

At the time, the humiliation had only aggravated the emotional turmoil I had been struggling with. Losing Taamir, watching Leon die, and Jason's momentary betrayal before revealing he'd been on my side all along. I had been in no shape to give them the thorough explanations they wanted, let alone give any regard to the faces of the agents questioning me. Eddie's words penetrated the fog surrounding me, and I looked up at him.

"I didn't know. Thank you."

Eddie smiled. "I saw the photographs and readings the team sent back that analyzed the area around Palmyra. The abnormalities were too abundant to ignore." He stopped and twisted his mouth as if in thought. "Besides, why would you lie about having magical powers? No one wants that kind of attention from Division 12."

I let out a small laugh. "That's true."

"Well, anyway, since I haven't found any pattern to the timing of the earthquakes or the locations. All were random with no tie to the area or connections to volcanic activity." He opened another new window on the screen. This one showed lines streaking across it like stock market trends, and while I could detect different colors of each line, they all swooped up into a peak at nearly identical waves. "But then I figured out I was looking at it all wrong. The pattern wasn't in the timing. It was in the intensity." Eddie's voice reached an octave higher, and I worried if I should grab a napkin in case he was about to start drooling. "They all happened at different times and in random areas, but it wasn't until I compiled the data I saw it." He paused, letting his gaze sweep over Jason and me to make sure we were paying attention. No worries there, buddy.

"It was the intensity. The magnitudes of all the earthquakes in the past twenty-four hours were the same. It's not close, but precisely a magnitude of 3.355.

Jason crossed his arms in front of him. He'd rolled up the sleeves of the dress shirt he'd been wearing at the wedding to his elbows, and the white fabric pulled taut over his forearms and biceps, showcasing the well-defined muscles and momentarily distracting me.

"Fine," he said, his voice carrying a mix of skepticism and frustration. "Let me get this straight. An Earthquake shakes up the place, messing with the elevator and cutting the power. But what I don't get is why every Division research agent is now blacked out as if they were doling out free drink passes in Vegas?"

Eddie shifted uneasily, and a strange look passed over his face. After some time, his shoulders sagged. "I don't know," he said, and his voice sounded weary, tinged with sadness, and I wondered how often this ridiculously educated guy had ever uttered those three words in his lifetime.

Probably not many.

A long silence filled the air between us until, finally, Jason spoke. "Elly, stay here with Eddie. I have some calls to make."

Before I could protest about all the reasons we should stay together, he was out the door and striding to the door marked 'Emergency stairwell' next to the elevator.

Eddie continued to stare at the screen, biting the tips of his nails like they were his last meal.

Since Eddie seemed lost in his thoughts and didn't seem up to conversation, I found a rack of spare lab coats and went around, folding them and placing them like makeshift pillows under people's heads. It wasn't much, but at least it felt like I was doing something to help them. By some miracle, no one seemed fatally wounded, just nicks and bruises, although the man by the elevator might have to learn to live with a missing earlobe when he woke up. If he ever woke up.

That was the most puzzling part of it all. I'd been around lots of military, both private and public, and there didn't exist an aerosol gas this potent that would knock someone out for what was nearing two hours. Whatever had affected these people lasted much longer. How long, I couldn't guess.

Forever was a very real possibility.

When I'd done all I could to keep myself occupied, I returned to the lab where Eddie was keying away at a keyboard.

"None of my readings are making sense," he said, clearly talking out loud to himself. "There's a lot more going on here than I thought. The statue, it has to be..." he murmured.

"What about the statue?" I asked, my throat clenching. "It's broken. The power it had is gone. How can you think it's connected to all of this?"

"Look at this." Eddie's fingers swiped on the keyboard, bringing up a live video feed looking into the padded box with the broken statue.

He switched the filter to what I assumed was an infrared camera, so it cast a reddish glow over the fragments. Instantly, the edges of the statue illuminated in gold light as if glowing from the inside.

"Wait... what is that?" I said.

Eddie didn't answer right away, his eyes fixated on the screen. "You seem certain there isn't power anymore inside the statue, but I fail to agree."

I leaned in, captivated despite myself, then glanced back at the screen as the statue glowed. The spike in the graph was unmistakable like shadows punching through the light in a black-and-white photograph. "You mean the statue reacted to the earthquake?"

Eddie nodded. "Yes, I believe so." His voice was practically crackling with excitement now, and I could tell he'd been planning something grand all along. "I suspected there might be some kind of force inside the statue - something we couldn't detect with our current technology - and this confirms it."

He tapped away at his keyboard, bringing up a new set of data points on the monitor. "Look here," he said, pointing to the screen. "This isn't just an ordinary earthquake; there's something else going on here—a low-frequency energy wave that seems to be emanating from within the statue itself."

When Jason returned, we examined every angle and every inch of the statue to determine how it was sensing the subterranean vibrations. I could offer very little insight, as this was so out of my wheelhouse, and so I made myself useful by either rotating the camera or the box so Eddie could keep his eyes glued to the monitors. The infrared produced the most interesting effects, but ultraviolet as well seemed to be getting some responses. However, while the different video filters made the pieces light up and look pretty, we learned nothing new and proved to be as useless as a pixel-perfect snapshot in an unmarked folder. Existing but without context enough to make it valuable.

I found it hard to concentrate with all the people lying like corpses around us, and when Jason told me that medics were on their way, the low-grade tension headache that had formed in my temples eased slightly.

"The agency is going to have the staff transferred to a private facility where medical personnel has already been notified and can begin thorough examinations." Jason sighed. "Director Ferguson had no choice but to contact the CDC and has me on point to keep the shit storm from completely blowing up with the Feds' involvement."

"Once everyone is transferred," Eddie said, swiveling in his chair to face us. "The agency can analyze blood and tissue samples, their vitals, and any other signs of trauma that you missed."

If Jason had hackles, I would've seen them rise. If there was one thing Jason hated more than being told he was wrong, it was being told he hadn't done his job well. Failing to be thorough as an agent for Division 12 didn't mean he wouldn't get a Christmas bonus; it meant people were dead. Himself included.

Mistakes just weren't allowed.

"I'll make sure they do so." Jason's jaw shifted, and he turned his eyes to me. "It'll take several days for the agency to regain control and get it cleaned up. Once I've got the clearance, though, I'm going to take you back to California."

Instantly, I protested. "No, no way."

Jason's lips formed a thin line, and I knew this was one argument I couldn't win. Something bad had happened here, something no one knew anything about or whether it was going to keep happening, and no world existed where Jason would knowingly put me in danger—seeing as I was more than willing to do that to myself.

"Please, Elly," he said. "I promise I'll keep you posted. Share whatever I can when we've had a chance to get a handle on this."

I looked at Eddie, who was, once again, bent over his desk, squinting at the screen with his glasses perched on his nose. Indecision tore me in opposite directions. If I went back to California, I could start the process of repairing the damage I'd done to my family.

On the flip side, if I stayed, I'd be more at hand if Eddie had a breakthrough by uncovering more of how the statue was connected to everything. Eddie had proved the frequency of the earthquakes was increasing, which meant another one was imminent. So far, no deaths had been reported since they'd all occurred in unpopulated areas, but it was only a matter of time.

Eddie hadn't yet found a pattern to the earthquakes besides their intensity, so it was complete luck that they hadn't yet landed in a major city.

Even as weak as they were, given the proper placement in a city full of buildings not engineered to withstand any sort of seismic activity, and…boom. The 'little hiccups,' as Eddie had called them, would cause massive damage. Could I honestly take a plane home, sit by my condo's pool, sunbathe, and wait for the news to break about an earthquake cracking open and killing hundreds?

Jason's eyes weighed on the side of my face as he awaited the answer I'd settled on. I shook my head before I could change my mind.

"No. I know you're looking out for me, but I want to stay here. I might not have my abilities anymore, but I still know more about that statue than anyone." Jason frowned, and his blue eyes darkened from their usual steel to cobalt. "All right. But if I get wind from the CDC that this is contagious, you'll be first on the list to a quarantine zone, even if I have to carry you there myself."

I smiled and rested my arms around my middle. Clearly, our time spent together over the summer had only encouraged his protective side. It didn't matter that I'd hid in bunkers with refugees or dashed through minefields with NATO soldiers.

It was him at his very core to guard those he cared about, which made him an incredible agent for Division 12 but a controlling albeit adorable side for a boyfriend. Jason moved to the computer on the table behind us and opened the window to access the agency's network. He keyed in an extremely long series of numbers and letters for a passcode and hit enter. The Division 12 logo, a golden D with a black number 12 inside, formed at the top of the screen, and a single search bar appeared. Jason began with earthquakes plus sickness, then earthquakes plus illness, and continued searching through all the records the agency had collected for the half-century it'd been in business.

While Eddie and Jason worked, I couldn't feel more useless. As if the universe sensed my growing fear that I'd made the wrong choice to stay and would only be in the way or, worse, a distraction for Jason, the stairwell door beside the elevator opened. A team of six or seven paramedics stepped out, carrying medical bags and gurneys.

I stood, and Jason caught my movement and followed. He greeted the paramedics, and together, we led them through the offices and hallways, showing them where the most severely injured employees were. Immediately, IVs were placed, vitals were checked, and lights were shined on pupils for responses. Jason shared the names of the ones he knew and did his best to share any information he had about them, their ages, backgrounds, and any medical conditions he knew of.

Once they were checked, they were safe for transport, they were placed on stretchers, and with a two-person lift, they carried them one by one up the stairs. Even if the elevator was working, I didn't blame them for not trusting it after the malfunction. As they worked, I assisted where I could, handing bandages or helping remove shoes and clothing. Some of them were National Guard, while others sported navy jackets with the Marion County EMT team. I had to applaud Division for reaching out to local authorities for something like this since they seldom liked to play with others, as it proved that they were, in fact, serious about their employees and staff getting the quickest medical treatment possible.

However, their out-of-character reaction only amplified the fear that was growing inside me. They were in the business of dealing with the unusual and risky missions and assignments the world governments wouldn't dare touch. So, their response meant that this was indeed something beyond their scope. Perhaps it wasn't an isolated incident, and Jason hadn't yet been privy to that information. When the last of the unconscious workers had been carried upstairs, Jason reappeared by my side. "The director is five minutes out, and I have to meet her. She's going to want you at the debriefing, too, so you should prepare yourself."

"Prepare me?" I asked, raising an eyebrow. "For what? It's not like we did anything wrong."

Jason's mouth twitched. "She's... well, you'll see. Let's just say when they called the meeting after the incident in Palmyra, Director Ferguson was the hardest to convince."

I licked my lips, finally understanding. "She doesn't believe that I had magic."

He nodded. "So, I'd keep that little bit to a minimum unless she asks, okay?"

"Okay." I glanced to where Eddie was still typing away at the computer, oblivious to the commotion of the medical staff swarming through the lab as they swabbed samples off the backs of chairs, windows, and keyboards. He had never witnessed my abilities either, yet his lack of surprise regarding the existence of such powers struck me as curious. A comforting warmth settled within me. Quirky as he was, his acceptance of both me and my story was a definite plus in my book.

Eddie suddenly stopped typing. He looked up, locking eyes with me for a moment that felt longer than it was. "You know," he said. "I'm very good at keeping secrets in this lab." Then he gave me a cryptic smile before turning back to his computer.

CHAPTER

SEVEN

"What a clusterfuck," Director Ferguson grumbled. The agency research director was middle-aged with light brown skin and strawberry blonde hair bobbed short above her shoulders. Her nose was covered in a smattering of freckles, adding a touch of intrigue to her appearance, although her intense brown eyes dispelled any notions of innocence. She was dressed in a dark blue blazer, complemented by white wide-legged pants, and donned designer heels that made my own feet ache.

She laced her fingers, resting her elbows on the desk, fixing Jason and me with her glare. Jason had come to fetch me once her helicopter had arrived and had led me up the stairs to the top floor and into a rectangular-shaped office, which had taken not one but two agency personnel to key in codes, too.

A large window overlooked a lush forest of trees and bushes, their trunks and roots submerged in a wetland teeming with birds swooping down to catch the flying insects that hovered above the surface of the green water.

"Sit down, will you?" she said with an exasperated sigh. "It's not like any of us are going anywhere anytime soon."

Jason and I hurried to take the pair of chairs in front of her desk.

"Now," the director said, leaning back in her chair. "In an effort to contain this situation and keep it from growing feet and walking out of here and into the grubby hands of the media, I will need you two to remain here until we have more details. During the preliminary medical examinations, I received reports that the victims' vitals were within normal ranges. They're just...unconscious."

Jason shifted from where he sat beside me, and his fingers gripped the arms of the chair, looking like he was about to spring to his feet at any moment. I couldn't blame him. The warning he'd given me about the Director had been an understatement. I'd met some powerful people in my lifetime, Generals, diplomats, even a few senators, and this woman could've stood toe to toe with any of them. Her very essence exhibited control. Power.

"Ms. Dawson," she said, directing me with a look that sent a trickle of cold down my spine. "You were brought here on behalf of the research department requiring a second opinion on an artifact. Is that correct?"

"Yes," I said, then added, "Ma'am."

Her mouth formed a tight line, her face unreadable. "And this artifact, you share a particular history with it from the Palmyrian event?"

Palmyrian event. So that's what they were calling it. I bristled with irritation. Just an event. Another file in their database. That's what Taamir dying, me being attacked by their own agents, and Jason nearly getting trapped in an underground temple meant to them. An event. "Yes," I said, keeping my voice steady. "I was the one who found the statue originally and used it to find where the temple of Ur was."

"And the other findings in the report..." She trailed off,

leaving the question open for me to answer so I would be the one to say the word magic. She wanted me to play the fool, fine. I'd been called worse and had accepted that most of what I said these days sounded certifiable. "The statue showed me visions." I held up my hand, revealing the silver eight-pointed star that had been branded on my palm. The faintest of silver lines remained, but it was still there. Proof. The one lingering reminder that I clung to in order to keep from completely spiraling into gas-lighting myself that the whole thing had been all imagined, a fever dream.

"This was given to me, a symbol of the Sumerian goddess Inanna. It allowed me to control natural elements, carbon specifically." The entire time I spoke, the Director's expression never wavered, her eyes remaining fixed upon my face, listening as if absorbing every word. It was as unnerving as it was reliev-ing. Maybe I'd misjudged her. Maybe she was more open-minded than Jason had said.

"But your power, as you called it," she said, smoothing invisible lint from her pants. "It's gone now, correct?"

I nodded, and the tight twinge in my belly that usually accompanied me when I admitted I no longer had my powers was smaller than before. The resentment toward Enheduanna and Inanna waned with each passing day. They'd given me the power when I needed it, and I'd accomplished what I'd been tasked with doing. Who was I to demand more? Hadn't that been their warning since the beginning? Humans weren't meant to access the power of the gods. Too long of exposure to it from Enheduanna had corrupted her father, the king, and destroyed their empire. How could they assume I was any different? That I wouldn't be corrupted too, in time, if my magic remained with me forever.

"So, if it's gone," she said slowly. "What use are you to supplying the agency with information?"

Her words were a hard slap to the face, and I fought back the whiplash from the sudden shift in her tone.

Nope. Jason had been right. This lady was exactly as he'd said. A real b—

"Because Ella has spent more time with the artifact than any of us," Jason supplied. "Division 12 research knows that the statue's vibrations are connected to the earthquakes, which we now know are additionally tied to people falling into comas." Director Ferguson sighed, long and slow, as if she were a bartender serving the slippery nipple shots to the fourth group of giggling newly turned twenty-one-year-olds.

"Very well, never the matter. The statue is clearly a threat to the safety and security of the agency. I'm having it removed and sent to a secure facility with limited personnel access."

"Wait," I said, getting to my feet. "You can't do that." The director's eyes darkened, pinning me with their glare. She wasn't used to being told no, and she wouldn't dare let me undermine her authority, especially in front of Jason.

Jason argued. "You can't be serious. Director, if you'd just listen for one second—"

"Enough. I've heard everything I need and made my decision. If you want to continue to press the subject, I advise you to choose your words carefully or find you've talked yourself out of a job, Agent Price."

The Director's shrewd eyes drifted over our faces. "Unless you can provide me a definitive answer as to why the three of you aren't currently among the victims that the CDC will actually buy, it's the only option."

The furrow in her brow deepened. "Don't be petulant. You should be grateful I'm keeping in Division 12 possession. If I really wanted to be an ass, I'd pass it off to the CDC, where I can guarantee it'd be immediately incinerated."

My stomach clenched at the threat. She had us backed into

a corner with no ground to stand on for defense. At least at Division, there was potential we could gain access to it again if the need arose.

Still, she might take the statue, but that didn't erase the fact that something had protected the three of us, even if we weren't next to each other. My subconscious had been working over-time ever since we'd stepped out of the elevator, attempting to sift through how we'd been unaffected, and yet the only answer I'd settled on was I still had a tendril of my magic. Buried some-where inside me that I'd managed to summon and shield us. However, there was no way in hell I could convince someone as pragmatic as the fierce redhead director standing in front of me. So, I lifted my chin, refusing to let my voice waiver, and answered. "I don't know."

Jason started to say something, an attempt to come to my defense, but the Director's raised hand stopped him.

"What you're saying then is that you and Agent Price were still en route when the earthquake occurred, and the elevator's malfunction was merely coincidental."

"Yes," I said definitively. I got it. She was covering the Agency's ass, and if I had to play into her little lie, then so be it. I'd do whatever it took to stay on her *and* Division 12's good side. Their connections and resources were too valuable to throw away on pride alone. If I wanted to know more about the statue, find out what disease had affected these people, and potentially restore my power, I couldn't be left out in the cold. Not to mention where Division was, Jason was, and I rather liked the idea of being a part of his inner circle than being left for days, not knowing where he was or what dangerous thing the agency had him on.

Director Ferguson closed the folder on her desk. A label had been affixed to the front with only the day's date and the word Ocala.

"As for what happens next, I'll need the three of you to remain here until we've had you cleared as well. While I have my doubts about this condition being contagious, the risk remains. Find a medic and get tested. I'll let you know if I need anything else."

It was as close to a dismissal as we were going to get, and after Jason murmured, "Yes, Director," we shuffled out of the room. Eddie's nose was buried in the notes on his iPad screen, and it was obvious he'd never stopped working since being called into her office.

With nowhere else to go, we started back down the stairs to the lab.

"I'm isolating the vibrations the statue produced," Eddie said as if we'd never stopped the conversation. "But since the statue wasn't being monitored when it was in my possession in the storage closet, I have no data to pull on from the exact moment of the earthquake."

"It's over," Jason said. "Ferguson has her mind made up, so we'd be better off dropping it." Resignation weighed his words, and I hated seeing this side of him. He'd surrendered.

I, however, was far from waving the white flag. I turned to Eddie as we continued making our way down. "When we first spoke, you said the vibrations coming from the statue were weak, and there was a chance I could amplify them. Nothing about that has changed, except in less than thirty minutes, you'll never get the chance to test your hypothesis again."

Eddie's eyes snapped up from the tablet; hook, line, and sinker, I'd snagged a scientist's attention. I'd witnessed many meteorologists risk their lives to capture anemometer or humidity readings in the middle of a hurricane. Scientists were more baller than society tended to give them credit for. "If I set the metrics to equal that of the seismic readings, I could set the thresholds to be equal for the algorithm..."

"Great. In English, for those of us who spend more time looking through sniper rifles instead of microscopes," Jason chided.

Eddie pursed his lips as if dumbing down his words was truly an effort. "I could set up an alert that would give us an advanced warning of when and where another earthquake will strike."

Jason halted as his left foot stepped on the landing. "No shit," he said, looking impressed. "Right. Let's get to it."

Back in the lab, Eddie's fingers flew furiously with keystrokes, and lines of code flashed over the screen. When he seemed satisfied, he reached into a drawer and pulled out a box of nitrile gloves.

"Here," he said. "The oils on your skin will react with the sensors."

I plucked two gloves from the box and slid them on while my stomach somersaulted with anticipation. After months of wondering and dreaming, I was going to finally know if the statue still contained any of the magic I hoped it did.

Eddie instructed me on how to correctly place my hands and fingers on the pieces of the statue before typing in the command that would activate the sensors. I followed his instructions, barely daring to breathe, and reached inside the box.

Gently, I placed my fingers on the idol's head and pressed the pieces together so it reformed the statue. The beeping monitor, the whir of the computer fans, and the steady beep of the seismograph all faded into the background. A silence fell upon my ears as a calmness blanketed me. A relaxed state of consciousness I only ever felt when I was tucked snugly against a sleeping Jason in the dark stillness of night.

The edges of the statue illuminated, causing the breath in my chest to freeze. The ancient power awakened, fusing the bronze and stone, blurring the lines until the stone was once more whole.

"Fuck yeah," Jason said, his voice distant as I remained focused on the fantastical scene unfolding before me.

The monitor lit up with a flurry of numbers and symbols as Eddie read them off, sounding more excited than I had heard before.

My vision blurred, and a tremor in my right hand caused my hand to cramp. Involuntarily, my hand curled into a ball, and I released my touch, and the statue crumbled, not into large fragments as before, but into actual, literal dust.

My pulse thundered in my ear, fear consuming me as I desperately reached out to scoop it into a pile. "No, no," I shouted, tears stinging the backs of my eyes. "What have I done."

A hand gripped my elbow, Jason's hand. "Stop. It's okay, Elly."

My frantic movements slowed, even as the pit of my stomach twisted. That was it. The last chance I'd had to restore my power was gone.

I turned and buried my head into Jason's shoulder, and he wrapped his arms around me. The warmth from his body seeped into me, easing the ache in my heart. Now that the door had closed, it felt more real than before, and I realized I'd been clinging to the hope that I could restore my power more than I'd known. A tether. A connection to my previous duty as Guardian. A duty I'd fulfilled yet wasn't yet ready to accept it being over. There was still so much good I could do in the world, people I could help, lives I could change if only I could tap into the magic.

Jason broke the embrace and stared at me; his eyes clouded with concern.

"I'm fine, Jason. Really," I lied.

"I don't believe you." His hands moved lower until they rested on my wrists. "You don't have to pretend with me. These past months, I've seen how not having your magic anymore is tearing you up inside. It's eating you alive, Elly. You need to let it go."

The first twangs of the champagne hangover I'd been dreading, combined with the jet lag and exhausting day, induced a throb in my temple. I didn't have the strength to argue with him or deny that his intuition had been wrong, so I simply nodded.

"With or without your gifts, you're still the fearless, determined, and obnoxiously stubborn woman I know. The woman I love."

Love.

He'd said it.

The word we'd danced around for weeks. The word neither of us dared speak, whether it be for fear of jinxing whatever good thing we had going or worry that it wouldn't be reciprocated, I couldn't say. And yet, he'd spoken it. Knowing my dream had been crushed, my heart broken. Jason loved me.

I blinked, trying to clear the tears from my vision, and reached up to gently caress his cheek. His eyes watched me expectantly, waiting for me to say it back, but Eddie, clearing his throat, interrupted us.

"So, uh... there's going to be another earthquake. And it's not going to be like the others. If my calculations are correct, which I'm certain they are, it's going to be a big one."

CHAPTER

EIGHT

"How big?" Jason asked in response to Eddie's announcement that another earthquake was imminent.

Eddie switched from his thumb to his pointer finger, his teeth gnawing at the edges of his thumbnail. "The pattern has changed. Something changed it, and where the others were 3.4 on the Richter scale, this one is predicted to be over a 5."

"Where?" I breathed.

"Thirty miles outside of Columbus."

"Ohio?" Jason asked, and Eddie responded with a nod. "Get me a detailed map of that area and identify any potential populated areas we'll need to evacuate." His eyes returned to mine, questioning whether I was okay or not. I pressed my lips together and flashed him a small smile, reassuring him I was okay. Although his gaze remained skeptical, he nodded and took out his phone. "I need to notify Ferguson."

My mouth had gone bone dry from the whirlwind of feelings wreaking havoc on my emotions. The statue turning to dust, Jason's admission of love, and now this, another earthquake, only bigger and potentially more deadly.

Jason sat the phone on the desk, hitting the speaker so we could all hear.

"Cancel it.," the Director said. "Whatever you're about to do, don't."

Jason rested his hands on the desk and stared down at the phone. "Director, we might have an impending disaster. It's not the time for subtlety."

"I heard. Steinberg with you? Is your data solid?" She said, not bothering to wait for him to answer.

Eddie sat up. "It's as solid as it can be. The seismic anomalies—"

"I said solid, not scientific," Ferguson interrupted.

"Yes, Director. It's solid," Eddie confirmed, swallowing hard.

"Good. Price, I want a clean mission. No toes out of line. Take a team of ten to evaluate and, if need be, evacuate. I'll reach out to my contacts and keep them on standby. But I want this handled discreetly. If we send in the cavalry and there's no earthquake, Division 12 loses credibility."

Jason's jaw tightened, but he nodded. "Understood, Director."

Jason ended the call, leaving the three of us in silence. A quake above five on the Richter scale was no joke. It had the potential to cause significant damage, maybe even fatalities. But then there was Eddie's hypothesis. Something had changed the pattern. What did that mean? My gut writhed with a cocktail of dread and skepticism.

My eyes drifted to one of the crates of supplies, and I stalked toward it.

"Elly," Jason said, his voice low like a warning. "What.? No. You're not going."

"Yeah, I am," I asserted, stopping in front of the plastic totes

I knew contained bulletproof vests. "You got a problem with that?"

"No, it's just—" He hesitated, his eyes shifting towards Eddie as if he would back him up. "We still don't know what it is we're up against. You're not an agent. I can't do my job if I'm too worried about protecting you."

My fingers paused on the strap of one of the vests, and I looked up, facing him. "Then don't," I said with a finality.

Jason groaned and strode toward me. "Please. This is just a reconnaissance mission."

"Exactly," I snapped, lifting my chin. "I heard the Director too. Evaluate and evacuate. Both are things I have done before. Twice in Pakistan and once in Ukraine. I can shoot a gun if I must, but this doesn't seem like that kind of situation, does it? So, what if there is an earthquake? Then you'll need all the more help you can get to get everyone to safety, and I don't need to be an expert marksman to guide people away from danger."

"Or read maps," Eddie chimed in.

Jason shot him a glare, and I couldn't help but smirk. "That too," I said.

Jason frowned, his jaw hardening, and for a split-second, I thought he'd stand firm, but then his eyes softened just a hair, and he let out a deep sigh. "All right, all right. You can be on my team. But stay close. I don't want you out of my sight for a second. Are we clear?"

"Crystal," I said, trying to contain the glee in my voice. The monotony of being stuck here was driving me crazy, with no other tangible ways to make any progress. I was another set of eyes, ears, and hands that could all be of use to the mission. Eddie caught my eye briefly; he looked hopeful yet tinged with unease. I looked away from him, focusing on the array of computer monitors displaying geographic data and schematics.

Jason moved with purpose, handing out gear from the stockpile of crates He helped me don a vest that was snug and laced with hidden pockets, gloves that gripped like a second skin, a radio, and a combat knife that felt reassuringly heavy. As I stashed the knife into one of the pockets, Jason was already filling another bag with tech gear and assorted essentials, his actions meticulously precise.

Before I could tease him about his having fantasies about seeing me in combat gear, the sound of footsteps resonated in the room. Other agents from Division 12 filed in from the central doorway, some two or three at a time, others by themselves. Jason greeted the first woman, O'Malley, with her sharp bob and sharper gaze, who was next to Davis, a burly guy whose muscles seemed to ripple as he walked. Wilson and Henry followed, both portraying fierce stares and a quiet intensity that made me glad they were on my side.

Jason, now laden with his own set of gear, stepped up to address the room. "Listen up, everyone. Thanks for coming on such short notice. I'm not sure how much the director relayed to you, but we've been alerted to the potential of seismic events targeting particular locations. Our job is to find out what's causing them and neutralize the threat. To do that, we'll need to split into two teams."

"Ah, so Price is running the show now?" O'Malley smirked as she checked her sidearm, her voice tinged with sarcasm. "Director Ferguson finally took your training wheels off?"

Jason didn't flinch. "I can assure you; the training wheels came off a long time ago. So, buckle up. Any other questions?"

Kevin chuckled. "Fate's a funny thing, isn't it?"

"Only when it doesn't get you killed," Jason replied, pulling a tablet from one of the crates and firing it up to display a map. "Team One, you're going to the epicenter of the most recent quake. Linda, Kevin, you're with me. Team Two—Taylor, Henry, Miller—you're headed to the university campus to secure the statue for study. Both locations have shown abnormal energy spikes. Ella, you'll be with me, coordinating communication between the teams."

I nodded, as he watched me, waiting for me to argue, but I'd gotten what I wanted. To be out there, at ground zero, and hopefully find out more about what was happening.

"Gear up," Jason then continued, "Standard issue weapons, but also bring EMF detectors and thermal imaging cameras. If these events are supernatural, we need to document it."

Everyone moved, a sense of urgency filling the room as agents collected their gear. I watched Jason interact with them, his eyes focused, the lines of his face hard. Yet, when he looked at me, something in his expression softened as if seeking reassurance or perhaps offering it. My heart squeezed; we were in this together, yet worlds apart.

Taylor strapped on her vest before joining Miller, Henry, Jason, and me as we made our way toward the exit.

I glanced at Eddie, who was supporting an uneasy smile with a thumbs up, before looking away to refocus on the computer monitors.

***

The van ride to the country club from the Columbus airport was nearly silent, only occasionally interrupted by commands from Jason regarding intermittent data updates from Eddie, who was monitoring the situation remotely.

The closer we got to the site, the tighter the knot in my stomach grew. We pulled up to the rendezvous point, and I saw the other agents riding with us, faces taut with concern but eager to get started.

"Remember, clean mission," Jason reminded everyone as we disembarked. "We get in, assess, and get out. Any questions?"

No one spoke.

"Good. Then let's go," Jason ordered.

CHAPTER
NINE

"So, what exactly am I supposed to be looking for?" Jason asked Eddie's face on his phone's screen. "All I'm seeing is over-fertilized grass and a bunch of rich white guys probably discussing which mutual fund to add to their 401k."

"The seismograph says coordinates are 23 degrees, 35 degrees."

The director's face appeared, blocking Eddie from our view.

"Getting everyone evacuated is the first priority. The board forced my hand to put a call into CDC, FBI, and the National Guard, so I want anything interesting picked up and bagged before they show up and get their hands on it."

"Noted," Jason said, as if he completely understood, although I was left at a loss for what defined "interesting" these days for Division 12.

Jason and I filed out of the back of the SUV, while behind us, the other team of six Division agents exited theirs. With their face masks, black jumpsuits, bulletproof vests, and weapons belts, they were hard to discern as individuals. Which I suppose is the idea. Anonymity gives power. If I were an enemy and recognized the agent as an individual person, I might also recognize their weakness or assume I could.

And now I was one of them, attired in the all-black uniform, with my own vest strapped around my chest.

"I'd feel better with a gun," I said as Jason closed the door to the truck and moved to where I was standing.

He shook his head. "I'm sure, but we're here strictly on info collection and evacuation orders. I don't see any need—"

"Just give her a gun already, Price," a woman said, and another agent appeared beside my shoulder. "The Director sent her on the mission with us. She should be prepared like us." Over the top of her gray mask peered deep brown eyes with lovely long lashes. I tried to picture her without the mask, wondering if I'd seen her before, but it was no use. There had to be hundreds of agents at Division, most of whom worked especially hard to keep themselves out of the public eye or fraternize outside of missions for any number of safety concerns.

Jason glared at the woman before rolling his eyes. "Fine." He pulled open the passenger's door and popped open the glove compartment. He took the small Beretta with a silver grip and held it out for me. As I reached, his fingers closed over it, and I looked up.

His brow furrowed, worry clouding his blue eyes.

I forced a smile, trying to reassure him. "I'll be careful. Promise."

At first, Jason didn't move, and there was a split second I feared he would rescind his offer and take away the gun, but instead, he let out a sigh and unfurled his fingers.

"For the record, I'd feel better if you stayed in the truck."

"For the record, that's never gonna happen," I replied, taking the pistol from him, which was surprisingly heavy for its small size. I clipped it into the holster at my belt. Another fun accessory these tactical uniforms came with—fashion and functionality. Maybe I should join Division 12. The second the thought crossed my mind, I recoiled internally. And take orders without question from people like Ferguson?

Nope. I liked doing my own thing very much.

Jason, now mildly irritated but resigned to my being armed, ushered the other agents over to him.

"You've all been briefed on the mission. We have thirty minutes to get everyone within a two-mile perimeter evacuated. It's a simple job, everyone. Beckett, you take Alpha. You take the north end of the course and sweep back. Bravo stays with me, and we'll work our way from the south to the clubhouse. Do what you need to do to get these people out of here before the earthquake hits. Let's not fuck this up."

The woman, who'd taken my side to convince Jason to give me the gun I now knew to be Beckett, stepped up and called out the names of three other agents.

Jason summoned two others to come with us. A Black woman with a scar just visible down the left side of her face, and a pockmarked face man with forearms bigger than my thighs.

Jason's eyes swept over us and lingered on me a second more. "Stay close." He started down the grassy slope that descended onto the eighteen-hole golf course. The perfectly manicured green of the golf course was lush and inviting, punctuated by a half-dozen ponds as it dipped and carved into the land. The wind blew through the willows and palms, rustling its leaves, causing shadows to dance on its velvet-like surface, and it was hard to fathom those hundreds of feet beneath them. The crust of the earth was compressing, compounding against itself, and building pressure of immeasurable force that would soon cause the ground to shake and crack violently.

We descended onto the seventh hole, Division 12 agents fanning out like a tactical comb on my flanks. Jason beside me studied the screen of the seismic reader Eddie had given him, occasionally glancing up and altering his direction. As promised, I stayed close to him.

He shifted the device's dial as Eddie's voice cut into my earpiece.

"There, right where you are now, drift a little more North. Vibrations are spiking. See anything?"

"Negative," Jason replied next to me, and a split second later, I heard his voice echo in my earbud. Over a small hill, we approached a golf cart, and a pair of startled golfers clutched their clubs, preparing to tee off. "What's going on here?" the first man said with a Titleist ball cap and golf shoes that cost more than my monthly rent. "We were told this was a private course," he continued, "Who authorized you to be here?"

"National security," Jason flashed his Division 12 ID quickly, too fast for them to read it, but long enough, it caused their annoyance to turn to trepidation. Jason straightened his shoulders, taking up his full six-foot-three height. "There's a possibility of an environmental hazard, and I'd advise you to leave. Now."

Before they could complain further, a loud crack of thunder erupted from a grove of trees enveloping one of the ponds no more than a hundred yards from us. The sound reverberated off the landscape, and an enormous bolt of lightning struck nearby. The odd thing was the sky was clear. Not a single cloud drifted above us. Jason and I locked eyes just as the ground roared.

Every muscle in my body tensed as the world trembled beneath my feet. Division 12 agents darted past us, shouting for the people to run and take cover.

"What the hell is happening?" someone yelled. My nose caught the stench of sulfur, and an acrid tang clawed at my throat. I pulled my shirt collar over my nose, trying to filter the air.

Trees collapsed like surrendering soldiers, their leaves a blur of green as they fell. Rocks and gravel burst from the splitting earth as though mini-volcanoes were erupting around us. Dodging the showering dirt and debris, Jason charged ahead, and I followed, but I'd barely managed twenty steps before the ground buckled beneath me, tossing me sideways where I fell and tumbled down into a sand trap.

Gritting my teeth against the jolt of pain, I scrambled to my feet. It seemed to me as though I were on the verge of a sinking ship, desperately clutching at the shifting ground, struggling to find balance and stand. Jason's voice, his shout, cut through the cacophony of cracking tree branches and frantic screams, "Elly! Where are you?"

I turned, searching for him through the billowing dust and ash. The earth shifted again, a widening crevice zigzagging between us like a snake. "Jason!" I screamed, but he was gone, swallowed by the ashen haze.

Heart pounding, I stared at the place where he'd been, my mind racing.

As the earth continued its dance of destruction, I pivoted and ran, the crack's widening maw chasing me like a hungry predator. I felt more than heard the rumbling now, a deep vibration that sang in my bones, in my soul.

I keyed my earpiece, coughing against the sulfur-infused air, "Eddie, talk to me? What do we do?"

"Still figuring that out," his voice crackled in my ear. "Get everyone away from the trees and buildings. Try and find higher ground!"

"Will do!" I retorted as I sprinted uphill, dodging falling branches and agents directing dust-covered golfers and country clubgoers to the parking lot.

Something loomed ahead through the dust—a boulder, newly birthed from the earth's tremors. I made for it, leaping atop its rough surface just as another crack split the ground where I'd stood moments before. I caught my breath, my heart drumming a frenetic rhythm in my chest.

As I scanned the scene for signs of Jason or any other Division 12 agents, a dark figure materialized through the swirls of dust and ash. About a hundred feet away, it stood like a beacon of shadow. At first, I thought it was a disoriented golfer who had become paralyzed in terror, but then I realized he wore a billowing black coat that seemed to absorb the ambient light. While it was humanoid in shape, tall and without hair, it was his eyes—or rather, the dark pits where his eyes should have been—that seized my attention.

The world around me became a muffled echo as if someone had turned down the volume. It was just him and me, or *it* and me. I couldn't assume anything about this *thing* at this distance.

"You, Guardian. *You* are the one who opened the bridge," his voice resonated directly into my mind, deep and gravelly as if spoken through a layer of earth.

"I am," I answered mentally, not sure how I was doing it, but confident that I was. They were here. *It* was here. The thing causing all the earthquakes and the strange disease forcing people into comas. I couldn't let them escape, not without getting some answers. I swallowed the rising fear in my throat. "Who the hell are you?"

The figure knelt, placing his hands on the ground. As if in response to his touch, the earth cracked open, a new split forking outward from him like lightning captured in soil. "I am Asag. But it does not matter, for I am one of many."

"Why are you doing this?" I shouted, "What do you want?"

"My brothers and sisters know I am free, and they cry out to me," he pounded his chest hard like they were trapped inside it.

"They long to be free, too, and I will not stop until it is done. The seals must be broken. The vessels must be ready."

Vessels? What vessels?

This had gone on long enough. I needed to see him, *face* him so I could recognize who it was or rather *what* it was we were fighting. Before I knew it, my legs were moving, propelling me toward him with a mind of their own in an attempt to get a better look. The distance between us shrank as I sprinted, my adrenaline-spiked blood erasing any awareness of the trembling ground or the sulfurous air. His face came into clearer focus, and just as it felt like I could almost touch him, he vanished, evaporating into the thickening haze.

But I didn't stop. I couldn't. My legs were on autopilot, carrying me farther into the chaos. Ash and dust filled my vision, each inhalation becoming a battle. I stumbled, disoriented, my ears filling with a cacophony of disembodied voices and guttural roars. I felt like I was running through a maze of smoke and illusion, the world itself playing tricks on me.

And then, just as abruptly, I burst free. The air cleared, and I found myself at the entrance of the country club, overlooking the path that led to whatever version of civilization existed beyond this hellish landscape. I gasped for air, doubling over with my hands on my knees.

I straightened up and clenched my fists. Asag had communicated with me and singled me out as the one who had "opened the bridge." The ramifications sent a shiver down my spine. And what did he mean by his 'brothers and sisters'?

I reached for my earpiece, eager to hear a human voice, even if it was Eddie nattering on about seismic anomalies. But before I could make contact, I paused. A sensation crawled up my spine, an unsettling awareness that Asag—wherever or whatever he was—was still watching me.

"My brothers and sisters know I am free," his voice echoed

again in my head. A chill shot through me, freezing me to the core. If Asag was just one of many, then this was far from over. He had plans, and something told me those plans were about as stable as the ground beneath my feet had been minutes ago.

I started to turn back toward the devastation, considering the need to find Jason and regroup with Division 12, but then a voice stopped me.

"Please," a woman said with a whimper.

I moved under the grand entrance to the country club. Wooden columns and beams soared overheard, and several luxury sports cars parked at the valet station. Adrenaline slammed into my veins as I burst into the splintered remains of the country club's foyer and further into the dining area. What was once a chandeliered symbol of affluence was now a war zone—the floor covered in broken glass, shattered tables, and twisted beams.

The air smelled like spilled wine mixed with burning wood and the sharp tang of blood. Moans stifled screams, and the ominous creaking of a compromised structure filled the air. My eyes flitted around, taking it in. That's when I saw her—a middle-aged woman in an olive-green golf outfit, with her left arm pinned under a massive wooden beam.

I sprinted over and immediately was soaked through by the emergency sprinkler system attempting to put out whatever fires had started inside.

The woman peered up at me and smiled weakly. "My arm," she murmured. "I can't feel my arm."

My pulse quickened, an odd mixture of dread and determination filling me. "It's okay," I said, squatting beside her and examining the extent of the damage, where the four-inch chunk of ceiling lay over her shoulder. Ignoring the trembling in my hands, I groaned as I tried to lift the mess of Sheetrock and wood.

It barely moved.

"Damn it!" I snarled, and the trapped woman let out a mournful whine. "Don't worry," I said, "I promise I won't leave you." I started to stand, intending to find another board to use as a lever, when a man's voice made me jump.

"Need a hand?" A young Black server, blood trickling down from a gash on his forehead, appeared next to me.

"Yes, please," I said. Together, we grunted, our muscles burning with the effort, and finally lifted the piece of ceiling just high enough for the woman to crawl out. As soon as she was free, the man crouched next to her and helped her get to her feet.

I covered my mouth, coughing at the dust and intensifying smoke drifting in the air. "You need to get to the parking lot now!" I commanded her. The floorboards groaned beneath us as if in warning.

"There's more people, though," the server said, looking over his shoulder. "Inside. There was a tournament, and they're in the banquet room."

"This whole place is a death trap," I yelled over the sound of a loud rumbling from what I assumed was another section of the building collapsing. "Any second, this whole hill could slide. Go, take her to safety! I'll get the others."

He swallowed, weighing my words as he hesitated, but something in my eyes must have convinced him because, finally, he nodded and took the good arm of the shaken woman. Half carrying her, he hustled them out of the dining room and toward the front doors.

I spun on my heel and ventured further into the dining room, keeping my breathing even as I listened and looked for any signs of life. My gut wrenched as I spotted two lifeless bodies near a toppled display case. The wood frame splintered, and the broken shards of the window showered their faces and bodies with glass. I kept moving, and the acrid stench of smoke led me to the kitchen, where licking flames were now visible through the bar. Three people stumbled past me under the haze of smoke lingering on the ceiling. Their faces were maps of dust and blood, and their eyes were wide with terror as I shouted at them to get to the exit.

The building gave a deafening groan. My mind spiraled with images of the entire building splitting in two and sloughing off the hill with me trapped inside.

Forcing my legs into motion, I sprinted through the kitchen and found four guests shouting from the other side of a locked storage room. A rack of pans had fallen in front of it, blocking them in, and I frantically hurried to heave it backward, allowing them to pry open the door a foot and squeeze through. They didn't bother to thank me as they bolted out of the kitchen and disappeared. The earth grumbled again, a low, dangerous sound that made me think of monsters under the bed. Only this monster was real, and it was about to consume everything in its path. Eddie's voice crackled in broken fractions of words in my ear, and I tore it out, wishing to keep my ears alert for any more sounds.

Clambering over toppled furniture and splintered doors struck too close to home as it felt like navigating a war zone. My heart pounded like a jackhammer in my chest, and each beat syncopated with the blaring of the fire alarms. Smoke choked the air, a noxious blend of burned wood and melting plastic that filled my lungs and blurred my eyes, making it harder to see the further I went.

"Move, move, move!" Frantic people surged past me, shoving and scrambling in their desperation. From the corner of my eye, I caught sight of several individuals leaping through shattered windows, landing on what I hoped was solid ground not too far below.

Finally, I staggered into the banquet room, drenched in sweat and gasping from the thick air. My eyes immediately locked onto a banner hanging lopsidedly on the wall: "Twenty-Second Ladies Luncheon and Summer Golf Tournament."

The sprinklers above still sputtered, casting a fine mist over everything. People were strewn across the room, some nursing injuries, others in a daze of disorientation.

I hurried over to a woman clutching her wrist, her face contorted in pain, and helped her to her feet, steering her toward the door. "Go, now!" I shouted above the din of alarms and human distress.

An older man's voice sliced through the din. "Help! Someone, help!"

My gaze located him; he was doubled over, his hands on his knees, coughing as if trying to expel his lungs. I reached him in seconds, my own breath coming in ragged gulps.

"Can you walk?" I grabbed his arm, hoisting him upright.

He nodded weakly. But as we took a step, the wood floorboards beneath us let out a groan of surrender, splintering violently. Instinctively, I pulled back, toppling backward to avoid tripping him.

My eyes widened in terror. A gap had appeared on the floor, revealing a dark crawlspace teeming with a mess of broken pipes and twisting wires. It was like staring into the mouth of some subterranean monster waiting to swallow me whole.

My body went into overdrive, hands scrabbling against the floor as I tried to claw my way backward. Desperation to not plunge into the dark pit induced a surge of primal fear to rocket through me—this was it. I was going to be buried alive in this hellhole.

Just as the heel of my boot slipped over the ledge of the splintered floor, a hand shot out, gripping my elbow with iron strength, and yanked me back onto solid ground. I shoved myself away from that gaping maw in the floor, and only when I was a safe distance from it did I finally allow myself to breathe.

My fingers ached where I'd torn several nails in my attempt not to slide down, and my shoulder ached where I'd collapsed onto the floor. Finally, I looked up, wondering who my savior was, and my breath caught in my throat. A teenage boy—dressed in a black suit and apron, the attire of a caterer stood looming over me. His dark brown hair was wavy and badly in need of a cut. His hazel eyes looked almost calm amidst the chaos, but what caught my attention most were the intricate designs of iridescent blue tattoos snaking up his left arm, visible only through a torn sleeve.

"Dude, finally," he said, his voice tinged with a strange enthusiasm. He fist-pumped the air as if he'd just scored the winning goal. "What's up, Guardian? I'm Gavin."

TEN

I blinked, disoriented.

He'd called me a Guardian?

"Wait, what?" My mind raced, trying to catch up like I'd missed the first half of a movie and was confused by the twist.

Gavin just grinned, a little too smug of a smile that seemed completely out of place, and in that bizarre moment of mutual recognition—amid sprinklers and sirens and the ever-present scent of danger— I felt a subtle shift in the air.

Things had just gone from catastrophic to surreal. My gut churned with a swirl of emotions. "I'm Ella," I said abruptly, shaking off my daze from the waning adrenaline and climbing to my feet. "I have so many questions, but first, can you help me get everyone out?"

Gavin's grin widened as if he'd been expecting just that sort of response, then blinked as if suddenly remembering where we were. "Uh yeah, sure."

A second later, I'd recovered enough and plunged back into action, scoping out more survivors. The room was a mess of strewn chairs, spilled food, broken glass, upturned tables, and disoriented people. We set to work, hoisting tables and shoving aside debris, our movements synchronized in the unspoken language of urgency.

Somewhere back toward the dining room, a loud explosion erupted, and I imagined one of the gas lines had burst.

"Are there any other exits?" I hollered over the noise.

"Yeah. Emergency exit, one room over," Gavin shot back, pointing toward what looked like a service door half-obscured by a fallen bookshelf.

"Let's go, people!" I yelled, my voice carrying over the alarms and the continual hissing of the sprinklers. I locked eyes with a middle-aged man in a tux, his face marred with soot. "You, help her," I ordered, pointing to an older woman clutching her arm.

Gavin led the way, his tattoos catching the flickering light like some kind of ethereal armor. We reached the door, yanked it open, and found ourselves in another room, this one smaller and less damaged but still showing signs of the catastrophe—cracked walls, broken vases, a few people crouched under tables.

"Come on!" Gavin bellowed, waving them over. "Through here!" Gavin called out, already wrenching open the emergency exit.

We corralled as many as we could find, and I shoved down the sinking sensation that there were more people we were leaving behind. However, our time had run out, and there was nothing more to be done.

The world outside hit me like a slap in the face—bright daylight, the tang of fresh air mixed with the smell of burning wood, and the stark contrast was disorienting. We spilled out onto the lawn, an uneven, staggering wave of humanity.

Behind us, the building let out a final, agonizing groan, a sound so deeply unsettling it seemed to reverberate in my bones, and then, with a roar that drowned out even the loudest of screams, it collapsed inward and down, spewing a monstrous cloud of dust and debris into the air.

My heart seized in my chest, realizing how very close we'd all been to going down with it.

The earth gave a final, low rumble, and then the shaking ceased. As we stood there, panting and bewildered, watching the mushroom cloud of dust settle over where the building had once stood, Gavin turned to me. The soot and sweat that streaked his face couldn't hide the gravity of his expression. "Guess we've got a lot to talk about, huh?"

"Yeah," I managed, my voice tinged with awe and something else I couldn't quite identify. "We sure do."

I looked around at the shell-shocked faces of the people we'd helped save, then back at Gavin. Whatever the hell was going on, whatever I was, or he was, or we were supposed to be, would have to wait.

For now, I needed to find Jason. My insides twisted as worry gnawed at my skull that something had happened to him. Quickly, I pressed the earbud back into my ear. I pressed the talk button. "It's Dawson," I said, "can anyone hear me?"

An eternity of a second later, Jason's voice reverberated inside my head. "God dammit, Elly," he said, his voice thick with overwhelming relief. "Thank god. Where are you? Are you hurt?"

"I'm at the top of the hill. I got as many people out of the country club as I could."

"Stay there," he commanded, and I felt a warmth spread across my chest at the protective edge in his voice. I hated the idea that I scared him, but my god, was he sexy when he was worried about me.

The black Division 12 SUVs roared up the hill like knights in shining, mechanical armor soon after. The doors popped open, and agents I recognized—Maria, Kevin, and Liam—spilled out. Faces covered in soot and ash, Kevin limped to the back door, taking out first aid kits and emergency gear. Without a word, they scattered among the survivors, their hands skillful and swift as they tended to wounds, applied makeshift splints, and performed triage.

Jason, however, darted straight toward me. His eyes met mine, and everything else, as it often did when he was around, faded away. He wrapped his arms around me so tightly it was almost painful, breathing into my hair as he murmured, "I told you to stay right next to me. God dammit, Elly, I thought I fucking lost you."

His voice broke, and that crack in his stoic façade stabbed me more deeply than any physical wound. "I'm here. I'm fine," I assured him, even though the skeptical look he shot me when he finally stepped back said he was far from convinced.

His eyes skimmed over me, assessing me from head to toe to confirm that I was okay. "Really, I'm fine." I insisted. "A few bruises are all, thanks to him, actually," I said, my gaze going to Gavin perched on a stone bench a few feet away.

Just as he opened his mouth to say something, the wail of approaching sirens drowned out any further conversation. Local county ambulances, fire trucks, and even a couple of news vans rolled up, turning the putting green into a makeshift emergency zone. Paramedics took over from our Division 12 agents, administering oxygen, rolling out gurneys, and taking blood pressure. Firefighters focused their hoses on the now fully engulfed remains of the country club. We watched momentarily as emergency services began to swarm the parking lot. Sirens wailed, people shouted, but I was enveloped in a sudden, eerie calm. The waning adrenaline was sending my body into shock, and I suddenly didn't trust my legs to hold me. I sidestepped to the bench beside Gavin and collapsed.

Jason rushed to me, and his face visibly paled. "Holy shit. Your hands," he said, fear punctuating his words.

I peered down at where they lay on my lap, and in the light of the day, the jagged and torn edges of the broken fingernails caused nausea to pool in the back of my throat. Jason disappeared, then reappeared with a paramedic carrying a blue medic bag, demanding she disinfect my hands, which were caked in dried blood. Not all of which I was sure was mine.

There definitely were other people far more injured than me who needed her attention, but Jason's crossed arms. She peered at him curiously, her mouth twisted in annoyance. "I'll tend to hers if you let me look at yours?"

Jason's jaw shifted as he lay his right hand over the back of his left, clearly trying to hide something.

"Elly first," he said.

The paramedic gave his hand a final look, then turned to me. "Fine. You should get a tetanus booster just to be safe."

She ripped open the Velcro pouch on her bag, and reluctantly, I held out my hands for her to clean and bandage them. She barely spent a minute before she was done, and Jason stepped aside, letting her move on to the rest of the injured.

"What happened to your hand?" I asked when she'd gone.

"It's nothing," he said.

"Jason," I replied, leveling him with my best 'don't bullshit me' look.

Jason sighed and slowly lowered his hand, revealing a small scrape no more than an inch across above his knuckles. "I couldn't see shit in the smoke. I must've cut it on something. A tree branch or rock or—"

"Or a rusty piece of metal fence."

"Possible," Jason said, idly scratching the wound. "Division has my immunization records. I'll check when my last one is when we get back to base."

I nod, pleased he was taking this seriously.

I heard Gavin talking with a paramedic right behind me, receiving similar treatment, though he kept stealing curious glances in my direction. The questions hung between us like a magnetic force; I could feel their pull but wasn't sure how to broach them.

Finally, I took the plunge and cleared my throat. "Jason, this is Gavin. He helped me get people out."

Gavin extended his hand, that strange, indigo tattoo still catching my eye. "Nice to meet you, man. So, you're like CIA or something?"

Jason looked at me, a moment of silent communication passing between us. I wasn't going to decide for him whether he could be trusted or not. Sure, he knew I was a Guardian, but I'd only just met him.

"No, not CIA. Division 12," Jason finally said, extending his hand to shake Gavin's. "It's a private security firm. We collaborate with various government agencies."

Gavin's eyebrows shot up. "Security? Isn't that for spy stuff? This was an earthquake," He paused, licking his lips with a little too much enthusiasm. "Or wasn't it?"

"We're still looking into it," Jason answered cautiously. "Anomalies like this are only a part of what we investigate."

Gavin shrugged. "Sure, sure. I get it."

"What were you doing here?" I asked. "Is there someone we need to call for you?"

Gavin took out his phone. "I already texted my grandparents and told them not to freak out and that I'm good. Since I graduated, I've been working here over the summer."

"So," I began, turning back to Gavin, "you called me a 'Guardian.' How did you—"

"Ninurta told me," Gavin interrupted as if it was the most natural thing in the world. "He's the one who gave me these tattoos." He glanced at his left arm, the intricate designs shimmering slightly. "You see, I'm a Guardian too."

My world, already tilted on its axis, seemed to shift yet again. I looked at Jason, then back at Gavin. What the hell was going on?

Gavin looked both ways nervously, like a kid about to jaywalk, then said, "Look, I can do some stuff, okay? But I don't want it to become, like, a big thing, you know?"

Jason and I exchanged glances as if daring the other to speak first. I mean, we'd seen our fair share of "big" stuff, so what could this kid possibly do to scare us?

"What kind of 'stuff' are we talking about?" Jason finally asked, ever the professional.

Gavin's hazel eyes narrowed for a moment, gauging whether he could trust us. "Well, the first thing is I can control electricity. Like Thor only without the hammer?" He watched us, trying to determine if we were familiar with the reference.

"We know who Thor is," I said, gesturing for him to continue.

Gavin smiled quickly. "Cool. So yeah, I won't do it here because, well, because first the power lines are down and I need electricity to control it, I can't make it. And second," he hesitated, scratching the back of his neck. "Well, I'm not the best at controlling it yet."

"I suggest you don't," Jason interjected, seemingly unfazed by Gavin's admission he had magical powers. "There are enough hurt people already."

Gavin's mouth turned up at the corner with a timid smile. "No worries, I won't, but there is one other thing." He stared up at us, then, sensing he had *our* full attention, bent down and pressed his hand to the green turf. Tiny white flowers bloomed around his palm, sprouting like nature was answering his beck and call.

"Not sure how that'll ever be useful, but it's still dope, right?" Gavin said, grinning proudly.

My eyes widened at the show of magic, and I chuckled. "Sure is," I said, though my mind was racing a mile a minute.

Gavin's eyes met mine, and my stomach clenched, anticipating his question. "So, what about you? What's your superpower? Control the wind? Go invisible?" His eyes widened, and he clapped his hands together like he'd just had an epiphany. "No way, can you fly?"

I opened my mouth to answer, the familiar lump forming in my throat at the prospect of admitting my lack of powers, but before I could utter a word, Jason cut in, saving me.

"We have reason to believe that there's still a threat present. For your safety, we need you to come with us back to the Division 12 base if that's alright?" Jason's voice was authoritative, commanding even, but there was an undertone of concern there.

Gavin's eyebrows lifted, a mixture of surprise and intrigue painting his face. "Uh, sure. But I have to ask—am I being arrested or something?"

Jason shot him a stern look that didn't reach his eyes. "No, you're not being arrested. However, we *do* need to figure out what's going on. And I'm not comfortable with the idea of letting you return home if your powers are uncontrolled."

Gavin nodded, seemingly okay with not having all the pieces of the puzzle. Hell, none of us did. "Alright, cool. Lead the way."

We piled into the SUV, Jason taking the driver's seat, and I hopped in the passenger's side while Gavin took the back. For a moment, my eyes lingered on Jason's hand, resting protectively on my thigh, and I felt warmth flush through me, remembering how he'd hugged me like he'd never let go.

Then he shifted and went to the key in the ignition to start it. Soon after, he was steering the SUV back toward the Division 12 base, weaving through the emergency vehicles, and the world outside seemed oddly quiet, as if it, too, was holding its breath, waiting for whatever came next.

During the airplane ride back to Florida, I kept stealing glances at Gavin. His expression was unreadable, a quiet sort of pensiveness clouding his features. How did he fit into all this? Who—or what—was Ninurta? Was there another statue out there like mine that he had found and been gifted his powers? If so, where was it now, and why had it chosen him? And then there was the part that weighed on me the most: why did Gavin already seem to know more about what was going on than I did?

I felt Jason's hand squeeze mine gently, pulling me back from my whirlpool of thoughts. When I looked up, he was watching me, his eyes full of questions he was holding back for the moment. As reassuring as his touch was, it also served as a poignant reminder of how much was at stake and how quickly things had spiraled beyond our control.

Finally, we disembarked and were loaded into another awaiting SUV that drove us to the Division 12 warehouse.

"Welcome to Division 12," Jason said, gesturing toward the entrance as if presenting a grand palace.

Gavin looked up at the building, then back at us. "So, do I get a badge or something?"

"No, no badge," Jason replied. "But if you're lucky, I'll let you flicker the lights on and off during power outages. Trust me, it's a coveted position here."

Gavin snorted and shook his head while I rolled my eyes. We'd met another Guardian, like me, and Jason had taken it all in stride, not missing a beat and acting like this was the most normal thing in the world. And to be honest, I was grateful for it because every waking hour felt like we were heading into a new kind of normal, a reality where battling demons and closing otherworldy gates was as commonplace as complaining about traffic.

I reached for the door, and Gavin's eyes landed on the faded silver scar of the eight-pointed star on my hand.

"Looks like we've got more in common than we thought," Gavin said, tugging up his right sleeve to reveal an eight-pointed star inked into the space above his right wrist. My eyes immediately focused on the little symbol, and a cold shiver zipped between my shoulder blades. "Guess the gods have a flair for the dramatic, huh?"

Gavin smirked and lowered his sleeve. "Certainly seems that way."

Jason's steady gaze met mine. "Once we're inside, let me take the lead with the debrief, okay?"

Gavin and I nodded in unison. I smelled of ash and sweat, and the pain medication the paramedic had given me had worn off, leaving the tips of my fingers throbbing. I also hadn't eaten anything since early that morning, but a shower and meal could wait. But first, we had a lot of talking to do, and I had a feeling it was going to be one hell of a conversation.

CHAPTER

ELEVEN

As Jason led us through the maze-like corridors, I couldn't shake the sense of unease. I had my own shit to deal with, my own powers to recover, and here I'd found another with the same fate as me. A boy. A *kid* whom an ancient god had blessed to be their champion.

Never could I have imagined I'd find someone else with this connection, and yet we couldn't have been more opposite. I couldn't remember the last time I'd had to make small talk with a high schooler, and since my mom had sent me to an all-girls school until college, even at twenty-five, it felt beyond awkward.

I glanced down at the name-brand high tops and took a stab in the dark. "So, do you play basketball?" I tried.

Gavin stuffed his hands in the front pocket of his hooded sweatshirt. "Yep, ever since I was five."

"You any good?"

"Full-ride offers from three colleges," Gavin replied, a hint of pride lacing his voice. "But when Ninurta appeared to me and made me his champion. Kind of made college sorta seem pointless now?" He paused and held the door open for me as I stepped into the steel catwalks crisscrossing the old garment factory warehouse, illuminated in places by buzzing fluorescent lights. They were wide enough for two people to traverse side by side, but even then, they shook and creaked in protest as we navigated our way down the three flights of stairs. A single layer of plywood divided me from what seemed like an infinite abyss below. My pulse quickened just as a cold sweat soaked into my clothing with each step closer to the edge.

"What about you?" Gavin asked, seemingly unaffected by the precarious pathway. "When did you get your superpowers?"

His question was a sucker punch, but it also distracted me from the creaking of the century-old bolts that were all that held the stairway aloft. "Actually, I lost my powers recently. My connection to Inanna, well...it broke," I confessed.

Gavin laughed, and a wry smile formed on his face. "Broke?" he said. "These are gods we're talking about; they can't just break." His expression shifted, and he arched an eyebrow. "Oh shit, did you do something to piss her off?"

I frowned and shook my head. "No," I replied, "I didn't piss her off." At least, I didn't think I did. "There was this statue, a bronze idol of her that acted like a battery, and when I stopped the Bridge from opening, it broke."

Gavin stopped at the next landing and met my eyes. He was so tall, even with a two-stair advantage, he met me at eye level. "So, I get I'm new to all this, but I didn't have a battery or anything like that. Ninurta said I was his champion, and the next day, *bam*, powers. Are you sure that's why they're gone?"

I looked at Gavin, studying the sincerity etched into his face and the question he'd just asked that had haunted me for months. "I honestly don't know."

Gavin tilted his head, considering my words. "We can figure

it out. But until then, you're still you, aren't you? Powers or not. That's got to count for something."

I smiled, touched by his kind words. "I guess it does." *I hope it does.*

Gavin started once more down the final flight of clanging stairs. "You know, last summer, when I crashed my dirt bike, I broke my arm a month before the division championship. So, coach told me if I wanted to play, I had to learn to shoot with my left hand. I spent every hour before school or on the weekends in our driveway, taking shot after shot at the hoop on our garage, and when I got frustrated, my grandma would say that sometimes we find our strength when we're at our weakest."

He paused, allowing his words to hang in the air, giving me the space to consider them. Could it really be that simple? Perhaps the statue had been a crutch I'd been leaning on, and I needed to learn to walk without it. Okay, running was more like it if we wanted any chance at stopping these demons, but I'd settle for crawling on all four at this point. I wanted to believe him, but self-doubt was a fickle bitch, especially when you relied on something that no longer existed.

We stepped off the last step and onto the warehouse floor. Gleaming steel and glass loomed everywhere; the central area having been transformed with the humming with the sounds of technology. Along one wall were banks of computers teeming with information, while in a nearby corner, security cameras monitored every movement within its walls. In another area lay folding tables with various machinery and electronic equipment. Within hours, Division 12 had transformed this decrepit building into a sanctum secluded from the prying eyes of the government and where they could continue their work without interruption.

A circular table had been set up with various snacks, fruits, and coffee, and Gavin and I made a beeline for it. After loading up a plate with a bag of chips and a banana, I strode past a dozen agents in suits and ties, tapping away on keyboards. While a few gave me a curious glance, most ignored me. I doubted many knew I was Jason's girlfriend since personal life was supposed to be kept secret. Still, I recognized a few faces from the country club. I found Eddie wearing tennis shoes, flannel pajama pants, and a white MIT shirt.

"Evening," I said.

"Is it?" he said, standing up from where he'd been hunched over the seismograph. He glanced at his wristwatch and yawned before looking at Jason. "The Director wanted a full report, and I have some new readings to chart."

Jason put his phone to his ear, requesting an update on the condition of the agents who had been injured at the golf course, and stepped away to an empty computer.

The vision of Asag's dark form flickered in my mind's eye. I can't believe I'd forgotten to tell them.

"Um, Eddie, there's something you should know."

My words did the trick, and Eddie stopped typing long enough to look at me.

"I saw it. *Him,* I guess. The thing that is causing the earthquakes. They said their name was Asag."

Eddie didn't say anything, but I noticed he'd ceased at the biting of his left thumb, and his hand was slowly lowering to his lap.

"Some, *thing,* a person is causing entire earthquakes?" His words were distant, as if he couldn't believe what he was saying.

I nodded. "Yes, but they definitely weren't human."

"What did they say?" Gavin asked.

"They knew I was a Guardian, and they said that..." I hesitated briefly, deciding at the last minute to skip the part about it being my fault they'd been released. I'd tell them eventually after I'd dealt with the guilt on my own. "They said that they were trying to free the others by breaking seals."

"What kind of seals?" Eddie asked this time.

I shook my head. "I have no idea. That's all they told me. Seals."

"Seals could mean doors, maybe? Or locks?" Eddie said.

"It'd make sense in the way he was talking about it and the need to literally break them like the ground."

Eddie pursed his lips. "Let's say these seals are like locks. Then, there must be a pattern to their locations. Magnetic coordinates or lay lines?"

He paused, opening a window on his screen and taking notes. "I'll loop the other researchers in case they come across any new information about patterns of the seismic activity. This information changes everything." He shifted a quick gaze to me. "But I am glad you're safe, too."

I flash him a quick smile. "Appreciate it."

Of course, there'd been injuries. I choked down the lump in my throat before risking asking the dreaded question. "How many were injured?"

Eddie chewed the backside of his thumbnail and stared at the laptop. "Numbers are still coming in, but two agents are in ICU, and the others just bruises and scrapes."

"And the people at the country club? How are they?"

Eddie turned to me. "Three people died, and several are in surgery for broken bones." His eyes narrowed on me before shifting to Gavin. "But for all the people that were transported to the hospital, not one coma has been mentioned in the reports."

A lead weight sank in my stomach. Three people had died because of that evil thing. That demon. I vowed the next time I was face-to-face with it, I wouldn't let it escape. It deserved to suffer just as those people trapped in the burning building had suffered.

"It is tragic," Eddie continued, but unfortunately, this does provide new data for us. No comas have been reported from the hospital."

"No one? The people were all right there, next to the epicenter." I paused, my pulse skyrocketing. "We all were."

"Yes," Eddie said slowly, almost as if he'd speculated on this for some time. "It's odd. Isn't it?"

"What's odd?" Gavin asked.

Eddie pursed his lips and explained to Gavin how the earthquakes were linked to people succumbing to comas like some airborne virus. "The impact zone is around a half mile, so everyone, agents, and country club members alike, should've been affected. According to my data, we shouldn't even be having this conversation right now. You should all have your own beds at the hospital. But you're not."

My thoughts whirled with the revelation that, once again, I'd dodged a metaphorical bullet, or should I say, a lot of people did. "Remember back at the agency building when I was with Jason in the elevator? Neither of us was affected, and neither were you."

"Yeah," Eddie murmured. "At the time, I'd thought you weren't just close enough, and I, well, I had the statue in a lead-lined storage closet, so I had gathered that had protected me, but maybe I was wrong." Eddie frowned as if the idea disgusted him. "No, I wasn't wrong. Just not completely right." His gaze swiveled to the laptop and then to me. "It's you, Ella. While I was protected in the storage unit or because of whatever the statue was doing, you somehow shielded Jason and yourself from the effects."

"But I don't have my power anymore," I retorted.

"But you're still a Guardian," Gavin said. "Ninurta told me.

He told me I'd recognize you when I saw you and that we would meet. And he was right."

I wiped my hand over my face, trying to sort through their words. I was a Guardian. I knew that, however, the title meant nothing without my gifts. My magic. Which had died when the statue broke, at least I'd thought it had, but when Eddie had me touch the statue, even for the briefest of moments, I had felt the connection. It was still there. A shadow, a wisp of what it had been, but there nonetheless. A renewed sense of hope rushed through me. "Okay, okay. Let's assume some fragment of my power protected Jason and me in the elevator, but dozens of agents were still unconscious on the fifth floor. So, it still doesn't explain how no one at the golf course is in comas?"

Gavin clapped his hands, startling Eddie, me, and a few neighboring agents working at their stations. "Oh, I have the answer to this one." He held up his hand as if awaiting a high-five. "It's because of me. I was there, too."

Eddie's eyes widened, realization settling over his features, and he adjusted the glasses on his nose. "Of course," Eddie said, shaking his head. "How could I have missed that? You're like her. Another Guardian, but still with all of your power. Together, you must have amplified each other, increasing the protection radius."

Eddie continued murmuring about magnetic impulses and energy arrays while pivoting in his chair back to his laptop.

"I'm going to be busy for a while with these calculations," he said dismissively. "My whole algorithm and database need to be re-calibrated."

Gavin and I exchanged confused glances. "Wait, so what can I do to help?"

Eddie ignored us.

"Eddie," I said firmly. "We can't just sit here. We want to help."

Eddie tore his gaze from the computer. "Uh, oh yeah. I guess you can—" his voice drifted off, and then he pointed to another open laptop with a display of North America on it. "The latest data from USGS should be uploaded now. The earthquakes have all been in rural countries, with no hope of cameras to catch them. What we need is a perimeter marked out as close to the epicenter as possible and then cross-check them with any names of people admitted to local hospitals who were unconscious. Cell phones, ring cameras, hell, I'd settle for a GoPro on a biker at this point." He passed me a paper with a list of over a hundred cities on them. "Anything to give us a chance at a video so I can give the Director something."

I took it and sat in the chair next to the laptop. "All right, easy enough," I said, clicking open the downloaded file. A spreadsheet with numbers and decimals appeared, and my stomach clenched at the incomprehensible data.

As if sensing my confusion, Eddie said. "They use coordinates, longitudes, and latitudes, so you'll have to look them up on the map individually."

I sighed. "Right. Got it." I opened another window and looked up the first city at the top of the list, Albuquerque, and then the geographical coordinates. I'd made it to the 5th name when my temples ached, and I desperately needed a cup of coffee.

Jason slid into the chair next to me, wearing a black Division 12 suit and tie and holding a cup of steaming coffee in his hand. "You look like you could use this," he said, sliding the cup over to me. "Eddie briefed me. We're matching times and names, right?"

I wrapped my fingers around the warm cup, welcoming the comforting heat and Jason's presence. "Yeah," I said, taking a sip and immediately feeling a bit more human. "It's tedious. We're trying to see if any cities were near the epicenter's coordinates. Eddie thinks we might be able to catch the earthquake on video."

Gavin twirled in the seat across the table from us, spinning a pencil in his fingers, staring into the middle distance, and clearly bored.

"Hey," Jason said, following my line of sight. "They brought a van with more cords, monitors, and supplies outside. You want to go give them a hand?"

His hand snapped out, and he stopped spinning. "Uh, sure," he said, and got up more than a little quickly and hurried to the main doors.

Jason laughed. "I could never sit still in class either."

"But this isn't class. This is serious."

Jason cocked an eyebrow. "Yeah, yeah, I know it is. But you can't deny this is the boring side of the work we do."

"Boring or not, it's still important, and he should accept that."

Jason frowned. "Don't be so hard on the kid. He's had to deal with a lot."

"Hard? I'm being realistic. We're dealing with life-or-death shit here."

"But that's exactly why we need to maintain some level of cheer, some form of hope," he retorted. "If we all become jaded, focused solely on the grim parts of what we're doing, we'll lose sight of why we're doing it in the first place. We're fighting for a better world, remember?"

I entered a new coordinate with unnecessarily hard keystrokes. The room felt smaller, the tension between us tangible. "I haven't forgotten why we're doing this. But I can't afford to be cheerful and lighthearted when I feel so... powerless." I glared at the computer, the numbers beginning to blur together. I clenched my jaw. "This is all any of us can do right now. So, I'm going to do it, and Gavin should accept that, too."

But that was a lie. Gavin still had all of his powers.

"Fine," I said, sighing. "Maybe you're right. But that doesn't change the fact that what we're doing here is important, even if it's not as glamorous or as exciting as shooting bullets or hacking into bank accounts."

Jason smiled a hint of relief in his eyes. "I never said it wasn't important. I just think you should focus on why we're doing it."

He was right. As much as it pained me to admit it, he was right.

"So," he said, clapping his hands together. "Want me to take over for a bit and give you a break?"

"Be my guest. The more eyes, the better," I said, shifting my chair slightly to give him room to slide his laptop next to mine.

Over the next hour, the room around us hummed with the subdued clatter of keyboards and hushed conversations. Division 12 was always busy and moving, and I felt like I belonged for a brief moment. Like again, I was a part of something bigger than just myself.

My stomach was growling when Eddie came over to check on us. "Director Ferguson's car is on her way. Please tell me you found something."

I returned to my list, now on name number 48, my eyes growing weary as they darted from one column to the next.

"We're still going through it," I said, feeling the weight of Eddie's expectations. "This is a lot of data to sift through, and we're trying to be thorough."

"Just find something," Eddie urged before hurrying off to another table where two other agents had rolled out a map.

I sighed, taking a final sip of my now-cold coffee and returning to the screen. Name number 49, number 50, number 51... It felt like I was looking for a needle in a haystack. And then, as my eyes skimmed the data, something caught my attention. One of the names, 'Lila Davidson,' was a social media influencer I recognized. "Jason, look at this," I said, pulling up her TikTok profile. "She was admitted unconscious to a hospital in Ohio last week."

Jason leaned in, watching as I scrolled through Lila's feed. Most were the usual influencer posts — dances to music, outfit of the day, life updates. Then I stopped on a video showing her dancing outside a diner, right in front of a rainbow-painted wall.

"Okay, she's in Ohio, at a diner," Jason said. "But what does that have to do with—"

"Wait," I interrupted, tapping the screen and freezing the video. "Look there, in the corner." The camera had unintentionally caught a shadowy figure, a cloaked man lurking near the edge of the frame. My blood froze in my veins.

"Is that it?" Jason whispered, his eyes widening. "It just looks like a guy?"

My breathing quickened. This was it; this was something solid. I hadn't been delusional when seeing him at the golf course. The cloaked figure *did* exist. For the first time in days, I felt like I was contributing meaningfully. "This is him," I paused. "I know it. We need to show this to Eddie and the Director."

Jason's phone buzzed with a text alert just as I was about to call Eddie over. It was from the security team outside. "Director Ferguson is here," it read.

"Get Eddie on this," Jason said, getting to his feet. "See if he can enhance it enough to get some actionable intel from it. I'll try and buy you some time."

Jason hurried to the door and passed Gavin on the way. The two exchanged a word before Gavin's eyes landed on mine. I redirected my attention to the computer as Gavin plopped into the chair across from me again. "Jason said you found something?"

Feeling quite pleased with myself, I tilted my chin. However, my legs felt like mush as I pushed myself from the desk and got up to locate Eddie. What if it wasn't something at all but just a random dude walking by, and I'd wasted everyone's time?

I went to find Eddie hovering over an older field agent who was struggling to open an Excel sheet.

"Eddie, I think I found something important. You got a sec?"

Eddie turned and raised his finger and began chewing on the quick. "Show me."

I led him back to the desk and pulled up the TikTok video on the computer. I paused at the exact frame where the shadowy, cloaked figure was visible. "See that? In the corner? I swear that's the same guy I saw at the golf course. The one that made the ground split."

Eddie's eyes narrowed as he looked at the image, then slid into the chair. "I'll try to enhance it, see if we can pull any details."

My heart was racing as I watched Eddie run the video through different types of software until the frames were isolated and he could enlarge the pixels while keeping it clear. I had to hand it to him. He knew his way around photo editing for a scientist, and the programs he used were top of the market. I was low-key jealous of the deep pockets Division 12 afforded him to use thousands of dollars worth of software.

Jason reentered the room with a weary-looking Director beside him. They paused, talking with agents as she strode through the op setup. Jason looked at me questioningly with the director's back to him, and I gave him a halfhearted shrug. His face relaxed a fraction, but the tension didn't entirely dissipate.

Finally, Director Ferguson approached us. "Updates?"

Jason took the lead. "We've been combing through hospital records to find a pattern. Elly made a potentially significant discovery, and Eddie is currently working on enhancing the footage for more information."

Her eyes turned towards me. "Good work. Get me everything you can on him. I want to know everything about this... person. Who he is, what he wants, how often he shits. And I needed it yesterday. CDC is threatening to declare another epidemic if we don't have proof these are isolated incidents. Time is a resource we don't have people."

"I understand, ma'am," I replied. My hands were clenched in my lap, silently urging Eddie to hurry.

Minutes stretched agonizingly long as the Director stood, literally breathing down our necks.

Finally, Eddie sat back in his chair. "I've got something."

Eddie moused over a window, and there it was. The enhanced image clearly showed the cloaked figure. His face was obscured, but it looked like a human man; although it was hard to tell the specific age, they had a bald head and dark, deep-set eyes. My stomach clenched, twisting into a hard knot, and I regretted only drinking coffee that morning and not eating something. I thought I'd prepared myself to see him again, and yet seeing him, it again, filled me with a cold sense of dread, and tiny black specks swirled in my vision. Did we honestly believe we could take on something like that...*unnatural?* That evil. It seemed impossible even with Gavin's abilities and if I still did have my own.

I'd only scratched the surface of how to use it when it'd vanished. It had been pure instinct alone when I'd shattered the altar, severing the connection to the bridge before Derek could cross it.

I inhaled deeply, attempting to calm myself. Once again, I

would just have to trust fate's plan. And meeting Gavin... that couldn't have been a coincidence. We were destined to meet, and there was a small comfort in knowing that I was still needed and I wasn't alone.

"Steinberg, get me the diner's location," Director Ferguson said.

Eddie nodded. "Easy enough."

Jason moved to stand behind me, and I noticed that we'd gathered a crowd of other agents, all eyes fixed on Eddie's computer.

It took another nerve-wracking fifteen seconds before Eddie shouted. "Got it! The mural is from a well-known diner in Akron, Ohio."

Director Ferguson wasted no time. "Agent Price. Prep a team. You're going to Akron. I want the video footage from every camera in a two-mile radius from when this was taken."

"Yes, Director," Jason said, and the group dispersed, each person breaking away to their respective tasks, some going to Eddie for further information, others going to the weapons crates and taking out pistols, bulletproof vests, and other tactical gear. Jason caught my eye and motioned for me to follow him, leading me away from the others and into a more secluded area in the warehouse under the stairwell.

"What's up?" I asked, my eyes searching his.

"Listen, I know you're worried about me going to investigate the diner," he said, capturing my moods almost as well as I captured them with my camera. "But I need you to know that I can handle it. I've got Sanders and Chapman on my detail. They're beasts, and I wouldn't want anyone else watching my six."

His hands came to rest on either side of my shoulders, his eyes locking onto mine. I felt the weight of his words, yet my stomach was knotted with tension. This world, filled with shadows and uncertainties, had made me skeptical of any guarantees, even from him.

"Jason, you know as well as I do that 'handling it' isn't a surefire thing anymore," I said, my voice tinged with worry. "Not with everything that's been going on."

He tightened his grip slightly as if he could shield me from the very fears I voiced. "I get it, Elly, I do. But you also know that this is the only way to get a step ahead of this Asag. It's the first real chance of finding and capturing him. Opportunities like these don't just fall in our laps, and if we falter, we'll miss it."

My lips parted, but no words came. Instead, I nodded, giving him a look that I hoped conveyed a mix of dread and trust.

"So, promise me you won't wait up. Have Harrison pick up some Thai food and try to get some rest, okay?" he said, finally letting go of my shoulders to cup my face gently.

My eyes met his, and in them, I saw his concern, his weariness, and a glimmer of something else—perhaps the shared understanding that rest was a luxury neither of us could afford.

"Rest?" I scoffed, laughing. "While you're out there tracking that thing? Not a chance."

With that, he rolled his eyes and sighed. Then, he leaned down to kiss me, which made my toes curl in my boots, before finally turning to leave. As I watched him walk away, I couldn't shake the nagging feeling that rest would be a long time coming for both of us.

CHAPTER

TWELVE

Eddie's hands shook as he fumbled with the DSLR camera. "I swear, these things are more complicated than trying to crack a firewall at the NSA."

Gavin chuckled from his perch on the stool. He was shirtless, and while I'd seen the tattoos on his arms, they extended beyond to his chest and back. The elaborate runes glowed faintly under the fluorescent light, eliminating all doubt that they were anything but magical.

"I've got an itch on my chin," Gavin complained and moved his arm to scratch it just as the flash went off on the camera.

Eddie lowered the camera, and worry furrowed the space between his dark brows. "You're sure you're okay with us documenting this, Gavin? These runes are a part of you, and—"

"Yeah. It's cool," Gavin interrupted. "If I'm stuck with tattoos I didn't want, I should at least know what they are, right?"

"That's the plan, yes," Eddie said, staring at the viewfinder and working the adjustments.

I shook my head, feeling that this was taking way longer than it should. I walked over to him. "Here, let me see."

Eddie looked relieved as he handed me the camera. With a few quick adjustments—aperture, ISO, shutter speed—and it was ready to go. "Try it now," I told him, handing it back.

Eddie shook his head. "I have a hundred and forty-seven IQ, which makes me smart enough to know when I'm out of my skill zone."

I laughed. "Fair enough. Move that lighting there? And then dim that one." Eddie did as I instructed, and once satisfied the lighting had improved the shadows and contrast, I aimed and shot. I flipped to display mode and showed the image for Eddie's approval. The lab tech chewed on his left thumbnail and stared at the LCD screen. "That'll work just fine."

Gavin flexed his arms as if that would somehow make the runes more visible. I scoffed, even as my eyes roamed over the runes. They were extremely elaborate, and the shading enhanced the curves and lines.

I moved to the opposite side, snapping photos on his left shoulder.

"Are these going to show up in the photos like they do in real life? Like how they're glowing?"

"The camera should capture the details well," I offered. "Especially now that it's adjusted," I paused, smirking to myself, "correctly. The glow, however, I'm not sure. If these were normal ink tattoos, then we'd be golden, but since they're not, we'll probably have to do some photo enhancing afterward."

I took a few steps back to frame the shot. Looking through the viewfinder, I saw Gavin sitting there, his glowing runes like pieces of a cosmic puzzle.

I realized that there was a bitter irony in all of this, and for a moment, knowing full well Gavin would hate it, pity welled up inside me. How do you navigate the challenges of being an eighteen-year-old, grappling with the precipice of adulthood, when you're also burdened with cosmic responsibilities you never signed up for?

But envy twisted within me, too. Envy for the sense of purpose those tattoos represented, a screaming declaration that he was part of something much larger than himself. How many people wander through life wondering if they're special if they're chosen for something grand? Gavin didn't have to wonder; the ink etched into his skin was proof enough.

Yet, I couldn't ignore the weight that 'being chosen' had felt to me when Enheduanna had spoken to me and now must place on him. It's one thing to be special, to be integral to some grand, cosmic plan. It's quite another to live up to it, especially when you're just trying to figure out how to be a human being, how to transition from the dredges of adolescence into the unforgiving world of adulthood.

I wished, not for the first time since I'd met him, that things could be simpler and that he could concern himself with fantasy football drafts and weekends with his Xbox rather than prophecies and battles against whatever it was we were truly up against.

But that wasn't our reality; this was. We were who we were, marked or not, chosen or not, and the gods that had gifted us had left us without a guide. Not even a fucking instruction manual on what we were supposed to be doing or how we were supposed to navigate this path while trying to balance an ordinary life.

I drew in a sharp breath, realizing that I'd zoned out, letting years of working a camera take over while I mulled over Gavin and mine's predicaments.

"I think that's all of them," I said, standing upright and passing the camera back to Eddie.

Eddie carefully took the camera from me, his fingers deftly ejecting the memory card. "I'm going to pass these on to my assistant to get started on piecing them together. The sooner we can analyze them, the better."

As Eddie disappeared into the main area where we'd set up a temporary workstation, I turned to Gavin. "You sure you're good with all of this?"

His hazel-green eyes met mine. "What choice do I have?"

"You always have a choice."

Gavin scoffed. "Do I? Look at me." He held out his arms. "Ninurta branded me. I have these runes in ink that glow like I'm radioactive. How am I going to go to school looking like I just came from a rave? Play basketball? All my friends are going to take one look at these and think I lost my mind over the summer. Sure, they're dope as hell, but also, like, I wish I'd had a say at least."

My throat tightened at his confession. I couldn't imagine waking up one morning covered in ink like that. The fear, the confusion. It must've been hell. And to go through it all *alone*.

Gavin picked up his shirt from the table next to him and slipped it over his head, the fabric draping over his runes, obscuring them from view but not from memory.

From the other room, Eddie's voice floated back to us, giving stern instructions to his assistant, whom I knew was named Amy. A petite, bright-eyed intern fresh out of Caltech with a quiet voice and purple highlights in her hair.

I turned my attention back to Gavin and handed him his hooded sweatshirt. "You said you live with your grandparents? How did they react to all of this?"

Gavin shrugged. "Of course, I tried to hide them at first. But when they started glowing at all these random times during the day, and when Grandpa saw me get out of the swimming pool after a late-night swim, it freaked him out. He's superstitious, always throwing salt over his shoulder and chasing off the neighbor's black cat from our lawn, so he said I brought a curse into the house and called the pastor from our church."

He scratched the back of his elbow as if he could somehow remove the magic ink from his skin. Even his nonchalant tone, however, couldn't mask the pain in his eyes.

My heart sank; it was a familiar tale. I put a hand on his shoulder. "I'm sorry, Gavin. But you're safe here. We'll figure this out. We're in this together."

He looked up and smiled, and for a second, I saw myself in him—the same fear, the same burden of powers neither of us had asked for.

An agent brought lunch for Gavin and me—tuna sandwiches, chips, a banana, and a wrapped package of Oreos. While we ate, Gavin scrolled through his phone. I was surprised the agency let him keep it but assumed they monitored the WIFI network here anyway, and a hundred alarms would go off if he did anything they didn't approve of, say, blast the agency's location all over social media.

While I chewed my sandwich, I watched him sift through web pages of Mesopotamian lore. I suggested a few sites I'd visited myself when I'd lost my powers that had great information but nothing of use to me.

"You said Inanna is the goddess of war, right?" Gavin said after some time.

I nodded. "Yep. There are poems and hymns of her being epic on the battlefield and incredibly brave."

"It says here, though, she was also the goddess of love, and Venus and Aphrodite were inspired by her."

I smiled. "Yep, she covered a lot of bases."

"Did you ever think that's why you lost your powers? Cause you're not in love?"

The earth tilted as he spoke the words, and the chip I was

holding cracked in half. My mind stuttered, unsure how to respond. It'd been the last question I'd ever thought he'd ask.

"I have a boyfriend," I said, my defense sounding weak even to my ears.

The corner of Gavin's mouth twisted up skeptically. "So? That doesn't mean you're in love."

Annoyance flicked at the back of my skull. This was stupid. I didn't need to defend myself to him. I dusted the crumbs off my hands and tossed my garbage in the empty paper bag. "My private life is none of yours or God's business. If you're done eating, we should meet up with Eddie."

Gavin didn't move at first, and confusion clouded his face, brought on by an abrupt end to our conversation. I swallowed the sour taste of guilt and stood. Sure, we both had been blessed by Sumerian gods, but I'd barely known him for twenty-four hours. He had no right to tell me who I did and didn't love. He didn't know me.

"Uh yeah, okay. Sorry," he stammered, getting to his feet. "Let's hope he has some good news."

My mind buzzed with a million thoughts and theories as I scanned the printed photos of Gavin's tattoos, maps, and diagrams plastered across the warehouse's walls. We knew a demon was behind the earthquakes and the illness outbreaks, but its motives and origins were like a maze with no exit. Each turn just led to more questions.

I glanced at Jason and saw my own unease mirrored in his steel blue eyes. His trip to Akron had proved a bust. The earthquake had happened a minute after Lila's video and had taken out the power and the security cameras along with it.

The team and he had returned looking weary, and the frustration hanging in the air was palpable.

We had to figure this out—and fast. So far, the casualties had been few, but the frequency of earthquakes was intensifying, leading to a...a what? An even bigger one smack dab in the middle of a heavily populated city? Or off the shore of a coastline, creating a record-setting tsunami? To what purpose? There had to be more behind this than meaningless destruction.

The images and maps on the wall were a mess, but we had to find a pattern, some clue to what this demon would do next. "We're in the dark here," I finally said, putting voice to what we all were thinking. "We don't even know what we're fighting against."

"Creating an earthquake is a big flex," Gavin added. "How can we stop something that can do that?"

"We can't," Jason added, looking as grim as I felt. "Not unless we know what *it* is we're dealing with. There must be a way to kill it or at least trap it."

Eddie tapped the computer monitor screen where the five-second video of the shadowy figure had been paused. My skin crawled at the memory, remembering the way he'd knelt and pressed his hand into the grass before the world split open and all hell broke loose.

"Well, those are some shitty odds," Gavin said.

"Except this isn't a game; it is life and death," I pointed out.

"Right," he nodded. "End-of-the-world prophecies, old gods, shadow demons. Just another Tuesday."

"Welcome to the team, Guardian."

Eddie laughed. "I prefer champion."

"Alright then," I said. "Champion."

Eddie's finger clicked on the mouse, opening and closing windows. "I'll keep analyzing the video we got at the country club and let you know if anything turns up. But there's not much to go on. We need more information. An expert."

Jason and I exchanged a look. Apparently, we'd had the same thought occur. "Dr. Katherine Mayberry," he said. "She's an expert on Mesopotamian lore and history. She could help."

Eddie's eyes glanced over Gavin and me before narrowing on Jason. "You think Director Ferguson will go for bringing another outsider in?"

Jason smirked. "I think she's grasping at straws and tired of looking like a fool in front of the directors. She'll go for it."

A glimmer of hope sparked within me. "Then let's get her in here."

"I'll see if we can get her on the next flight out," he said and put a phone to his ear.

THIRTEEN

The sound of footsteps heralded Kat's arrival, and just seeing her again in person eased some of the tension in my shoulders. She was brilliant, fearless, and kind, and if I could have anyone on my side sorting out five-thousand-year-old mysteries, it'd be her.

Kat's overnight bag was taken, she was given a visitor badge, and an NDA was shoved in front of her on a clipboard. When Jason introduced her to Gavin, her eyes scanned him up and down before settling on the tattoos visible on his wrists.

"Lift your sleeves," she commanded.

Gavin looked uncomfortable under all the scrutiny but did as he was told. I took pity on him, recalling how vulnerable I'd felt when Kat had insisted. I show the eight-pointed star burned into my palm.

"We have pictures of them," I said and pointed to the wall where they'd been pinned up in order.

"Fascinating," she said a little breathlessly. "These tattoos are more than just symbols. They're a story," Kat exclaimed, her eyes scanning the wall. She stopped, narrowing in on a particularly intricate section on the inside of his right forearm.

"Quick, fetch me a cup of tea. I need to make a phone call."

Kat wasted no time pulling out her cell, but Director Ferguson snapped her fingers, and another agent leaped forward, swapping phones with Kat before she'd hit call. "This is a secure line that can't be traced back," Director Ferguson said. "Can't be too careful."

Kat pursed her lips but took the phone anyway. She dialed the number and, keeping her voice low, asked to speak with the curator of the Babylonian collection at the Penn Museum. I realized she was trying to get more information about Asag and Ninurta without raising the director's suspicions.

My palms grew clammy as I watched Director Ferguson's scrutinizing gaze, and I was certain someone would forcefully take the phone from her should Kat begin to drift too far into details for her liking.

Kat, however, expertly danced around the specifics, vaguely referencing an archaeological find that went to auction from a private collection in 1977 containing an unedited version of the *Lugal-e*, an epic poem about Ninurta. I held my breath, hoping Kat's reputation held enough influence to convince the curator to scan and send over the parts we needed without asking too many questions.

When the conversation ended, Kat thanked the curator and hung up.

"He'll send them over. I gave him my personal email so as to not draw suspicions." She fixed Director Ferguson with a challenging look, and I secretly smiled inside. I'd hate to be in the same room with these two if ever they were at opposing odds.

"That's fine," the Director said after a pregnant pause. She tilted her head to the agent who had given Kat the agency cell phone. "Harrison. Get her a computer *with* a printer. Now."

The agent hurried to where a stack of black crates had been set to the side and took out a still-in-the-box printer.

"The rest of you, get back to your assigned tasks. We need to get eyes on it and pronto. We can't fight something if we don't know where it is."

Jason and I exchanged a glance, and he gave me a reassuring smile before making his way with the Director to a private room with a handful of the other agents.

Once Agent Harrison had set up the printer, he brought over the laptop that Gavin had used and connected it.

"Should be good," he said and stood, motioning to the chair for Kat to sit.

"And the tea?" she asked. Harrison looked at me, and his face paled. It was hilariously obvious he had no clue how to make tea.

"I'll get it for you," I said, coming to his rescue, and went to the food table.

Harrison appeared by my shoulder. "Thanks. I made tea once for my aunt who was visiting from England, and she'd been so angry that I'd oversteeped it."

"No worries," I said, spooning the loose-leafed tea from the tin. "I don't remember the last time I used a printer, to be honest, so you've got that skill on me."

Harrison laughed. "The Director likes her hard copies, so I make sure to have one on order when we set up field stations."

With the tea in the cloth bag, I set it in the paper cup and poured the steaming water over it, the mint and herb aroma instantly filling my nostrils.

"So," Harrison said, turning to face the main area. "I've got a wager that I need to settle."

I arched an eyebrow. "Oh yeah?" I said, knowing exactly where this was going.

"You and Agent Price. You're like seeing each other, right?"

I smirked, letting my eyes drift up and to the closed door where they were having a meeting.

"You'll have to ask him."

Harrison made a pained sound. "He'll never tell me. Division 12 regulations prohibit it."

"Ah. You thought I was an easy mark then 'cause I'm not an agent?"

He pursed his lips. "You got me."

I removed the tea bag and emptied a single packet of sugar into the cup, recalling how Kat took it. She'd preferred the actual sugar cubes when I'd see her make it at her enormous estate outside Baghdad, but this would have to do.

"Please, I've got three hundred bucks riding on this. But they won't pay up unless I have proof."

Three hundred. I should feel bad, but this was way too much fun watching him squirm. "Sorry, can't help you."

I picked up the tea and started back to Kat, feeling more than a little smug and wanting to throw an —"See? I told you so"— in Gavin's face. Although Jason and I were mostly careful about PDA around the other agents, our relationship had been more obvious than we'd assumed. If it was that apparent to other agents, it had to be love, right? Still, Gavin's words had buried a seed of doubt in my subconscious, and I worried about how long before it took root. I breathed in deeply, attempting to collect myself before confronting Kat, and assured myself that I would discuss it with Jason later when I saw him that evening at the safe house.

The monitor in front of Kat had pages and pages of scanned texts— some in Cuneiform, some in Latin, and some handwritten with blue ink, while the table had printed copies of Gavin's tattoos from all angles.

"Ah," she said, taking the tea from me. "These are the translations of the thirteen tablets that comprise the Lugal-e. A poem roughly translated means the 'Lasting Song or Praise of

Ninurta.' The poems are a series of legends, exploits of the god Ninurta."

I noticed Gavin had walked up quietly behind us, his eyes fixed intently on Kat's screen. I recalled the swirling emotions I'd felt when Kat had spoken about the legends of Inanna and Enheduanna. He was Ninurta's champion, and the answers he sought could be hidden in these texts.

"Does it say anything about my tattoos?" Gavin asked.

Kat pursed her lips, scrolling through the pages. "No. I'm afraid not."

"But what about Asag? Does it say anything about him?" I asked.

Kat steepled her fingers, studying the bound manuscript. "It refers to Asag down here, but there's only one line before the section of the tablet that broke off ends it." The creases around her eyes deepened. "It says Asag was one of the most powerful among the demons and had, with the aid of other gods, freed themselves and the hundreds of other demons from the underworld. It had been Ninurta and the mace that had driven them back underground, locking them in magical prisons so they could never escape again. But the specifics on how a god wielded powerful magic like this is anyone's guess."

"Oh, so Asag, the big bad," Gavin said. "Got it."

Kat chuckled. "It appears so, yes. Which means we should be all the more cautious when deciding how to deal with it."

"The funny thing is," Kat said, leaning back in her chair and twisting her mouth in confusion. "Long before they were driven to the underworld when the demons were free to walk the earth, they never acted on their own accord. They had no initiative. They were always used as tools or instruments by one of the other gods. They serve no other purpose than to bring death and destruction, famine, or disease. Their only existence was to inflict harm on humanity.

"There's a legend about one of the most powerful of the gods, Enlil, who was tired of all the noise humans made and was unable to sleep. He drew upon his power and caused a flood that lasted seven days and seven nights, which killed thousands. Inanna and Ninurta were the two that stood up for humanity to Enlil and argued that instead of causing floods, Enlil should ensure that humans never become overpopulated."

"The comas? How are they tied to this?" Jason asked.

"It is a disease." Kat shook her head slowly, dropping her gaze to the floor. "I'm unsure how the earthquakes are causing them, but there is certainly a connection. Gods, demons, and angels pick any of the religions or beliefs, and they share a similar pattern. The need to control or punish humans. Whether by famine, natural disasters, or disease."

A tightness formed inside my chest, constricting the space around my heart. "There's no hope for these people then. Is that what you're saying?"

Kat reached over and squeezed my hand. "There's always hope, Ella. You know that. And these myths are myths for a reason. They're always exaggerated to give the story more emphasis, even if there is an underlying truth to them. I believe that there is a cure for these people. Because I don't think I'd accept anything else."

I felt the same way, too. Imagining these people, this epidemic, continuing unfettered, uninhibited, well, let's just say it wasn't a future I was looking forward to.

So, if I figure out how to use my power again, then perhaps we could find a way to cure these people.

He nodded. "Yeah, I guess that's the idea, huh."

First things first, I get my power back. Then, we find out what these demons are doing and where we will find them next. Then we figure out how to stop them."

"Oh, yeah. About that, there is a way to stop them."

"There is?"

Gavin flashed me a toothy grin. "Yep. It's a weapon. Ninurta showed it to me in the last vision I had. He called it the 'Breaker of Mountains.' A mace so powerful it could smash a thousand skulls. Pretty dope, huh?"

"Very," I said.

Gavin's smile collapsed. "But there's a problem."

"Of course, there fucking is," Jason said, rolling his eyes.

"What's the problem?" I asked.

"He said I had to find it on my own, and then dude bounced before I could ask him anything else."

I chuckled, remembering how Enheduanna had been equally cryptic with her "help."

"Great, so we have an epic weapon that could solve all our problems, but we have no idea where it is. Perfect," I said and laughed.

"He had to have given you something, a clue to finding it?"

"Pretty sure that's what these are," Gavin replied, looking at the tattoos on his arms.

"Dr. Mayberry," Director Ferguson said, causing all of us except Kat to startle. She stood hovering over us, the room instantly growing tense. Jason shifted beside her, moving to her right shoulder and just where I sat.

"While these stories are interesting, I'd like to know if they say anything about how to defeat this Asag or, better yet, any weaknesses it might have. I want my agents to be as prepared as possible."

"I managed to translate more of the text," Kat began, "It's vague, but it mentions that the weapon is hidden 'where the sky kisses the earth.' It's poetic and frustratingly ambiguous, but it's something."

"Could that mean a mountain?" Gavin chimed in. "Or maybe somewhere in the sky?"

"Or perhaps it's metaphorical," Jason added. "Either way, it's a start."

"Then let's follow that lead," Director Ferguson said. "Kat, I want you to work with Eddie to narrow down possible locations. Jason, start prepping a team for immediate deployment once we have a destination. Ella," she paused, and her lips formed a thin line. "Assist where you can."

I caught Jason's eye, and he gave me an encouraging nod as if telling me that no matter what, I was still needed, but it did little to soothe the sting of resentment. I wasn't just another agent doing my work; I was less than that since I wasn't even trained, and I might as well be running to the food table. Grinding my teeth together, I opened the document Eddie had given me to find connections between victims and earthquakes.

By late that evening, we were exhausted. We'd made frustratingly little headway on locating the mace or analyzing Gavin's tattoos. Jason and I gathered our things, preparing to leave, when Gavin's phone buzzed.

He looked at it briefly, confusion flashing in his eyes when he read the caller ID and put it to his ear.

"Yeah, this is him," he said. "What? When?" I could make out nothing from the other end of the line, but Gavin's face had gone as gray as the concrete floors, and I knew whatever he was hearing, it wasn't good.

"Okay, I'm on my way." He ended the call.

"What is it?" I asked.

"It's my grandparents," he said. "They decided to take a road trip to Rock Springs Casino, and there was an earthquake. They found them in the parking lot in their car unconscious and were taken to Newhaven Medical Center."

CHAPTER

FOURTEEN

I walked into the sterile hospital room, my eyes immediately falling on the two beds where Gavin's grandparents lay. They looked peaceful as if they were merely asleep. However, the machines surrounding them told a different story. I felt a lump forming in my throat when my eyes landed on Gavin. Jason had gone in first and then came to fetch me when he'd helped Gavin complete all the intake paperwork.

Gavin looked shattered, his eyes red and puffy, his usual upbeat demeanor reduced to a drawn and exhausted shell.

Jason stood next to him, his face unreadable, as the doctor, a middle-aged man with graying hair, addressed him. "We had thirty-eight individuals brought in from that casino earthquake. It's puzzling, to say the least."

Jason intently listened while shooting Gavin a subtle glance. "Is there any sign of them waking up?"

The doctor shook his head. "They're stable, breathing on their own, but unresponsive. I've put in calls to other hospitals for consultations with other doctors but don't have any explanations at this point."

Suddenly, a tall man with a buzz cut and a suit walked in,

flashing a CIA badge. "Doctor, a moment of your time," he ordered, pulling the surprised-looking doctor aside but still within earshot.

Gavin moved like he wanted to intervene, but I saw Jason subtly shake his head. Now was not the time for outbursts, and the last thing we needed was to cause more of a rift between Division 12 and the government.

My mind raced back to earlier in the day when I'd snapped at Gavin. We were all stressed, all handling the pressure in our own ways, but Gavin was just 18, and in that hospital room, he looked like a young boy lost in a world he didn't understand. The weight of my earlier harsh words crushed me. This kid didn't deserve any of this.

"Gavin," Jason said softly, "why don't you stay here with them for a bit? I'll have a couple of our agents stay with you for security."

He sniffed and crossed his arms. "Yeah. Sure."

"We'll go back to Division 12," Jason said, looking at me. I could see he was torn between staying with Gavin and going back to handle the agency's response to this latest disaster.

"We'll let you have some time," I said. "And we'll figure out what happened, I promise."

Gavin nodded, his eyes still fixed on his grandparents. As we left the room, the CIA agent was talking quietly but emphatically with the doctor. Whatever he was saying, I'm sure, would be relayed to the agency.

Jason and I walked down the hospital corridors in silence, both lost in our thoughts. When we got to the car, Jason slammed a hand on the roof. "God dammit,"

"I know," I agreed, my stomach twisting.

Jason sighed, and we climbed into the car and headed back toward the Division 12 warehouse. "He's just a kid. We've got to make this right, Elly. Whatever it takes."

As we drove, the sun sank below the skyline, and the palm trees cast long shadows on the road. I stuffed my hands under my thighs, feeling a fresh surge of resentment at the power that had abandoned me. Every minute Gavin's grandparents were in a coma was another minute closer to them never waking up. The Asag was growing stronger, and we were running out of time, and the dozens in comas might soon become thousands.

Back at the warehouse, I could feel the urgency in the air. Eddie's grandparents were unconscious in the hospital, and we needed to find a way to help them soon.

Kat had utilized our time away, digging deeper into what Gavin could've meant when he'd said the weapon was called: "Breaker of Mountains."

"Sharur," Kat had proclaimed proudly once we'd joined her in the central area of the warehouse. "It is a legendary weapon, a mace, specifically in Mesopotamian lore. Ninurta wielded it when he struck down the demons during one of his many epic battles. However, the myths state it was broken into three pieces: the handle, the shaft, and the head." Kat flipped through various digital archives on her monitor, letting us follow along.

As I looked at the screen, at the illustration of a bearded man carrying a spike-shaped mace, my heart skipped a beat. There it was: Sharur, broken down into its three components— the mace's head, the wooden shaft, and the leather-wrapped handle.

"The Breaker of Mountains is Sharur," Kat announced, her voice tinged with awe. "If the legends are true, reassembling these pieces could change everything we know about history. About power."

My mind whirred with fascination, concocting all sorts of scenarios and possibilities.

"I need to make some calls," she said, picking up her phone.

Eddie picked up the ball and ran with it. His fingers danced across the keyboard like a virtuoso pianist. Every so often, he'd exclaim, "This photo matches the handle's engravings," or "I think I've found a black-market listing for something."

I watched as pieces of the puzzle came together on his screen, and each match stoked the fire of my excitement.

Kat finally hung up, scribbling notes furiously. "According to my contacts, the shaft was last seen on a ship owned by a wealthy lord in 1723—a ship that pirates attacked."

"And guess what?" Kat continued. "That ship never reached its destination. It was either sunk or the pirates took everything, but it vanished, along with the golden shaft."

I felt a surge of hope. If the ship had sunk, maybe the shaft was still out there. If the pirates had taken it, well, then we were kind of screwed.

"The handle has been to various auctions and is believed to bring prosperity in business."

I glanced at Jason; his eyes were on fire, a fierce intensity that only surfaced when someone he cared about was in trouble. "Where is it now?"

One of the agents, Mortimer, I thought his last name was that, was eating a bagel near us and observing, "That necklace, I've seen it."

Everyone stopped what they were doing and turned to him. "We did a money transfer for a hostage situation a few months ago," he said, licking the cream cheese off his fingers. "An Italian mob boss goes by the name of Marco, was wearing it. He said it's been in his family for a long time."

Jason's eyes narrowed. "Marco Lombardi is a notorious womanizer and drug dealer."

"*And* he likes blondes and is a sucker for antiques," Mortimer said and slid a not so-subtle-gaze my way.

Jason sat upright as if a rod had been shoved down his spine. "Fuck no."

"Hold up, Price. Hear me out. He never goes anywhere without the necklace, and time it right, it'd be an easy snatch and grab."

Director Ferguson's eyes darted between the agents. "It's a risky play, Mortimer. Even for you."

"Wait," I asked. "What's going on?"

Jason rubbed the back of his neck, looking uneasy. "Mortimer wants to send you in undercover."

"Me? But I'm not an agent."

"Exactly," Jason said, thrusting a hand in my direction.

Jason seemed uneasy, and what he said next stung more than I'd like to admit. "With all due respect, ma'am, Marco is smart. He'd smell an agent a mile away. Sending in someone with Ella's lack of field experience could be dangerous."

Agent Hansen, who had been quiet until now, spoke up. "Actually, ma'am, I think it's the best plan we've got. Ella is an unknown variable for Marco, and she'll look better in a skirt than Price."

"Hey, wait a minute." I tilted my chin up. "Just so we're clear, I might not be an agent, but I tagged along with seals in Kuwait and was one of the first journalists on the ground in Ukraine. If this is the way to get a piece of the weapon, then I'll do it. I can handle a handsy mobster."

Director Ferguson sighed. "Thank you for that, Eleanora," she said, plucking a loose hair off the sleeve of her jacket. "But Jason's right. Marco will be suspicious of anyone he doesn't know coming into his circle. But we're short on time *and* agents. Your girl is our best play."

While the feminist inside me should've balked at the nickname,

I was no one's property. The phrase 'your girl' released a dozen butterflies soaring in my stomach, making me feel way too good for someone agreeing to go undercover for a dangerous assignment.

"One wrong move," the director continued, her eyes on Jason, "and we'll lose him." Her head swiveled to me. "That is if you're not dead first."

I forced down the golf ball-sized lump in my throat and seized the moment. "I get it. I'll be cautious. And just for the record," I said proudly, "I can speak Italian and have experience dealing with guys like this."

Jason's left eyebrow raised slightly, clearly intrigued by some secret history I hadn't shared with him and then sighed. "If she believes she can do it, and Hansen's backing the plan, then maybe it's worth the risk."

Director Ferguson made her decision. "All right, you're going in. But we're providing maximum backup."

I smiled, both vindicated and excited. "Understood, ma'am. I won't let you down."

"And *I'll* lead the op team," Jason added.

Hansen nodded in agreement. "Then it's a plan."

Director Ferguson locked eyes with me. "We're putting a lot of faith in you. Don't underestimate Marco, but don't underestimate yourself either."

Though I felt a twinge of resentment toward Jason, I understood his reservations. This was risky, but while I wasn't an agent, I was trained and ready. And I was going to prove it.

Director Ferguson stared at the live satellite feed on the screen. "We're in luck. Marco's yacht is parked at the Miami marina."

Hansen swiped open her tablet and read the screen. "There are three clubs he frequents when he comes to port. I'll send a team ahead and see if we can't get eyes on him.

Hansen took charge of the logistics. "I'll coordinate with local law enforcement to keep an eye on the marina. We'll stay low-key."

The Director then turned to Jason. "Put together a team, get Eddie to set up a van, and get out there. If this weapon is the only way to stop this demon, I want it in our custody before Marco disappears again."

Jason nodded. "Understood, ma'am."

Her voice was firm, a steel underlining that reminded me how high the stakes really were. The word 'force' rang in my ears. While the agency had the power and resources to execute such an operation, the cost would be tremendous. The situation would go public, other agencies would step in, and who knew what would happen then? Not to mention, it could put Marco and his associates on high alert, making future missions exponentially harder.

"If your cover is blown, that's it," she continued. "We will go in and take the necklace by force. Understand that this is an absolute last resort. I don't want to escalate this situation further."

I met her gaze squarely. "I understand, Director. I won't let it come to that."

She nodded, her eyes meeting mine for just a second longer than necessary as if she were trying to impart something more. "See that you don't."

Hansen led Jason and me to one of the side rooms before leaving us alone as she went off to find wigs and different clothes for my disguise. Jason instructed me on how to wear the nearly invisible earbuds and a crash course on agency code words that I could use without blowing my cover.

Halfway through the notecards with words like Hemlock and Stardust, I paused and set them on my lap, looking at where Jason sat in the chair facing me. "Are you sure you're okay with this?"

The weight of the situation was overwhelming, a knot of tension pulling at my stomach.

"No, of course I'm not fucking okay with this," he said, his voice hard. "I'd never do anything to put you in harm's way if there was an alternative." His jaw shifted. "But I know it's the best option we have, and I wouldn't ask you to do this if I didn't believe you could." His eyes locked with mine. "And I promise I won't let anything happen to you."

His words, heavy with the unspoken emotions that he so rarely revealed to me, hung in the air. Yes, the mission was dangerous. Yes, there was a lot that could go wrong. But the chance to finally make a difference, to finally get us that much closer to stopping these earthquakes, and further to help Gavin's grandparents. That was worth it. The thought that I could do something even without my abilities ignited a fire within me, pushing back the cloud of doubt.

"Okay then," I said, exhaling a breath I hadn't realized I was holding. "Let's do it."

As Hansen worked her magic, transforming me from *me* into a glamorous club go-er who had a passion for antiques, I couldn't help but feel a mix of excitement and trepidation. This was my chance to finally help, to do something besides stand in the background.

Jason watched the makeover from the corner of the room, his arms crossed and a strange look on his face. For most, they'd see his usual impassive mask, but for me, it wasn't hard to read. His gaze portrayed a blend of concern, pride, and the undeniable look of desire glinting in his eyes.

As Hansen put the finishing touches on my makeup, he stalked over to me, the tension almost palpable between us. "I hate sending you out there looking like this," he said, his voice a low murmur only I could hear. "But remember, if anything goes wrong, I'll be right there with you." He tapped my ear.

It was the reassurance I needed, the final push to silence the creeping doubt. Jason had always had way more faith in me than I did and had a way of amplifying my courage. I peered up at him, batting my lashes playfully. "I know."

Later that night, I sat in the passenger seat as Jason navigated the neon-lit streets of Miami. We stopped a few blocks away from the club. Checking my makeup and disguise in the rear-view mirror, I took a deep breath.

Jason handed me a small, discreet, flesh-colored earpiece. "Remember, we're monitoring everything. If things get risky, say the code word, and we'll come in."

"Got it," I said, my heart pounding. "See you on the other side."

As I stepped out of the car and walked towards the club, my nerves were a mix of anticipation and fear.

With every step, I felt the weight of the mission. And when I went into the nightclub, it only grew heavier. With every beat of the music, with every step I took closer to Marco, I felt it: a potent blend of excitement and purpose. This was my mission, my responsibility. I was going to get that necklace, come hell or high water. The alternative, as Director Ferguson had laid out so starkly, was not an option. I would succeed; I had to.

To prepare, Kat fitted me with a blonde wig and helped me pick out a stunning red dress that would turn heads but not raise eyebrows. "Remember, Marco loves talking about antiques," she reminded me, handing over a purse fitted with a concealed weapon. "Be engaging, but don't let him suspect you know too much."

The nightclub was a pulsing mix of light and shadow, a place where secrets were just another form of currency. Jason's eyes met mine as I prepared to walk in, a silent exchange of trust and fear. I took a deep breath and stepped into the lion's den. Walking into the nightclub, all dolled up and blonde felt like stepping onto a live stage, except my audience was one of the most dangerous men in Italy.

I approached Marco, keeping my eyes open for the little details, the way his men eyed the crowd, the almost imperceptible nod he gave one of them as I approached, the swagger that masked a carefully calculated demeanor. My journalist's instinct kicked into high gear.

We exchanged pleasantries, the conversation flowing toward safe topics before I cautiously steered it toward antiques. I had to be tactful; prying too blatantly would set off alarm bells. Journalism had taught me that getting someone to open up required a delicate dance, especially if your subject was a guarded individual. You had to make them feel like they were in control, even when you were leading.

Spotting Marco was easy. He was surrounded by laughing and drinking women in tight skirts and men in expensive suits and ties. However, even with all the company, he seemed alone, a king in his castle. I waited for the right moment when several of his entourage had left for the dance floor and then 'accidentally' bumped into him holding a cocktail.

"Oh, I'm so sorry," I apologized, spilling my drink on the carpet.

The annoyance resting on his face faded when he looked me over, clearly intrigued. "No harm done, Bella. You seem to need another drink?" He waved a waitress over, and I smiled as she took my order for another martini.

"That necklace you're wearing," I said, "Babylonian?" I shook my head. "No, Akkadian."

Taking the bait, his eyes lit up, and he ran a thumb over the four-inch piece of bronze wrapped in leather. "Ah, you have an eye for antiques." He lowered his voice and whispered. "Did Sergio send you?"

I played along. "Oh yeah. You got me."

"I hope you asked him for double." Marco chuckled and winked, which surprisingly didn't make my skin crawl. If I hadn't seen the mile-long rap sheet Division 12 had on him, he genuinely seemed like a good guy. Still, I was on a mission, and I couldn't let a guilty conscience stop me from doing what I had to.

He asked me to sit next to him on the semi-circle couch in the VIP section, and as we shared drinks, he seemed more and more relaxed. Eventually, I half-sat on his lap and laughed with him when one of his group of friends got into an argument that ended with a glass of champagne in his friend's face. I used his distraction to lean closer and rested a hand on his chest, feeling the heavy necklace against my fingertips. I was inches away from my goal.

A glass tray was placed on the table with a telltale white powder. Marco was first to go, and as he leaned over, I unclasped the necklace smoothly and slipped it into my purse. The entire time, I knew Jason was listening through the earpiece, probably scrutinizing every word, every pause, every shift in tone. And strangely enough, that awareness added another layer of excitement to all of this, the tension sparking between us even though we were apart.

It was a fucking rush.

By the time I secured the necklace, my pulse was racing for more reasons than one. He sat upright, wiping his nose, and I needed to make a break for it before the surge from the cocaine wore off, and he felt the necklace missing.

"Uh, sorry," I said, getting to my feet and pretending to stumble. "I really need to use the ladies room."

"Don't stay too long," he said, flashing me a toothy grin.

"The party is just starting." He gestured to the two little white lines of powder on the table.

I giggled nervously, tucked a loose strand of blonde wig behind my ear, and made a beeline for the exit. As I stepped outside, blending into the night, my heart was pounding with adrenaline and relief. And when I slipped that necklace into my purse, when I finally stepped back into the cool night air, I felt it —a rush of exhilaration, relief, and a fierce, triumphant joy. I had done it. We had done it.

Jason was the first to greet me in the back of the van and leaned down to kiss me. "I knew you could do it." And for a moment, in the cool night air, I truly felt invincible. Almost, but not quite, like I had my power back.

FIFTEEN

Back at the warehouse, after I'd handed over the necklace with the artifact, Jason led me through a labyrinth of dim hallways and creaking metal until, finally, we'd found the break room. The space was a mishmash of old couches, a snack vending machine that had seen better days, and a couple of tables scattered with yesterday's newspapers. I plopped down on a frayed sofa, my limbs feeling like they were made of molten lead, and kicked off the heels and my wig. I ran my fingers through my hair, trying to sort out the tangles from under the mesh cap.

Jason took the chair opposite me, pulling it closer.

Kat's voice still echoed in my mind. She had looked more wired than tired when we left her in the makeshift lab downstairs, and we'd honestly been surprised she was still awake, even outlasting poor Eddie, who had wandered off to crash on one of the cots. "I'll examine it tonight," she had said, referring to the ornate handle we had risked our necks to get. "Eddie's databases might have something. I'll finish up in the morning."

Jason interrupted my thoughts. "You sure you don't want to go to a hotel? You look beat."

I raised an eyebrow, the muscles in my face almost too tired to manage even that. "If Kat's still sifting working, I'm not about to get room service and a bubble bath. Besides, if she finds something, I want to be here."

He leaned in, his eyes searching mine. "Fair point. But we've been running on fumes, Ella. Even Guardians need to rest."

"I know," I muttered, my mind buzzing with unanswered questions and the adrenaline finally draining away, replaced by a bone-deep fatigue.

He seemed to have sensed my restlessness because his hand reached for mine. The second our fingers touched, a spark had jumped between us—literal or metaphorical. I couldn't tell, and honestly, I didn't care. At that moment, the chaos of the day had condensed into this single point of contact, grounding me.

"I've been thinking," he started, pausing to read my expression, "about us."

I held my breath. Our relationship had never been simple. A complex weave of duty and personal entanglement had torn us apart before we'd crash-landed into each other's lives once again, and lately, the lines were blurring more than ever.

"These past few months, Elly," he continued, his voice tinged with something that sounded like awe. "In this wild mess that's our life, you're the one constant I never knew I needed."

His words struck chords deep within me, each syllable sinking into my skin, rooting itself into my bones. His hand lowered to his right pocket, and my soul left my body.

Oh, shit.

He leaned closer, his lips finding mine. The kiss was a slow burn, pulling us both out of our heads and into this pocket of peace we'd somehow managed to carve out for ourselves in a world brimming with the unexplainable. The sensory overload from the heist at the club had dulled down to a murmur, replaced by the intimacy of the moment.

When we finally broke apart, Jason's face was flushed, eyes clouded but intense. "Wow."

I laughed, the sound light and free. "Wow, indeed."

He leaned back, a content smile still lingering on his lips, and I assumed I shared a similar expression as well.

As he moved his hand to rest on his knee, the oxygen whooshed back into my lungs, and the panic that he was about to propose subsided.

"You were amazing out there tonight, you know. You might have a career at the agency if you ever decide to put down your camera."

"Not gonna happen."

"You don't have to work in the field, you know. They need analysts like Eddie. Work somewhere mostly safe, like at the headquarters or the research lab."

I scoffed. "Are you serious? Sitting at a desk all day? I'd get bored so fast." I smirked, "Besides, I've hit platinum level on my frequent flyer miles. Which credit card are you using, anyway?"

Jason's brows pulled together. "Why do you do that?" he said, the levity leaving his voice.

"Do what?" I shook my head.

"Deflect when I try to talk about the future? About our future? About us?"

I swallowed and turned away, not wanting to face him. He'd made a series of comments about what we'd do differently at our wedding since we'd been so involved with Cara's, which was expected, of course. However, I'd thought it'd been an idle conversation at the time. So I'd hoped all the espionage, legendary weapons, and shadow demons had been enough to distract him from this topic, but apparently, I had been wrong.

"I guess... I guess I'm just focused on the present. We're kinda in the middle of something big here, and it's hard for me to think that far ahead when I'm worried about today."

"But we can't just live in the *now*, can we? At some point, we have to consider what's next. Don't you ever think about that?"

"I do, Jason, but it's complicated. We can't just plan a future when our present is so messed up, can we?"

"That's just it, Elly. The present will always be unpredictable, but it's the possibility of a future that makes facing that uncertainty worthwhile."

Jason's words floated through the air, settling heavily between us. My mind raced. The present was indeed a wild, unpredictable thing, but what about the future? Was it just a series of these 'nows' stitched haphazardly together like a patchwork quilt? I felt like I was on the edge of a cliff, staring down into an abyss of uncertainty.

If I had been the old, pre-Jason Ella, the one who had loved recklessly and without reservation, I might have jumped right into that future, he was selling feet first. However, *that* Ella was long gone. My past mistakes, along with his, had left scars and deep grooves carved into my soul. How could I think about the future when the ground we were standing on was not just metaphorically shaky but literally quaking beneath our feet?

The room closed in on me as I hesitated to respond. Words hung in the air, heavy and unspoken, words that could either fix the cracks between us or tear us apart.

Then Jason said it. "I love you, Elly."

There it was. Just three words and my heart was pounding as if I'd just got off the bike at an advanced spin class.

It felt like someone knocked the wind out of me. Emotions I couldn't even begin to untangle tightened vice-like around my chest. Part of me instinctively wanted to echo his words. *That's what I should do, right?* I was his girlfriend. I should tell him I love him, but the words stuck in my throat, imprisoned behind layers of doubts and reservations.

I stared at him, his face a desperate mix of hope and vulnerability. It was heartbreaking, like watching a storm and a sunset collide, and I understood that I couldn't walk that path with him. Not yet. Not when I was still trying to find my own way.

"I'm sorry, Jason," I whispered. "Really, I am. I like what we have right now, but I'm not ready to promise a future I'm not sure of."

Silence filled the room, heavy and final. We were stuck on a cliffhanger, a pause in a story that had no clear ending. We were left with nothing but a chain of what-ifs, and for the moment, that was where we had to leave it.

Jason stood, his eyes piercing daggers into mine. "You sleep in the same bed with me, you fuck me, you share a goddamn toothbrush with me, but you can't say it?" Although his voice was barely above a whisper as he continued, it might as well have been a scream. "What the hell are you so scared of?"

Without waiting for me to answer, Jason stalked out of the room and shut the door behind him.

I was left alone sitting on the pullout couch that had seen better days. the breakroom suddenly felt like the set of a sad indie movie, devoid of warmth, echoing with the silence left in the wake of our broken conversation.

God, what have I done?

My mind was a whirlwind, spinning with the conversation that had just transpired. A conversation that had started with a toe-curling kiss and then plummeted so very far south. Should I run after him?

I put my head in my hands, elbows digging into my thighs. This was our second shot at this, and we'd both sworn that things would be different this time. We'd be open and honest, so how could I live with myself if I lied to him and broke the promise that our relationship was founded on?

There was no denying I cared about him deeply. He was my rock. My center. My world... but love... *Did I love him?*

A hollow feeling settled in my stomach as if someone had scooped out all the hope and left a crater. I didn't deserve Jason. The man who accepted me as everything that was Ella *and* as everything that was a Guardian. He deserved someone complete, someone whose soul wasn't twisted with the fates of ancient gods and prophecies. A whimper snagged in my throat, and tears prickled the backs of my eyes. I had just squandered my shot at something that even remotely resembled happiness.

The room weighed down on me as if the walls were closing in, wanting to compact all my emotional garbage into a neat little cube. How I wished the door would burst open and Jason would walk back in, tell me that his 'I love you' was retractable if it meant we could hit the reset button on this whole messed-up situation. I'd throw my arms around him, inhaling the familiar scent of his cologne, and tell him I was ready. Ready for a future, uncertain but ours.

But the door stayed shut.

No dramatic re-entrance, no last-minute declarations. It was just me and the aging couch that creaked like it was sharing my pain.

I hugged my knees to my chest, becoming a human ball of regret. What would it take to make things right? Could they even be made right? My eyes drifted to my phone lying on the coffee table. I could call him, text him, beg him to come back. But was that fair to either of us when I couldn't promise what he so clearly needed?

I leaned back, my spine pressing against the worn-out

upholstery of the couch. As if on cue, the breakroom light flick-ered above me, casting fluctuating shadows like it, too, was unsure of what lay ahead.

SIXTEEN

I woke up gradually, feeling every muscle in my body protest against the lumpy pullout couch I'd spent the night on. I rubbed my eyes and then glanced at my phone —7 a.m. God, even the time felt like a physical weight pressing down on my chest. I stretched my limbs, grimacing as last night's argument with Jason ricocheted through my mind. The words, the tension, him storming out, the throbbing in my skull, and my sick stomach felt like a terrible hangover.

I forced myself off the couch and shuffled into what had been the employee's bathroom. The splash of cold water on my face was like an unsolicited reality check, and the scratchy paper towels irritated the scratches that still lingered on my face. Just as I finished braiding my hair, my phone chimed. My heart shuddered in my chest as I read the notification: a text from Jason.

I'd always been a rip-it-off-like-a-band-aid kind of girl, so fingers trembling, I clicked it open, preparing myself for whatever it might say.

"Found a lead. It's urgent—meet me here ASAP."

An address was tacked on below the message.

I stared at the screen, bewildered. After the emotional grenade we'd lobbed at each other last night, I'd assumed he'd want some breathing room. The text told me something else: his professional duty still held sway, even if, personally, we were dancing on a fault line.

Taking a steadying breath, I grabbed my phone and jacket and slipped out of the room. My nerves were frayed, and the last thing I wanted was to bump into anyone who might question where I was going and why Jason wasn't here with me.

Just as I tiptoed down the hallway, Gavin's head emerged from the employee lounge like a prairie dog on alert. "You getting breakfast?" he said, yawning.

Damn it. I'd assumed he'd be staying at the hospital. "Uh, hi. I thought you were staying at the hospital with your grandparents?"

His face paled. "The doctor said I should take a night off and told me to take a shower and get a good night's sleep. He promised he'd call me if anything changed."

"Oh, yeah, that makes sense." I started forward again. "Well, I've got an errand to run," I replied, forcing casualness into my voice and keeping my momentum forward.

His eyes narrowed. "What errand? Can we stop and get breakfast on the way?"

Thinking on my feet, I sighed and decided to toss him a bone. "Okay, so Jason's found something about a piece of Sharur. I'm going to check it out, but it's probably nothing."

Gavin perked up. "A lead? Why didn't you say so?"

No easy way out of this one. "Fine, but we should hurry."

"Give me five to get my shoes," he said and disappeared back into the room.

Thirty minutes later, the Uber I'd called pulled up to the address Jason had sent me. I'd spent the ride nervously scrolling through Google, only to find out that the place was a pawn shop, one of Florida's oldest. However, it looked as sketchy as you'd expect. Gavin wouldn't stop talking, speculating on whether this lead would, in fact, pan out and what finding the shaft might mean. However, I was only half-listening; my thoughts tangled up with the memory of last night's fight.

Stepping out of the car and onto the sidewalk, I took a deep, grounding breath. Okay, Ella, you can do this. We had a mission to focus on, and if Jason could set aside our mess for the sake of that mission, then so could I.

As I approached the door, hand poised to push it open, I immediately sensed something was off. The door was locked, and the windows revealed it was pitch-black inside.

"Gavin, do you see this?" I pointed to the locked door and darkened windows.

"Yeah," he squinted, peering through the glass, "It's not even 8 a.m. though. Maybe they're closed?

I shook my head. "Look at the dust on the handle. No one has been here for days."

My gut clenched with worry. Something *was* wrong. Maybe I'd gotten the address wrong? Or the Uber driver had? I stepped back toward the road to get a better look at the sign on the building. No. This was the right place.

Frantically, I pulled out my phone and dialed Jason's number, my thumb hovering over the call button like it was a detonator. Voicemail.

Damn it, Jason, where are you?

I was just about to dial one of our contacts at Division 12, feeling a surge of unease, when I heard the sound of a lock disengaging. The door creaked open, and there he was. Jason stood in the doorway. He was wearing a black shirt and camo pants, and his face had its usual light stubble on his chin and jaw. His steel blue eyes met mine, and a wave of relief washed over me.

"Sorry. I came in from the back and thought I'd unlocked it," he said, ushering us inside.

I stepped in first, followed by Gavin, my eyes adjusting to the dim light. But as I did, questions swarmed my mind like bees around a hive. How had he found this place? Why had he come here alone without backup? And the one that was at the forefront of my mind: where did we stand after the emotional earthquake of last night?

Gavin breezed past me, blissfully unaware, as I locked eyes with Jason. The air was thick with words left unsaid, and yet, at that moment, the mission had to come first. Personal issues would have to wait; we had work to do.

As Jason closed and locked the door behind us, I realized this wasn't your run-of-the-mill pawn shop. The gleaming mahogany counters and the meticulously organized shelves with printed labels. And then my gaze landed on the items themselves—this was something else entirely. It was like walking into a museum of modern-day treasures.

Signed photos of Taylor Swift, framed with care, hung beside what looked to be one of her tour outfits, preserved in a glass case like it was a Renaissance painting. My eyebrows shot up at the dozens of designer labels on shoes and handbags.

Gavin let out a low whistle and bolted toward a display that had his eyes widening like saucers. "No way is this real," he exclaimed, pointing at a football encased in a glass box. A small placard beneath it claimed that it was signed by the entire team from last year's epic Super Bowl.

"Yeah, it's legit," Jason confirmed, coming up behind us.

Gavin looked like he'd just discovered the Holy Grail. "Wait, so how did you find this place?"

"It's not what I found; it's what we're here to find," Jason replied cryptically, throwing me a glance that was heavy with unspoken words.

I met his gaze, and for a moment, the tension of our personal drama filled the air again, but Jason broke eye contact, directing his attention to the task at hand.

"We can admire the merchandise later. Right now, I have something else you need to see," he said.

I nodded, shoving my swirling thoughts and anxieties to the side. As much as my heart wanted to dwell on last night, I needed to concentrate.

As I followed Jason deeper into the opulent pawn shop, I couldn't help but marvel at the certified treasures here. So, why did it look like it hadn't had foot traffic in weeks?

"How did you say you found this place?" I found myself saying, the uneasy feeling growing into suspicion.

"Well, it's a bit complicated. You see, I met this guy, and he worked at the museum in Philadelphia. He said that the owner here had a customer that would buy all the old stuff. Anything thousands of years old, coins, pottery, you name it."

"And where's the owner now?" Gavin asked, glancing toward the space behind the counter.

"Vacation," Jason replied without a look back and continued walking. "The piece is up here in the back. They hadn't even unpacked it." Jason's laugh this time was tinged with an edge that made the hairs on the back of my neck stand up.

My eyes remained fixed on Jason's back, and it occurred to me that he had changed clothes from when I'd seen him last. Had he come back to the room when I'd been asleep? Or had he changed them elsewhere? A hotel, perhaps, or another place in the warehouse? But why? If this had been so urgent, why had he taken time to change?

Then I noticed the lack of a lump at his hip, and the creeping unease slithered to the front of my thoughts. He never went anywhere without the rare and pricey custom Pit Viper.

He'd probably be buried with them someday. Hopefully, it's not too soon, of course.

"Jason, where's your gun?" I asked, my eyes narrowing at the empty place at his hip.

His gaze faltered for just a second, but it was enough. "Ah, I must have left it behind."

I exchanged a glance with Gavin. He sensed it, too; something was definitely not right.

"I'll show you what I found," he said before I could press him further and led us out into the back junkyard. We entered the maze of discarded treasures and garbage, and in the early morning light, the junkyard took on a spectral quality, the twisted metal and rusting cars like beasts from another world. Jason led us deeper before stopping and turning toward us.

"Here it is, in this crate," he gestured vaguely towards a pile of rusty auto parts and broken furniture.

It was that sentence—so calm, so eerily confident—that confirmed my suspicion. I peered at him, and his blue eyes had an unnatural sheen in the muted light.

This was not Jason, at least not the Jason I knew.

"Who are you?" I demanded, my hand inching toward a crowbar that was discarded beside a stack of wooden crates.

Jason—or whoever he was—laughed, and the sound was guttural, almost demonic. "You may call me Asag."

The air shifted, becoming dense with a dark energy I could almost taste. My heart pounded as realization set in; we were dealing with something—or someone—far beyond human.

"Where's Jason? What have you done with him?" Gavin's voice was tight, and I could see the tension ripple through his body, ready for conflict.

"The human you call Jason is of no consequence," Asag sneered. "His form, however, was a wise decision to obtain on my part.

I felt a rush of anger and fear coalesce inside me. This creature has done something with Jason to disguise himself to look like him. Hurt him. Kidnapped him. My stomach hardened. The scratch on his hand from the golf course. He'd had no memory of how he'd gotten it, only that something had cut him in the chaos of the smoke and ash.

It had to have been Asag. He'd disappeared into the smoke after speaking with me. Had Asag seen me arrive with Jason? Listened to us talk before the crack had separated us. He'd known Jason had meant something important to me. Enough to trust him implicitly if he'd said he needed me.

"Where the fuck is Jason," I said, emphasizing each word through clenched teeth. "If you hurt him, I swear to god I will—"

Jason's grin widened, revealing an evil, malice-filled thing, and I hated myself that I could've ever believed that this was actually Jason.

"Do what, *Guardian*?" he said, "I smell nothing but fear on you. Fear and disappointment." He tapped the front of his teeth. "Tell you what. You tell me where Sharur is, and maybe—just maybe—I'll let you walk away."

Beside me, the air crackled with electricity as Gavin waved his hand threateningly. "Tell us where he is."

Asag/Jason's smile faltered. "A boy, as champion? Ninurta mocks me."

"Mock this." Gavin unleashed a blast of blue lightning at the creature, even as I screamed at him to stop.

The creature's body arched back as if struck by a taser, and sparks danced along his face and arms.

"Gavin, no!" I shouted, placing a hand on his arm. "If he dies. Jason dies."

Gavin's chest heaved as he willed the electricity back into submission.

Asag/Jason leaned over, recovering from the onslaught of magic, then laughed. "The one you call Jason is dead."

My heart dropped to my stomach; each beat a painful thud against my ribcage. Traitorous. That's what my heart was. How dare it continue to beat unaffected, unfazed by the gut-wrenching truth that Jason, my Jason, was gone. A thick fog of regret and fear clouded my thoughts, choking me more effectively than if I'd been submerged under the ocean.

But before I could respond, a bolt of light and wind tore through the air as Gavin, face twisted in rage, shook off my grip and extended his hands. Bursts after bursts of lightning streamed from his fingertips as he spat curses of hate at the creature that were as if speaking my mind.

This time, however, the demon was ready and lunged at us. I may not have had my power or Sharur, but I had the crowbar, my resolve, and most importantly, the desire to kick some demon ass.

A surge of adrenaline burned through my veins, like a jolt of electricity supercharging every cell. Screw it, what did it matter now? If Jason was gone, and I had to go down, I'd go down swinging.

He'd tricked me, lured me here. Although it was a monster in front of me, the betrayal stung as if it had been someone I'd cared for, as if it actually had been Jason. As I raised my crowbar aloft, the world began to quake beneath us. The ground itself roared open as if the Earth were angry. I staggered, clutching a rusty fender for dear life to keep from losing my footing.

When I looked up, I was met with a visage from my darkest nightmares. The man standing there was not Jason, not anymore. His features twisted and elongated into something hideous, a creature nearly double my height with glowing embers for eyes, pale, hairless skin, and claws instead of fingers. This creature was not meant to walk in the light of day. This was a thing of terror that should be left in the shadows.

Asag's elongated arms lashed out, and an invisible force swept toward us, churning the ground like a giant burrowing worm. Gavin tried to leap out of the way but was a split-second too late, and the force slammed him into a pile of wrecked cars, his leg pinned beneath twisted metal.

My eyes shifted to the rusty crowbar in my hand. It felt absurdly inadequate, like bringing a water pistol to a gunfight. But as I met Gavin's gaze, I knew we were thinking the same thing. We had to try. We had to fight, even if the odds were laughably against us.

Because if we didn't, Asag wouldn't just kill us, he'd use Jason's body to do unimaginable things. And that, I realized as I steadied my grip on the crowbar, was something I couldn't live —or die—with. My eyes darted to Gavin, then back to the demon. Adrenaline turned my fear into fuel, and I lunged, crowbar aimed directly at Asag's head, convinced that if I could just make contact—

Thwack!

The crowbar hit, but Asag didn't even flinch. Instead, a shock of pain radiated up my arm, jarring my wrist and elbow as if I'd just tried to demolish a concrete wall. I staggered back, gripping my throbbing arm.

Still, I struck again and again, stuffing down the pain from each hit.

Finally, with the fifth assault, Asag spun, and the rumbling ground rose under my feet, and I was tossed backward, my side and shoulders slamming into the side of a dented truck. Pain radiated up my spine, and my chest heaved from the exertions.

Asag stood still, its eyes pivoting to focus on Gavin, who was rising to his feet.

I scanned the cluttered yard for anything else to use. Broken glass, wooden shipping crates, and fragments of old machinery lay strewn about like the discarded toys of a giant. Asag's dark aura seemed to swallow the muted light, making him look even more monstrous.

I sidestepped a heap of old tires, and my gaze locked onto Asag. But for all the junkyard's hazardous offerings, I was struck by a devastating realization: I was woefully unprepared to face this demon. I wasn't armed with sacred relics. I couldn't call upon celestial aid; hell, I didn't even have a pocketknife. It was just me, a Guardian with her power on the fritz, taking on an ancient creature of unimaginable strength.

But giving up wasn't an option. I tightened my grip on the crowbar, its cool metal the only reassuring sensation in a spiraling situation.

"Get ready!" Gavin called out. His hands were cupped, electricity crackling louder, swirling with the wind that had picked up. He looked like he was trying to capture a storm in his palms.

Asag roared, lunging toward us with monstrous speed. My pulse vibrated in my eardrums; this was it. It was now or never. Arm muscles screaming in protest, I swung the crowbar, aiming for Asag's side this time. Again, it felt like hitting a wall, but I had no time to nurse my stinging flesh and pivoted on my heel, dodging their retaliatory strike that splintered the wooden crate beside me.

Gavin unleashed his stored electricity just as Asag turned his attention back to me. Lightning lanced out, brightening the dark lot for a split second before striking the demon squarely in the chest. Asag's scream pierced the night, a sound so unnatural it made my skin crawl.

But he was still standing.

Asag's eyes—those terrible, burning voids—locked onto me, and I knew he was far from defeated. I glanced at Gavin, whose face was a mask of exhaustion and desperation. We were out of time and dangerously low on any chance of walking away from this.

From behind me, Gavin grimaced, and while favoring his left leg, electricity crackled around his fingertips, and then he threw his head back and yelled.

The sky erupted. A bolt of lightning, as if pulled by an invisible thread, struck Asag from a nearby power pole. Sparks exploded, a miniature fireworks display gone horribly wrong, and for a second, Asag twisted in agony, roaring in pain. Then, the security lighting fizzled and died, plunging us into an eerie twilight, lit only by the glow of Gavin's electrical charge and the ambient city light filtering in through gaps in the junkyard fence.

I gripped the crowbar, paralyzed by what to do. The metal was conductive, and if I hit him now, I, too, would be electrocuted.

Gavin and Asag were connected, bonded by the thousands of volts of electricity he was drawing from the grid.

I could do nothing but wait and watch and hope. Beside me, Gavin's body arched, and his arms splayed out as if surrendering himself to the sky, to the power. How long could he keep this up? Was it hurting him? Damaging his nerves and boiling his blood?

Every second could be killing him. If I'd already lost Jason, I couldn't lose him too.

Without thinking, I reached toward his shoulder.

"Gavin!" I screamed, trying to break his concentration, but the instant my hand connected, my body exploded in a torrential downpour of pain.

Gavin's head swiveled to me; the hazel flecks of green in his eyes, ignited with miniature thunderstorms, met mine, and there was a split second of recognition.

But it was too late. The uninhibited electricity surged into me, searing my veins and paralyzing my muscles. My vision clouded, and I collapsed to the ground. As I sunk into an abyss, I looked up at Gavin. Even in his pain, he was mouthing a word I couldn't hear but understood—fight.

I tried to fight the rising tide of fear and despair, but it was overwhelming. I was useless. Gavin's power had offered a brief glimmer of hope, but even he couldn't subdue Asag. The realization of our helplessness settled in like a weight, unbearable and heavy.

Asag taunted me, mocking my vulnerabilities and weaknesses. "Inanna has abandoned you, Guardian. You are pathetic. You cannot dare defeat me." I grimaced, looking at Gavin, still struggling against the weight, pinning him down. He was our last hope, and I was going to lose him too.

"No, Ella!" Gavin's voice reached me, but I was already slipping, caught in the allure of blacking out to avoid the agony that was consciousness.

I wanted to scream, to fight, to do something, but all I felt was pain and defeat.

As darkness claimed me, my last thought was an echo of my failure. I'd failed Jason, failed Gavin, failed myself, and now I was falling, falling into an endless tunnel of darkness, leaving behind a world still trembling, still breaking, just like me.

SEVENTEEN

When I opened my eyes, I was unsure if I was actually awake or still drifting through some surreal landscape of the mind. The air weighed heavily around me, like the atmosphere right before a storm broke. I found myself standing on a vast plain ringed by mountains so tall they seemed to graze the sky. Above, dark clouds churned, lit intermittently by flashes of red and blue lightning.

Beside me was Gavin—only it wasn't the Gavin I knew. Here, he was Ninurta, clad in bronze armor intricately hammered. We exchanged a glance, a mutual recognition darting between us, wordless yet full.

I peered down, recognizing that I, too, was clad in bronze armor and a white tunic. In my hand, I gripped Sharur, its vibrations humming into the marrow of my bones and echoing the rhythm of my heartbeat. Although I had yet to test my theory, I somehow sensed in this realm, this place, that my powers to manipulate carbon materials were restored. Yet they felt more intense, augmented by the essence of Sharur to create something entirely new, something stronger. It was as though my every cell had been supercharged, buzzing with an almost electric intensity.

I wasn't just human anymore. I wasn't even a Guardian.

I was a goddess. Inanna, reborn.

The embodiment of the goddess herself recreating a memory, an epic battle. Perhaps one of the ones Kat had told me about when we'd researched the statue and, later, Gavin's tattoos.

Just then, a powerful voice threaded its way through the howling winds. "Unite them, the essence of Earth and Sky, for only then can you banish the darkness."

"Ready?" Gavin/Ninurta's voice quivered with a newfound urgency as he rested his hand on the hilt of a sword that emitted a glow, a foil to the darkness around us.

"As ready as we'll ever be," I replied, the words lifting from my lips and vanishing into a gust of wind.

The demon surged, a tidal wave of malice, a gargantuan figure of living darkness. His roar rippled through the ground, juddering into my bones, filling my insides with a visceral dread that felt like liquid lead.

"This is it. No turning back," Gavin/Ninurta declared, and I tightened my grip on Sharur, feeling a binding of willpower— mine and the weapon's—as if we'd become extensions of one another.

Side by side, we charged, and Sharur was like an extension of my arm, each swing a release of kinetic energy that scattered the shadows like a wrecking ball crashing through a wall of darkness, sending shards flying in every direction.

I felt invincible.

Transformed.

Gavin/Ninurta beside me was a dance of light and lethal grace, his lightning blades slicing through dark flesh as if parting shadows.

Beside me, Gavin/Ninurta fought, a flickering embodiment of the god Ninurta. The air rippled as he swung his lightning sword, a glinting arc that cleaved the smoggy dark. A mound of smoke descended upon him, twisting around his throat, and he snarled rather than roared, his voice tinged with desperation.

The ground underfoot shifted with each step, loose sand spilling out from beneath my sandals. Gavin/Ninurta was a streak of lightning beside me, his blades crackling with electrical energy, leaving tracers in the air as they cut through the darkness. My grip tightened on Sharur's hilt as I lunged forward, twisting my wrist at the last moment to cleave through a writhing mass of shadow. It disintegrated with a hiss, evaporating like mist under sunlight.

Another shadowy figure lunged, bypassing Gavin's defenses, and it latched onto his arm, and he hissed in pain. A jolt of concern shot through me; we were strong, *very* strong; however, we were not invincible; we were both nearing our limits.

"Keep alert!" he yelled at me, ripping the shadow from his arm and reducing it to wisps with a flick of his blade.

"I'm trying!" I huffed back, thrusting Sharur into a wall of oncoming darkness. The shadows recoiled, but not enough. One broke through, its talons slashing across my arm. The sensation was like being branded, searing through skin and muscle and bone as though the demon knew where to cut to make me hurt the most.

Gavin shouted in rage, crossing his swords and releasing a burst of energy that vaporized the attacking shadows.

"Thanks," I gasped, using the momentary respite to reassess. We were holding our ground, but barely. Every demon we cut down was replaced by two more. The sense of being overwhelmed crept into my thoughts, sowing seeds of doubt and fear.

No. I was a goddess—the goddess of war itself. Inanna would never surrender. She would not concede.

With a rallying cry, I gripped Sharur tightly and charged back into the fray. Shadows surged toward me like a tide, but I was a breaker, splitting them apart, scattering them to the wind. Each swing was a symphony of destruction, each connection a burst of cathartic release.

Still, the shadows kept coming, relentless and insatiable. It felt like I was trapped in the level of a video game and with no idea how to move past the next one. Each step forward was countered by a pushback, each victory marred by a fresh assault. I felt myself tiring, Sharur growing heavier in my hands. It's once invigorating energy now a weight dragging me down.

"Uncle!" I called out as I swung Sharur. For a fleeting moment, the din ceased. Shadows recoiled, morphing into ever more grotesque shapes.

But then they retaliated. Talons of darkness reached out, lashing across my chest and neck, each welt burning like molten metal.

"They're too strong," I yelled, my voice edged with fear and frustration, barely audible over the sound of our desperate combat.

"I know," he shouted back, his blade severing yet another shadow, which disintegrated into a wisp of smoke but not before it clawed at him, leaving its mark. "I know."

Every clash, every swing felt like the dying gasps of a battle waged across eons.

The demons weren't retreating, just regrouping, their wails filling the air with a blood-curdling whine.

"Do we go after them?" Gavin's voice was hoarse, tinged with very human-sounding fatigue.

"No," I shook my head, spent and disheartened.

A mirthless chuckle escaped his lips. "A god and a goddess, yet we bleed and tire."

One particularly resilient shadow coiled around Gavin, almost pulling him off balance. "Ninurta!" I screamed, whirling Sharur with all the strength that remained. The mace met the shadow, tearing it apart like crepe paper.

His face was a grimace of pain and relief. Yet the evil shadows remained insurmountable and relentless. Finally, Inanna's voice filled the spaces within me once more: "Together."

In perfect harmony, as if choreographed by destiny itself, Gavin/Ninurta unleashed bolts of celestial light as I raised Sharur high above my head. With a scream that seemed to rupture time, I brought it down. The universe stilled for a split second before an explosion of blinding light erupted.

When my vision cleared, we were alone. The demons and Asag vanished as if wiped from existence. Exhausted but alive, Gavin/Ninurta transformed back into Gavin beside me. We exchanged looks with each other, both panting and dripping in sweat.

Just then, the landscape began to dissolve. Gavin/Ninurta, now a mere outline, began to fade, swallowed by some unfathomable mist. The woman's voice ebbed away: "Remember where your power comes from, Guardian of Vela. Remember."

As the battlefield dissolved and Gavin/Ninurta began to fade away, I found myself transported once more. My surroundings shifted, landing me in a place that felt like an ethereal version of the Middle East where sands were golden as if touched by Midas, vast skies tinged with shades of coral and lavender, and palm trees with fronds that shimmered like an emerald in the twilight.

I was in a desert, yet this was no ordinary desert. The sands beneath my feet felt like silk, and the air carried the scent of spices and unknown blossoms, adding to the dream-like quality of it all.

I walked, feet sinking softly into the gilded sand, toward a horizon that seemed both close and infinitely far. As I walked, I could see the silhouettes of ancient ziggurats and statues framed against the sky like haunting memories.

It felt like the essence of the region's rich history had been distilled into this single, extraordinary dreamscape—a tribute to the cradle of civilization, yet also a glimpse of some other-worldly realm. Every step I took was cushioned by the sands, as if the Earth itself was protecting me, caressing my feet, and an unseen force propelled me forward. The winds whispered secrets, not in words, but in feelings, waves of serenity washing over me.

In the distance, an oasis appeared surrounded by tall, reed-like plants with tassels that glowed like fireflies. The water in the oasis sparkled, reflecting a moon that was neither full nor crescent but shaped like an ancient symbol I couldn't quite place. As I approached the water, my reflection stared back, yet the image began to shift and change. I saw not just my face but countless others—faces of people I had known, some I had lost, and others that were strangers. It was as if the pool held within it the essence of countless lives, each connected by an invisible thread of fate.

Then, I heard the voice of the woman once more, but this time, it echoed all around me, coming from the sky, the sand, the very air. "Remember, you are a single note in the cosmic symphony, but even a single note can resonate with the power to change the world."

As she spoke, the landscape around me began to tremble, ripples spreading across the oasis. The ancient structures, magnificent as they were, crumbled into the golden sands from which they'd risen. With its unearthly hues, the sky started to darken, each shade deepening as though absorbed by an unseen void. The dream was collapsing, yet it felt like a necessary dissolution—and a pang of sadness seeped into me.

Then, I felt myself being pulled back through layers of sleep and the veil separating dreams from reality. The scents of spices and blossoms turned into the sterile smell of antiseptic. Plain walls and fluorescent lights replaced the lush landscape. And yet, as I awoke, laying there in what I now realized was a hospital, the last tendrils of the dream persisted.

And just like that, I was ripped back to consciousness. But something had shifted. I flexed my hands and felt it—a dormant power that had somehow awakened. One thing became clear as I sat up, tingles of energy still dancing at my fingertips.

I was never powerless. I never had been.

EIGHTEEN

"Finally awake?" Gavin said. "You were sleeping harder than my grandpa after he had his knee replacement."

I wiped the sleep from my eyes and licked my cracked lips. "Water?" I asked.

Gavin handed me a plastic bottle, and I removed the lid, my mind still reeling from all that had happened.

I sorted through my memories. We'd met Jason at the Pawn Shop. He'd found something related to Sharur—a piece of the weapon. Gavin and I had gone there, but then... Oh my god.

"Jason?" I stammered, worry clogging my throat.

"Don't worry. He's okay." Gavin sat back on the couch and rested his hands behind his head. "After you blacked out, I called Eddie. And Jason, the *real* Jason, showed up with a whole squadron of Division 12 guards. They had you checked out by a medic before moving you, and then when it was clear you had a mild concussion and just needed to rest, they brought you here."

The water soothed my dry throat as I slowly sipped from the bottle, trying to absorb and fill in the blank spots in my memory. Soon, they washed over me—how that creature had deceived me. How it mimicked Jason's voice, touch, and eyes, only to unravel into something dark, twisted, and terrifying.

My side hurt from where Asag had thrown rocks, and the left side of my face stung as if I'd fallen into a blackberry bush, but overall, I felt bruised but not broken. He'd been so strong. Unstoppable. My crowbar had been useless, equivalent to the amount of damage shooting arrows at a cloud would do.

I peered over at Gavin. He'd been epic. Summoning lighting from the nearby power poles, which seemed to be the only thing that *did* affect Asag/Jason.

And then I'd had my vision. The three parts of Sharur are a leather handle, a wooden shaft, and a bone head.

Carbon elements. All of them.

I was the one destined to find it, repair it, and wield it. I knew it as I knew my own name.

Still, the vision had meant more. Gavin had a huge part to play in this as well, and I shouldn't leave him in the dark with what I'd seen.

"Enheduanna," I started. "Or at least a version of her came to me when I was unconscious."

Gavin's eyes widened, and he shifted in his seat. "Really? What did she say?"

I relayed everything she had shown me. The mace, the great battle, the power, the way Ninurta had been a part of Gavin, all of it.

When I'd finished, Gavin was grinning. "Epic shit." He raised a hand, and I tensed, preparing for him to summon the electricity from the room, but then he lowered it to his lap as if remembering the harm it could cause, and his shoulders slumped.

"What is it?" I asked.

"How stupid is it that I think I can have a normal life now? What if I have a bad dream and can't control my magic and burn the house down?" He sniffed and placed his head in his hands. I leaned forward, wanting to reach out and comfort him, but found my side ached where I'd been hit.

"I'm sorry, truly," I said. "But I believe you can have both. This life and those gifts don't cancel out the old life you had. It's still there, waiting if you choose to go back."

"That's bullshit," he said, peering up at me with bloodshot eyes. "I can't go back. Not after what I've seen. What I'm capable of. Sitting in college classes feels pointless. Why learn algebra or write essays when the world could literally be ending?" He paused, his chest heaving. "Everything I thought was wrong. Gods. Demons. Magic. All of it is true, and pretending like it isn't like I'm some normal person, it's impossible."

I scratched the side of my face, feeling the tender scabs on my cheek that I must've gotten when I'd fallen. Fragments of memory shuffle forward in my brain, and I remember Gavin standing beside me when Asag's brutal attack had thrown me backward.

Maybe he could be right. Maybe I was the one mistaken. I had so desperately been clinging to the idea that once this was over, everything would go back to normal, with or without my magic. I could keep my everyday life *and* be the Guardian of Vela. Indecision tore at my insides, and I felt like there was nothing more I could say to comfort him except, "We'll figure this out. But right now, I need you to hold it together, okay? I know this isn't what you asked for, but the world and thousands of people in it are counting on you. On us."

Gavin sat up, grimacing. "Okay," he said after a long moment.

"Okay," I breathed and rested my hands on my thighs, trying to sort through what had happened before I'd been knocked out.

Asag had been desperate, frantically escaping Gavin's electrical wrath, but he'd been far from defeated. A question surfaced on the tip of my tongue.

"What happened after I passed out?" I asked.

Gavin leaned forward and shrugged. "The fuses blew on the block, and everything went dark, so I grabbed you and ran."

"You carried me?"

"Yep, like a fireman all the way down the block."

I laughed dryly. Athletic shit.

"And then took you to the bathroom of the gas station and called Eddie." Gavin's eyebrows raised to emphasize his point. "And the rest is just like I said."

My lips pressed together, confusing, still nagging at the edges of my skull that Asag would just let us go so easily like that. I should be thanking Gavin instead of questioning him. He'd saved my life. We'd caught a lucky break. Ridiculously fucking lucky. Things could've easily turned out differently; turned out wrong. In another parallel universe, I was sure we weren't having this conversation at all because we were both dead.

"Well, thank you," I said, smiling. "You saved my life, you know."

A flush appeared on his cheeks. "Sure. You'd have done the same for me."

"Absolutely."

Our conversation was cut short when a Division agent medic came in to check my vitals and apply antibiotic ointment to my cuts.

Jason entered shortly after, wearing a solemn expression, and for a moment, a tense silence filled the room.

Finally, Gavin stood and clapped his hands on his thighs. "I'll go see if they need uh..." His sentence finished with an awkward, mumbled excuse before he rushed out.

Jason shut the door behind him, and the room felt eerily silent, a stark contrast to the chaotic emotions swirling within me. I glanced up and saw that his blue eyes were filled with concern but also something deeper. It was the same look I'd always found comforting, the steadfast reassurance that everything would turn out okay. I would be okay.

It was the look I thought I'd lost forever.

"How you doing, Elly?" he asked softly.

"How am I doing?" I laughed bitterly, fighting back tears, and dropped my gaze to where my hands were tangled in the blankets. "That's a complicated question."

He moved closer and sat down beside me on the cot. "Look, I can't even begin to imagine what you've been through. I already thanked Gavin for getting you out of that shit show."

Jason took my hand gently, snapping me out of the spiraling flashbacks that lingered at the edges of my mind. "Elly, look at me."

I looked up, staring into his eyes, and for the first time since I'd awoken, I felt like I could breathe.

"It wasn't your fault," he said firmly. "You couldn't have known it wasn't me. And you're safe now. That's what matters."

His words were like a soothing balm to my jagged nerves, but they couldn't wipe away the feeling of guilt, the ache that clung to my heart. "I was so afraid I'd lost you, Jason. When Asag transformed into you, I thought he'd taken your body. Possessed you somehow, and I was so angry, so broken. I thought you'd become something evil, and that thought alone was enough to——." My voice cracked as I found I was unable to complete the sentence.

Jason squeezed my hand tighter. "I'm here. I'm real, and I'm not going anywhere. We'll get through this, just like we've gotten through everything else. Asag made a mistake by underestimating just how much of an asshole I can become if someone threatens someone I love."

Hearing him say those words made the weight on my shoulders feel a little lighter, even as my throat closed. Love. He'd said it again. Spoke so freely. So easily as if he had no clue what it did to me. The way my pulse ratcheted higher when he said it. I leaned into him, resting my head on his shoulder, and breathed in his comforting scent.

"I'm sorry," I whispered, knowing it wasn't enough.

Jason kissed the top of my head. "There's nothing to be sorry for. We're going to get through this. Together."

As he held me, I allowed myself to believe in those words, to draw strength from them. I wished beyond anything we could take a minute to just *be.* To discuss and evaluate who we were and what we wanted, but for now, just being in his arms was enough.

JASON STAYED with me for the next hour, fetching an ice pack for my side and convincing me to eat some soup and half a sandwich for lunch. I told him about my vision of the mace, and he'd sat in silence, listening until I'd finished.

"Glad to hear Enheduanna has decided to reach out to you again. Did she say anything else to you about why your abilities are gone?"

I shook my head. "It was super intense. Different from my other visions she'd shown me. It felt like she was farther away as if this were a memory that had been dormant from when she'd communicated through the statue before." I chewed the crust of my sandwich and contemplated. "I think Asag awoke it or triggered it somehow."

Jason frowned. "That makes sense, but I also hate that you

had to get so close to it for it to happen. I'd never been more scared than when Eddie called me and said you'd been attacked."

It was my turn to squeeze Jason's hand. "All the more reason we need to find this mace and stop this demon. It's only getting stronger, and now it knows Gavin and I are Guardians; I think it's going to escalate its plans to break the seals."

"Fuck I hate this. Feels like we're three steps behind this thing." Tension creased the corners of his eyes, and he stood. "I'll see if Kat has turned up anything else. You rest for now, but when you feel up to it, you can come down too since lord knows we could use another set of eyes researching the locations."

While the weapon was desperately needed, we hadn't been utterly defenseless against Asag. Gavin *had* damaged the demon with his abilities. The magic-infused electricity had seemed to hurt it before the power had gone out. An idea struck me suddenly, and I stood. "Is Eddie around?" The room spun, but I remained upright. "I need to ask him something."

Jason smiled. "You're not going to rest, are you."

I scoffed. "No. Not until that asshole is dead."

Jason moved to open the door. "At least I tried. After you?"

I PERCHED on a stool behind a one-way mirror, peering into the lab where Eddie and Gavin were setting up. The space was brimming with all kinds of tech—thermal cameras, sensors, and what looked like a stack of miniature car batteries. Ever since Gavin had agreed to let him examine his powers, he'd looked like a kid in a candy store. After our confrontation with Asag/Jason, as expected, tensions had been running a little higher. Director Ferguson had given the green light for Eddie to do whatever needed to be done to get a leg up on this enemy, especially now we knew it could assume any person's form.

No one came in or out of the warehouse without passing through the thermal scanners, checking their temperature within normal ranges. A trained dog, too, was brought in and given pieces of my clothing that smelled the strongest, like the rot and decay of Asag.

"Alright, the camera will monitor the heat distribution in your body," Eddie said. "Especially any rapid changes that might occur when you use your power."

Gavin nodded, looking a bit nervous but also intrigued. "So, you want me to just shoot it?"

Eddie grinned, his eyes twinkling behind his glasses. "Yes. Try and summon electricity and focus on the target that metal plate over there. Do your thing, and let's see what happens."

Taking a deep breath, Gavin raised his hand, focusing intently. I watched the thermal imaging monitor next to me flicker into a spectrum of colors. Gavin's body temperature rose, shifting from green to yellow to orange. Then, as if sparked by some internal catalyst, his fingertips blazed a vivid red. Seconds later, jagged arcs of electricity leaped from his hand, zapping the metal plate with a loud crackle.

Eddie chewed vigorously on his nails, and his eyes were wide with excitement as he stared at the thermal display. "Did you see that? Your core temperature spiked right before you discharged the electricity. It's like you're channeling energy from within and converting it."

"Yeah, usually," Gavin said, rubbing his temples as if battling a headache. "But sometimes it's not enough, and I need a boost."

I folded my arms and leaned against the wall, remembering how the transformers had blown when he'd blasted Asag. It still hadn't been enough.

"That's why we're doing this. You got lucky; the wrecking yard had a powerful electrical service. However, we need to prevent you from knocking out an entire neighborhood if you try to summon your power in a city."

Again, Eddie was already lost in thought, scribbling equations and diagrams onto a digital pad. "Okay, so here's what I propose. What if you had a wearable power source, something that could feed you energy when you need it?"

"You could make something like that?" Gavin looked skeptical but intrigued.

"Yes!" Eddie said, bobbing his head. "I could design a bracelet embedded with a high-capacity battery. It could even have multiple settings to control the output. You could summon electricity whenever you need it without causing neighborhood blackouts. How does that sound?"

Gavin's eyes met mine through the one-way mirror for just a second, though he couldn't see me. I knew he was considering the potential ramifications, whether to trust the agency or not. But eventually, he nodded.

"That sounds... actually really helpful."

Eddie was beaming. "Okay then. Let's see if we can't dial in the parameters a bit more."

I left the observation room and strode back into the main area. Agent Hansen, a tall blonde with her hair twisted into a bun and eyelashes so pale she looked like she'd stepped right off a Viking ship, looked expectantly at me.

"Ella, I was just coming to fetch you. I have a video call in progress from London with Dr. Mayberry. She has made a discovery and requested you if you were available."

Jason had informed me that Kat had had to return to London for an important meeting to discuss potential buyers interested in her Arabians, and I'd been bummed that I'd been unable to say goodbye to her before she'd left. My footsteps quickened as I followed Hansen to a computer at the end of the room. A handful of other agents milled about, and I caught fragments of conversation discussing security measures, coordinating contacts, and logistics for bringing in more weapons and supplies.

I took a seat in front of the computer and saw Kat's smiling face on the monitor. Even though it was afternoon here, the windows behind her were dark, and I could just make out a few buildings and the setting sun in the skyline.

"Ella, dear. It is so good to see you up and about. Are you alright? I've been wrought with worry."

I smiled warmly. "A little banged up, but nothing I can't handle. How are you? Sell any horses?"

Kat waved a dismissive hand. "Of course. Three fillies and a colt. It'll be a good shipment." She winked at me, knowing that I knew the real philanthropic reason behind her selling horses internationally.

"I have dinner reservations at 8 p.m. to sign the paperwork," she said.

"That's great," I said, trying to sound as upbeat as possible.

Her eyes narrowed, and she muttered a curse in Arabic. Kat rarely resorted to cursing, and when she did, she meant business. "Asag has gone too far. Thank the blessed stars you're okay. I've been researching like a third-year graduate student since I landed here. I met up with a professor who specializes in historical artifacts in auctions. And Ella, you won't believe what I found."

I perked up, desperate for good news or at least a lead that felt like progress.

"Go on, I'm listening."

"So, after some digging, he found a prestigious antique auction that took place in Spain in 1717, and there was an illustration of a spiked ball that said it had been imported from

Persia and was constructed of sheep bone. Then, he brought me old shipping records of a Spanish merchant vessel that sailed to South America in 1718. Pirates attacked it, but before that, it had a fascinating inventory list. The Spanish lord who owned the ship had what he described as a magical orb of bone, packed amongst other items from the same auction."

I felt a jolt of adrenaline, and my eyes widened. "That certainly sounds hopeful."

"I've just sent you an email," Kat continued. "I've attached a navigation map and the coordinates where the ship is believed to have sunk. Since the captain and their journal sank with the ship, we have to just guess as to where it was actually taken down."

"Kat, as always, you're incredible," I said, wanting to hug her through the screen.

"I can't fight demons head-on, but I'll be dammed if I can't pour through every book, manuscript, or journal to find a way for *you* to do it," she replied, her eyes filled with the fire of determination. "I'll keep plugging away over here, but you keep safe, alright?"

"I'll see what I can do," I said, laughing.

Her eyes softened. "Give my best to Jason."

As the call ended, I found myself staring at the blank screen for a moment, absorbing the weight of the information. We had the handle and now had our first solid lead as to where another piece of the mace was. Sure, it was thousands of miles away at the floor of the ocean, but it was something.

I stood, hurrying off to find Jason and Gavin.

CHAPTER
NINETEEN

"Take a look at this," I said, already pulling up the ancient shipping records on my laptop. Gavin, Eddie, and Jason had all gathered around me, peering over my shoulder as I opened Kat's attachments. "I just had a call with Kat, and she said she found something that might lead us to the last part of Sharur."

As I flipped through the pages of records, a wave of gratitude for Kat washed over me. There were so many pages, hundreds, and I couldn't believe how she'd had the time to read through them all and find the metaphorical needle in a haystack. Or, in this case, a piece of wood in the ocean.

While Jason and Gavin were an extra set of eyes, I summoned Eddie first, knowing that we'd need his tech-savvy skills to make sense of all this data.

Eddie chewed the back of his thumb as his gaze flitted across the screen. "Those are the 18th-century maritime records. Keep going further."

I scrolled further in the scanned records of stained parchment and scribbled handwriting. "There," Eddie said, pointing at the screen. "Those are 17th century. Sort them by month?"

I peered up at him, confused, and he sighed and gestured for me to move. I stood, letting him take my chair, and Jason moved closer. The back of his hand gently brushed against mine. However discreet, it still sent a ripple of shivers up my arm, sending me back to the temple underground when he'd revealed that he'd been on my side and had pretended to be working for Derek Kane.

"We need to decipher these coordinates," Eddie said, eyes already scanning the jumble of numbers and antique navigational terms.

He leaned in, typing the coordinates into specialized software. After a few nerve-wracking minutes of calculations and adjustments, he looked up. "Based on what I can tell, and taking into consideration the ship speeds of that period, the most probable location would be about five miles off the coast of Caracas."

"Caracas?" Gavin asked. "Sorry, I barely passed Geography with a C."

"It's in Venezuela," I confirmed, a knot of anticipation forming in my stomach.

"We have to get this to Director Ferguson," Jason said, already dialing her number.

We all intently listened as Jason gave the director a quick rundown. When he hung up, he relayed the message: "We're going to Caracas. Ferguson says to reach out to any agents nearby for local support."

Gavin looked pale, almost sickly. "Uh, guys, I've never actually left the country before, And my grandma is the one who knows where my passport is."

Jason and I shared a glance. "Don't worry about the passport," Jason said. "Division will work the logistics out. What's important is—are you up for this?"

"This might be our only shot at finding what could wake

your grandparents," I added.

Gavin's eyes met mine, then Jason's. Finally, he nodded. "I'm in. I just," he hesitated, chewing the inside of his cheek. "What if something goes wrong? What if I mess up?"

"You're not going to mess up. We're a team. We stick together," I assured him, my voice steady, hoping to instill some confidence. "And we're going to find the head of Sharur, and hopefully, if its power is real, your grandparents *will* wake up."

Gavin took a deep breath, his earlier hesitations seeming to vanish. "Okay. Let's do it."

Jason's fingers quickly danced over his phone screen, messaging any contacts in the area as we started preparations to fly to Venezuela. Scuba gear, maritime transportation, weapons for potential underwater threats—there was no end to the list of things we needed to organize.

Through all the preparations, my thoughts kept drifting to Gavin's grandparents, lying unconscious in a sterile hospital room, and I couldn't help but imagine what I'd be feeling if it were my mom or Cara lying there. The worry and fear that he'd never speak to them again. That they'd be forever trapped in their shells of bodies, purgatory assisted by ventilators.

None of the victims who'd fallen unconscious from previous earthquakes had died yet, but it had only been three days, which meant it was still a possibility.

As we reviewed our plans one last time before heading to the airport, I looked at the team—Jason, steady and reliable; Gavin, young and anxious but brimming with newfound determination; Eddie, practically vibrating with excitement. And I smiled to myself as I thought, if any group could pull this off, it was us, but the hilarious truth was, there was no one else.

∼

ONCE THE WHIRLWIND of preparations had passed, I found myself in Jason's car, heading toward Gavin's house. I'd not-so-subtly suggested we offer to take Gavin home so he could pack a bag, check on the cat he'd mentioned, and just get a general break from the flurry of activity at the warehouse.

Jason had agreed at once, and although it was a simple act, it warmed my heart. That was the kind of guy Jason was—always looking out for others.

As we pulled up to Gavin's modest, mid-century rancher, I felt a pang of nostalgia. The small lawn with brown cedar fencing, potted flowerpots, and peeling paint on the shutters felt worlds away from the high-stakes, otherworldly life we'd been navigating.

The inside of the house was just as unassuming as the outside—filled with knick-knacks, framed photos on the wall, and a small, worn-out couch in the living room. I noticed pictures of a younger Gavin, involved in various sports. A normal childhood captured in pixels and ink, something that seemed so remote from where we stood now.

Gavin led us into the living room, and a black and white cat leaped off a tattered Afghan folded on a recliner. It veered around us, heading straight for Gavin, who knelt and scooped it up. The purring intensified, echoing around the silent room except for a grandfather clock that ticked steadily with each second.

"This is Oreo," Gavin said, scratching the cat's ear. "He honestly doesn't care much if anyone is here or not, but I should fill up his food and water and probably clean his litter box." He started out of the room and then stopped as if remembering some etiquette his grandparents must've ingrained into him regarding hosting guests. "Uh, there's some water and pop in the fridge if you want anything to drink, so help yourself," he said before finally leaving.

"It's cozy," Jason commented when it was just the two of us. He picked up a framed photo of Gavin and what appeared to be his grandparents. "Reminds me of my Aunt Verna's house. She never threw anything away and loved all this cutesy crap." His eyes swiveled to the series of framed photos. "He looks happy. Well taken care of."

"Yeah," I mumbled, my gaze too on the photos. "He's so young, and yet so much has already been taken away from him —just like that, everything can change." I snapped my fingers.

Jason turned away from the photos and fixed me with a deep gaze, the blue in his eyes swirling with emotion. "We don't choose the cards we're dealt. We only choose how we play them."

When a few minutes had passed, Gavin reappeared sans Oreo. "I'm beat," he said, yawning. "Do you mind giving me a few hours to catch a nap and shower? I have my car, too, so I thought I could go to the hospital to check on my grandparents and then meet you back at the warehouse?"

"Are you sure? We can stick around?" Jason asked, his tone concerned.

I glanced at Gavin; his face was pale, and there were indeed dark circles under his eyes. "He needs some time alone," I whispered to Jason. "Let's give him that."

Jason nodded. "All right, bud. Call if you need anything."

Gavin nodded, his expression one of gratitude mixed with overwhelming exhaustion. "I will. And thanks—really."

We left and returned to Jason's truck, and the drive back to the warehouse was a quiet one, as if we were both lost in our thoughts. The disconnect between normalcy and the world we were currently elbow-deep in was growing wider. Being in Gavin's house had summoned forth all the doubts and regrets with my own family I'd been wrangling with. For a fleeting moment, we'd seen the life that could have been his—*should* have been his—but it had been snatched from him the instant Ninurta had decided to choose him.

We pulled into the warehouse parking lot and were waved through by security to the thermal detectors. The place was just as we'd left it an hour prior. Abuzz with activity—agents hunched over laptops, crates being shuffled and moved, discussions being held in hushed, urgent tones, the air thick with a tension that seemed to cling to your skin.

Soon after, fatigue caused my eyes to burn, so Jason and I found a vacant cot near the far end of the warehouse in one of the private rooms. Even in the middle of the night, the place still had a relentless buzz of energy. Agents and analysts were glued to their screens, fueled by caffeine and urgency. Even though we were focused on finding the mace, there were still earthquakes occurring, collateral damage to control, data analyzing to predict where the next one would strike, plus camera feeds hoping to catch another glimpse of Asag. The constant whirl of activity felt jarring, but at the same time, I couldn't think of anywhere else I'd rather be. In the center of it, I was doing what I could to stop the catastrophe that loomed over all of us.

Finally secluded with privacy, we sat down, and Jason draped an arm around my shoulders, pulling me closer. "Hey," he whispered, leaning in to give me a gentle kiss. "I'm glad you're here with me."

A delicious warmth spread through me at his words, settling in the core of my being before radiating outward. "Me too," I replied, resting my head against his shoulder.

We snuggled under the thin blanket, our bodies aligning with a familiarity that never ceased to amaze and comfort me. Amid the chaos, we were a small pocket of serenity, two people finding solace in the chaos with the simple act of being next to each other.

Sleep washed over me slowly, the murmuring outside the door fading into a muffled lullaby that coaxed my eyes shut. It felt like I'd barely closed them, however, when Jason's phone buzzed, jolting me awake.

"What time is it?" I grumbled, rubbing my eyes as Jason scrambled for his phone.

"Almost midnight," he said, glancing at the screen.

I sat up. Well, we'd managed around three hours of sleep at least, and while my temples still were tight from exhaustion, it was better than nothing. Jason's face tightened as he took the call. "This is Price." My heart pounded as I watched his expression, attempting to glean whatever he was hearing from him.

At first, I worried something terrible had happened, but then Jason's eyes widened, and a look of pure disbelief washed over his face. "You're serious? They've both..." He paused. "Okay. Okay, yeah, thanks for letting us know. We'll be there soon."

He hung up and stared at me, and the vibrant blue of his eyes brightened. "They woke up. Gavin's grandparents, they're awake."

It took a moment for his words to sink in before a sense of tremendous relief rushed through me. "What? Are you serious? That's great!"

"I don't know the how," he said, shaking his head, "but it's true. We should get to the hospital."

My brain was struggling to catch up, but as the news settled, I felt a profound sense of relief. We'd been buried under a relentless barrage of challenges and setbacks, and for once, something had actually gone right. Gavin's grandparents were awake. That had to be a sign, didn't it? That what we were doing was making a difference?

"Let's go," I said, untangling my legs from the blanket as I swung my legs over the side of the cot. I pulled on my pants and boots and then stood as Jason did the same. Once Jason had checked in with his team and the director, we left the warehouse, both of us brimming with energy even at the late hour.

The sterile scent of antiseptic greeted us as we navigated the maze of hallways to the ICU but then were redirected to the recovery floor since his grandparents had been moved. The atmosphere was palpably different from our last visit as we strode down the more brightly painted halls of recovery with gentle classical music playing and nurses chatting happily at the central station. Gone was the heavy, oppressive tension that had surrounded us last time on the upper floor. When we reached Gavin's grandparents' room, we paused at the closed door. Through the window, I saw a nurse and a doctor speaking to two elderly figures seated upright in their beds, who were awake, alert, and very much alive. It was surreal that something like this could've happened. His grandpa had the same chin as Gavin, but he shared his grandma's eyes. Their relation was unmistakable.

The door swung open, and out came Gavin. He had changed into black athletic shorts and a shirt with an indie rock band I'd heard Cara mention wanting to see live. His face was flushed with a sort of bewildered joy. "You guys," he said, still grinning as though he couldn't help himself. "It's crazy. The doctor is calling it a miracle."

Jason and I exchanged glances before looking back at Gavin. "How are they doing? How are you doing?" I asked.

"It's unreal," Gavin replied. "I mean, they're still confused and foggy, but they're here, they're back. And I... I don't know. I'm still trying to wrap my head around all this."

Jason clapped him on the back. "I'm so happy for you. Any idea what happened?"

Gavin shook his head. "The doctor doesn't have a clue. He wants to run some tests to see if he can figure out why they woke up. He mentioned that he's got a dozen other patients in comas who haven't shown any signs of waking. He wants to know if this is some kind of anomaly or if it was a combination of medication they gave them." He pointed to the bandage on the inside of his elbow. "They took my blood too, thinking maybe there was a genetic resistance or factor to the disease not affecting them as severely."

I studied Gavin's face as he talked animatedly to Jason. This was a good thing. *Right?* So, then, why couldn't I ignore the sinking sensation in my gut that something was *off?*

Suddenly, Gavin turned an expectant look at me, and I shoved away the thought. "Wow, Gavin, this is the best news. I'm so happy for you."

"Thanks," Gavin's voice quivered slightly, the magnitude of the moment catching up with him. "It's just... it's hard to process. Yesterday, I was coming to terms with the idea that they might never wake up. And now... now they're asking me when they can go home and about Oreo. It's a lot."

Gavin ran a hand through his hair, looking far older than his eighteen years to me. His shoulders straightened subtly as if accepting that he was no longer staring down life on his own. Alone and orphaned for a second time. A swell of sympathy rose inside me. Good things did happen to good people.

Jason put a reassuring hand on Gavin's shoulder. "This is a lot. Take it one step at a time. You should go and spend some time with them. If you're not up to going to Venezuela now, I understand."

Gavin nodded, his eyes shining. "Yeah, I'm not sure now is the best time for me to leave the country." He paused. "They're going to need me while they recover and regain their strength. The doctor said something about physical therapy."

The nurse stepped into the hallway and asked if Gavin

would be available to sign some more paperwork. He thanked us again for coming and then followed her back into the room.

For a time after, Jason and I stood there, staring into the room as Gavin signed the clipboards the nurse handed him and then helped his grandpa with the remote.

I folded my arms, watching an overjoyed Gavin with his family. "It's a miracle," I said softly, echoing what the doctor had said.

"Yeah," Jason whispered. "It sure is."

CHAPTER

TWENTY

Back at the warehouse, I was too amped to sleep, although I did manage to lay down in the dark for a bit while Jason briefed the director and had meetings with the other teams.

I gave up on getting any real rest around seven a.m. and showered in one of the employee locker rooms, changed, and put on a fresh coat of makeup before joining everyone in the main room. I poured myself a cup of coffee and selected a muffin that looked like it was more than a few days old, and then found an empty seat to try and force down some nourishment.

I had just finished eating the last bites of my blueberry muffin when a hush fell over the room. Gavin stepped through the door with a security agent in tow, carrying a duffel bag. The muffled murmurs of other agents enveloped me as I stood and went to him.

"Gavin," I said, a little breathless, "is everything alright?"

He flashed me a toothy grin. "I changed my mind. I told my grandparents I'm going on a backpacking trip with some old high school baseball teammates," he explained.

I looked at him, my gut twisting. "Are you sure? What about your grandparents?"

Gavin shrugged. "They're moving to a rehab facility and won't be home anyway. And Oreo is good for a few days without me." His hazel eyes met mine, unwavering. "I want to help, Ella. You know I do."

Something felt off. It wasn't just the determination in his eyes; there was a layer of something else…uncertainty? Guilt? Or perhaps the pressure from Ninurta was too much? It was hard to pin down, but still, it was there.

Before I could argue further, Director Ferguson and Jason approached us. "I've just been informed about a Venezuelan contact who can assist you. Agent Martinez will meet you when you land in Caracas."

"I trust you're all set?" her eyes drifted to me, then Gavin, before finally Jason.

"We are," Jason confirmed. "Steinberg will send me the final coordinates en route, but we should be good to go."

"Excellent," Ferguson nodded, her mouth pressed into a thin line. "My contact at the white house told me the CDC will announce the earthquakes are releasing hazardous toxins into the air and declaring it a global health crisis. We've got twelve hours until they have a warrant at our front door and confiscate all our hard drives. Time is of the essence. Let's not waste a goddamn second of it."

HOURS LATER, the agency's private jet's tires screeched against the tarmac, and we disembarked into the oppressive heat of Caracas. The city's vibrant energy hit me immediately, and beyond the airport, skyscrapers stretched towards the sky, their glass surfaces reflecting the sunlight in a brilliant display. It'd been three years since I'd been here to work, but I had always been obsessed with the landscape and the culture.

My gaze shifted to Gavin, and his wide eyes and eager expression filled me with a sense of delight. He was like a sponge, absorbing everything around him. A woman in her mid-forties with loose curls of dark hair stood waiting for us just inside the airport. She introduced herself as Agent Martinez and was nothing like the buttoned-up agents I was used to— her vibe was different, more relaxed, but no less competent.

She told us she had arranged a car and shook our hands. "I'll brief you all in the car. If you'll follow me?"

Another agent beside her took our bags, and she led us to a sleek, black SUV where a driver was waiting.

She told us that the drive to the marina was set to be a long one—four hours east up the Venezuelan coastline to Puerto La Cruz.

Jason and I took the second row while Gavin climbed into the back, his long legs nearly reaching his chin, but he insisted he was comfortable.

Our sleek, black SUV wove through Caracas' busy streets, a hive of activity, with people moving with intent to their jobs or tourists stopping to take photos in front of the iconic locations. The Avila Mountain in the distance seemed to cast a protective shadow over the city, with its lush green peaks contrasting with the modern steel and glass structures. We passed the Central University of Venezuela and the National Pantheon, both land-marks in their own right.

Gavin's eyes were glued to the rear window. "That's the Teresa Carreño Cultural Complex," I said, pointing. "And the Caracas Museum of Contemporary Art." I turned to Agent Martinez in the passenger seat. "It was partially closed when I visited last."

"They're repainting some of the rooms," Martinez said over

her shoulder. "And designing new showrooms so they can take the art from the vaults."

"Can't believe I'm actually here, experiencing all of this," Gavin replied, his voice tinged with wonder.

As we drove further from the city towards the coast, the urban landscape gave way to rolling hills and dense forests. A vivid blend of wildflowers painted the landscape, their colors twirling in the breeze.

We had just taken an exit onto the highway when Agent Martinez, sitting in the passenger seat, pivoted in her chair and looked over her shoulder at me, grinning.

"Ella, querida, do you realize you're practically a celebrity at the agency?"

I blinked, not sure if I'd heard her right. "Uh, what?"

I pinned a questioning look on Jason, who seemed to have found something very interesting to stare at out of the window.

Useless.

Martinez shook her head, her dark curls bouncing. "No, but seriously. After everything the agency dealt with in Iraq with that pendejo Kane—"

I dug my nails into my palms at the sound of his name. He'd been punished not as much as I would have hoped nor as much as he deserved, and I couldn't deny the regret that plagued me from time to time that I hadn't told Jason to leave him behind, sealing him away in the altar room.

Martinez continued, unabated. "Word got around, Chica. Everyone's talking about how you pulled off some Harry Potter-level magic to stop him."

I glanced at Jason, who gave me a casual, disarming shrug as if to say, 'Hey, I'm not the one who's agency-famous.'

Martinez leaned back, smug. "They sent a whole team of investigators, you know. The smartest the agency had to offer and then contracting out when they weren't enough. And none of them could figure out how that stone door and altar got obliterated."

My blood turned icy in my veins as flashbacks of that harrowing night in Iraq flooded back, followed immediately by a swell of vindication. Did Jason know about this? Why hadn't he told me? I pinned a glare on the side of his face.

"I was there," Martinez went on. "When they first debriefed you. I feel like you should know. I've always believed your story."

A sudden, unexpected warmth spread through me. That made two. Eddie and now her, two people at Division 12, a place known for its cynicism and red tape, had taken my side from the beginning.

"Thanks," I stammered. "I appreciate it. That means a lot," I managed to say, feeling the emotional ground beneath me shift. A pillar of trust had erected itself, and Martinez and Eddie were both standing on it, waving a 'Team Ella' banner or something.

Finally, Jason chimed in, his voice tinged with warmth. "I could've told you you're special, Elly."

"Yeah, well," I smirked at him, "Maybe you should've mentioned that my 'specialness' is agency-approved."

Martinez chuckled. "Why am I not surprised you didn't tell her, Price?"

He shrugged, although his eyes widened slightly, sensing that we were cornering him. "A lot happened, and I figured you wanted to put everything with Kane and Ur behind us, right?"

I sighed. It was true. We had discussed it several times, actually, and bringing it up only made me feel worse that I'd lost my abilities. Jason had respected that.

"So," Martinez leaned her arm over the seat, "what's it like being legendary? Do you get any cool benefits? A special badge or secret handshake with the director?"

Jason and I burst into laughter.

Martinez winked. "Well, you *do* get to kick some serious culo, no? That has to count for something."

"I guess you're right," I said, smiling. "Kicking culo is sort of my jam."

Martinez's phone rang, interrupting our conversation, and I peered out of the window. Outside, the houses and stores gave way to more and more trees. Two hours into the trip, Gavin was asleep with his face buried in his hooded sweatshirt and his head perched against the window.

I turned to Jason, choosing my words carefully and keeping my voice low. "So, I was thinking, since it's hard to know who to trust right now. After everything that happened..." I trailed off, implying how Asag would disguise himself as a human. "And now we don't have the agency scanning our bodies."

Jason pivoted in his seat to look at me.

I hesitated before adding, "I'm also concerned about Gavin. Does something seem off to you about him?"

His left eyebrow, the one with the small scar, lifted an inch. "You think Gavin's a risk? Where's this coming from?"

"I don't know," I admitted. "But can you blame me for being paranoid? Everything is so messed up, and—"

"I'm sorry," Jason cut in. "Okay, fine. We should take precautions. How about we come up with a code word? Something we can say to confirm it's really us."

Was I paranoid, or was I prudent? The lines had blurred so much recently; it was hard to tell, but after a moment's thought, I nodded. "What should the code word be?"

"Penelope," he said.

I looked at him curiously. "Why Penelope?"

"It was my dad's mom's name. My grandma and I were really close. Actually, she was one of the few good things I had growing up."

My heart stuttered in my ribcage at the admission. Jason

rarely spoke about his military family upbringing, even less about his childhood. It was a guarded subject, and his sharing felt intimate, a little window into a part of him I hardly knew.

"Penelope, it is," I said, locking eyes with him and smiling.

While weaving through the Venezuelan countryside, heading for the coast, I kept glancing out the window, but the beauty of the landscape didn't register. My mind was too cluttered, buzzing with what lay ahead of us—a dive into dark waters to find a piece of Sharur, a dive into an uncertain future. As if reading my mind, Jason's hand found mine, fingers intertwining as if trying to create a tether in this floating world of unknowns.

"We'll get through this," Jason said, squeezing my hand. The confidence in his voice was only half-landed; I felt it mingle with the worry in my chest.

"I know," I replied, my eyes still lingering on the passing trees and occasional house or farm. "But what happens after? You know, saying we survive and manage to stop Asag, what happens then? After all this is over?"

"Of course I do," he looked at me, a small smile tugging at his lips. "I've got a realtor friend of mine keeping an eye out for apartments near New York City. You know, for us."

Touched he'd been secretly thinking about a future shared with me, the thought still terrified me. An apartment? A normal life? My pulse quickened. "Really?"

"Yeah. I thought maybe we could be one of those couples that jog together in Central Park. Hell, maybe even get a cat."

A laugh bubbled up from inside me, breaking the tension. "A cat? You?"

He shrugged, grinning. "Why not? And when we're old and gray, we can go on cruises like other boring married couples."

I smirked, my grip on his hand tightening. It was a dreamy

scenario, painfully normal, but one that felt miles away from where we were then. "That sounds...nice."

"And maybe a family too," he added softly, his hand moving up then, and his thumb caressed my forehead as if he could smooth away the worry lines etched there.

A family. The words dropped like a stone into the well of my thoughts, sinking fast and deep. My heart hitched up into my throat. "Yeah, a family would be...great," I said, but it tasted strange as the words left my mouth.

When I'd first returned to New York City after everything had gone down in the Middle East, and after Jason and I had picked up the pieces and were a 'we' again, my first appointment had been with my OB-GYN. Birth control. I was a Guardian. I had seen things. Things no one else in thousands of years ever had. A cold tendril of fear laced down my spine, remembering how it had felt to be near Asag. The embodiment of everything dark and evil. How could I bring a child into this world, knowing the dangers that lurked in the dark corners? Would it be fair? To them? To us?

Jason seemed to pick up on the internal struggle warring inside me. "Hey, it's just a thought. We've got time."

Time. A word so simple yet so complex, especially for us. Time was what we were running out of as we raced to stop Asag from releasing the other demons. Time was what I wondered about when I thought of us—our future.

"You're right," I said, taking a deep breath.

As the car continued its journey, I leaned into Jason. The warmth of his body against mine brought a sense of comfort, however fleeting, and I closed my eyes, dozing.

And despite the dread, the ticking clock, and the vast unknowns, I realized that I did want to find out what was on the other side, even if it scared the hell out of me.

TWENTY-ONE

Late in the afternoon, the SUV pulled into the parking lot facing an expansive marina and dock with the Venezuelan coastline stretching out before us like a mural painted in hues of blue and green. Fishing boats bobbed alongside larger tour vessels, all dwarfed by the expanse of the sparkling Caribbean Sea.

The air was thick with the smell of salt and fish, a sensory blend that I usually loved and found comforting but now only intensified the pressure of the ticking clock in my mind. Jason had heard from Division 12 of another earthquake occurring, this time just north of Tokyo. Thankfully, the death toll had been minimal, but the latest running tally Eddie had sent over to us of people in comas was three-hundred twenty-seven. Several hospitals were frantic with trying to secure more beds for the afflicted.

Every second, Asag was growing more powerful, and the weight of our mission felt as heavy as the ocean itself. The seals he seemed to be determined to break with the earthquakes were scattered at seemingly random locations. We had no idea how many seals he'd already broken and, more so, no idea how many more remained.

Agent Martinez, our Division 12 contact, was already there, waving us over. "I've got good news and bad news," she began without any preliminaries. "The good news is I've found a boat for hire. It's large enough for all of us and has the equipment we need for salvage retrieval."

"And the bad news?" Jason asked, his jaw tightening.

"The boat's usual captain is in the hospital, triple bypass surgery. So, we need to find another one, and fast."

The frustration was palpable, but we couldn't afford to lose more time. "So, then," Jason said, finally exhaling. "What's our next move?"

"Get some food," Martinez suggested, pointing to a nearby seafood shack. "I'll make a few calls and get a handle on the captain situation. In the meantime, you can head to a Division 12 safehouse nearby. It's a hotel, actually." She handed me a key and gave us directions.

We thanked her and made our way to the food shack. I could tell Jason was ruminating over our predicament as he stood back with a solemn face and allowed me to order ceviche and fried plantains for all of us.

The three of us ate quickly and mostly in silence, the urgency and anticipation of what was to come next hanging over us. We were so close to the next piece and yet could do nothing but sit and wait and hope Martinez found a captain soon.

The aroma of freshly brewed coffee surrounded us, and the restaurant was bustling with conversations from locals and tourists alike. As we ate, I couldn't help but notice Gavin's gaze wandering toward the waitresses, all dressed in low-cut tank tops and short shorts.

"Thinking of studying abroad?" I teased.

Gavin's face turned a shade redder, his eyes darting back to his plate. "Uh, yeah. I mean, it's not off the table."

Jason leaned in and added, "I feel you, bud. They certainly know how to make an impression."

"Wow," I said, playfully punching Jason in the shoulder.

He laughed and pulled me to him, kissing me on the head. "No one makes more of an impression than you, Elly."

After we'd eaten, or should I say Gavin and Jason had clean plates, while I had eaten the tortilla chips and picked out shrimp, we paid, got up, and left. With directions in hand, we navigated the streets until we reached the Division 12 safehouse, which Martinez had correctly assured us was only a block over and still in the line of sight of the marina. It looked like any other hotel, with painted block walls and only two floors spread out along the road so each room had a view of the ocean.

As we stepped into the hotel room, I took a deep breath and let it out slowly, my lungs still tingling with the scent of the sea. The room was an oasis of manufactured comfort—crisp linens, air conditioning, and muffled sounds to insulate us from the outside world. It was so jarringly normal that, for a second, I felt disoriented. It was as if the room didn't know it was a staging area for a quest that felt like something out of myth, something almost ludicrous when said out loud: a search for a fragment of Sharur, lost deep under the sea in a three-century-old shipwreck.

I threw my bag onto the bed and looked at the gear Martinez had brought in—oxygen tanks, diving suits, underwater cameras, lights, and what appeared to be specialized sonar equipment for salvage operations. Each piece of equipment brought a pang of excitement, tinged with the bitter aftertaste of fear. I had let my scuba certification lapse ever since taking a girl's trip to Cancun in my Junior year of college. It wasn't that I couldn't swim, nor was I afraid of the water. It was the fear that all of this effort to get here, take a boat out, and then dive down would lead to nothing. Three hundred years had passed since the ship San Juan Bautista had sank. Storms, hurricanes, and currents could've long since buried the wreckage under sand. The thought that the odds were very much stacked against us made my heart race, and I wiped my clammy palms on my hands, hurrying to the bathroom.

Inside the small space, I flipped on the faucet and splashed water on my face, attempting to ease my increasing panic. The forward momentum, the flight, the drive, and then being foot-steps away from the marina had done wonders to calm my nerves. But the abrupt halt caused by the trouble in securing a captain had allowed all of the fear and uncertainty to come crashing down on me, threatening to pull me under. I drew in a shuddering breath and stared at my reflection in the mirror.

And then there was Gavin. Although with Eddie's device, he had improved his accuracy with his powers, I was still uneasy about being in too close of quarters with him in a dangerous situation. He was young and cocky, and while he had Ninurta behind him, he couldn't have been more out of his comfort zone.

Thoughts composed, I left the bathroom and reentered the two-bedroom suite. Jason's concerned gaze met mine, and I gave him a slight nod. Gavin flopped back on the bed and rummaged through the nightstands. "Where's the remote? I want to see what games are playing."

But before he could locate it, his phone rang, and he answered. He sat up on the bed, and his voice remained hushed but discernible. When he hung up, he seemed buoyed by relief and wore a broad grin on his face. "So, my, they just moved my grandparents to a rehab facility. The nurse said they're doing much better."

The joy was contagious. I grinned back, genuinely happy for him. However, a sliver of suspicion nagged at me. Could it be a coincidence that his grandparents' health improved so drastically, so quickly? In this wild world of gods and demons we were currently navigating, could anything be chalked up to mere coincidence anymore? There was still much we didn't know about why these people were falling into comas, so why should I look a gift horse in the mouth? His grandparents were getting better. I should be happy. This *was* a good thing—one of the few we'd experienced lately.

Jason and I exchanged happy sentiments with Gavin, who then had to spend the next twenty minutes filling in the rest of his family and friends on his grandparents' update.

While he paced the room making the calls, Jason and I sat at a round table that sat next to the window, looking across the street and to the distant waves. He pulled his pistol from his hip, his treasured Pit viper, and began dissembling it and cleaning it. I checked in with Cara via a short message. However, I assumed she wouldn't reply since she was on her honeymoon in France, then browsed through media outlets, gathering the latest on the earthquakes that seemed to be intensifying as Eddie had predicted they would.

An hour later, as the sun sank low on the horizon, there was a knock at the door.

Jason stood immediately, clutching his pistol down low by his side and silently motioning at Gavin and me to move behind him. While my pulse stammered in my ears, I couldn't deny the fact that the demon Asag probably wouldn't knock. He'd just bust down the door.

However, that didn't mean it was an impossibility, and staying vigilant kept us safe.

"It's me. Martinez." A familiar voice came through the door a moment later.

"Prove it," Jason said.

There was a pause, and I imagined her giving an exasperated sigh. "Remember that mission in Warsaw we were on, and you had a glimpse of the afterlife after drinking way too much Spirytus and thought you could see and speak to ghosts."

With his back to me, I could only see his shoulder's hunch in response to this story that I would totally bug him for more details on at another time before he slid open the locks and opened the door.

Martinez stood in the doorway, her lips forming a thin line, and moved inside.

Jason closed the door behind her as we gathered around, and I took another deep breath, bracing myself for whatever news she was going to share.

"Got us a captain," she announced, tucking a thumb into the belt loop on her jeans. The dark freckles on her face made her appear younger in the low light of the hotel room, and a slight surge of jealousy flared inside me as I wondered how long she had known Jason.

"Thank fuck," Jason sighed. "Director Ferguson demanded an update, and I couldn't put her off any longer. I'll let her know we're moving forward."

"Any ETA on when we'll be leaving?" I asked.

"Captain Silvanas is organizing the crew now and checking the maintenance records for the mechanical. When I gave him the coordinates, he was hesitant since that area is notorious for shallow spots and rock outcroppings that are tedious to navigate. But when I offered to pay him double, he seemed more amenable." Martinez paused, her eyes bouncing between Jason and mine. "However, he said because of the hazards, it'd be safer if we leave at first light tomorrow."

My stomach sank. Tomorrow felt a million miles away right now, and yet I knew I should trust the professional who would be navigating a boat into waters I knew squat about.

"All right," Jason said, his voice also tinged with disappointment. "I'll update the director." He took out his phone and began dialing before stepping further behind us in the room.

"Do we need to do anything else? Find equipment or anything?" I asked, mostly because I hated the idea of sitting idle while there was still daylight left.

Martinez shook her head. "The captain has experience taking salvage and research crews out and has operated this boat more than once. He said he'd have a crew with diving gear, and there is an onboard crane in case we find anything heavy."

Martinez paused, glancing over to where Jason was on the phone. "She sounds pissed."

I followed her gaze, catching a glimpse of Jason's face as he turned away from us, pacing and gesturing while talking. His brow was furrowed, and the muscles in his jaw clenched tighter with each word.

Martinez seemed to sense the tension. "Alright, I'll get everything arranged for tomorrow. Meet me at the marina, 7 AM sharp. See you tomorrow."

"Sounds good," I said, grateful for her no-bullshit attitude. With a brief nod, she exited the room.

Gavin, who had been quiet for the most part, picked up the remote and started channel surfing. He finally settled on a soccer game, his eyes focused but distant, as if his thoughts were somewhere else.

Soon after, Jason was off the phone, and we retreated to the adjacent room. He closed the door behind us with a soft click.

The bed looked inviting, covered with clean sheets and fluffy pillows, a sharp contrast to the chaos that had unfolded earlier in the day.

"How'd it go?" I asked.

"Scale of one to ten. I'd say about an 11."

"That good, huh?"

Jason scoffed. "She thinks we should've paid the captain triple to take us out tonight. She needs us to find the mace so she can leverage the agency to be brought back into the fold. The UN called a summit today to discuss whether a worldwide emergency should be declared, and the director wasn't told about it until after the fact. Also, the CIA has severed all intel they were sharing with us. Everything we get now is via Eddie's no need for passwords, and Ferguson implied that it still wasn't enough."

Leaving Division 12 in the cold was the absolute worst thing they could do right now. We needed to all be on the same page to fight this. A united front from all government and military agencies was the only way to find Asag and stop it.

"What are you going to do?"

"Me? Not a damn thing until tomorrow." He ran a hand through his hair, looking frustrated as he sat on the edge of the bed. I climbed on the other side and rested my hands on his shoulders.

"I know of one thing we can do."

Jason laughed, a deep, comforting sound.

"I suppose there is."

We climbed under the covers, the warmth enveloping us like a cocoon. Through the window, the distant melodies of music floated in from a restaurant somewhere outside, filling the room with a dreamlike quality. As Jason kissed me, the fear and the worries seemed to melt away, leaving just the two of us.

We were just Ella and Jason, two people in love, seeking solace in a world that felt like it was about to combust.

The sunrise would come soon enough, but tonight, as our lips met and the world outside continued to spin, we found our own sanctuary, a respite from the storm. And sometimes, that's all you really needed.

TWENTY-TWO

The engines rumbled beneath my feet as I stood on the main deck, taking in the immense size of the ship. The RVS Titan easily stretched the length of a football field, its metallic surfaces glinting under the bright sun. I breathed deeply, smelling the briny scent of the ocean, mixing with the tang of diesel fumes as the early morning sun hovered over the rolling waves to the east.

Martinez and Jason were meeting with the salvage crew below decks and had said it'd be another two hours before we reached the coordinates Eddie had given us. Odds were low that the ship had sunk exactly there, so we'd prepared to do sweeps beyond it, spiraling outward and using sonar to search the ocean floor for signs of the San Juan Bautista.

The strong sea wind whipped my hair wildly about, carrying the cries of circling gulls hunting for leftovers from the galley. As I headed below deck, the smells of grease and stale coffee hit my nose. The labyrinth of stark corridors reverberated with the echo of footsteps on metal. Voices filtered from the mess hall and recreation areas as the off-duty crew relaxed.

Stepping into the mess hall, I claimed one of the only empty seats at a table filled with six of the crew members.

"Ah, Ella! Welcome, welcome!" Juan, a burly Venezuelan with a salt-and-pepper beard, greeted me. "I am Carlos. I work on the engines as well as here in the galley. Lunch will be served a little later, but you look like you need coffee. Or something stronger, yes?"

I laughed. "Coffee would be great, please."

Moments later, Carlos pushed a steaming cup of thick, almost sludge-like coffee in front of me. I took a cautious sip, grimacing as I swallowed the bitterness.

"Haha! It takes a little getting used to," a crew member who introduced herself as Maria laughed. "It's not Starbucks."

"Yeah, it tastes like it's been brewed with spare engine parts," I chuckled, stirring in a bit of sugar.

Carlos leaned back, propping his boots on another chair. "So, you're the photographer, huh? Never heard of one being needed for a salvage job, but eh, what do I know?" He paused, taking a toothpick from his shirt pocket and prying at something between his teeth. "My niece, Lacinda, is in high school looking for career paths. Is it a good job?"

I laughed out loud, drawing confused smiles from the others. "It has its moments," I said, stifling my laughter. "I like the traveling. Meeting new people. Capturing their stories with my camera. And often, I get a fantastic view from my office window."

"We have a great view here as well," Carlos replied, grinning. "Except, sometimes our view often includes sunburn and loud machinery."

"Y el pago es una mierda, pero al menos la vista desde la oficina es agradable," Juan added, the table erupting into laughter.

The pay is shit, but the view from the office is nice. I translated for myself, nodding in agreement.

"So," I shifted the conversation. "Why do you think ships sink so often around these parts?"

"Could be any number of things—bad weather, faulty engineering, or," Carlos lowered his voice, "pirates."

Juan leaned forward, clearly enjoying the topic. "Ah, pirates. You know, I am descended from a fearsome Venezuelan pirate, Guillermo el Salvaje."

"No shit?" I said.

"It's as true as the sea is salty, mi amiga," he said, his eyes twinkling. "Our family legend has it that Guillermo buried his treasure around here but never returned. Every salvage operation I join, part of me hopes to stumble upon that stash."

"And I thought being related to Mary Todd Lincoln was a flex," I said, savoring the last drop of my coffee.

Carlos laughed loudly.

"If you find the gold, Carlos," Maria said, stretching her arms. "We could all retire then. Sipping piña coladas instead of this motor-oil coffee."

Juan lifted his cup. "To hidden treasures, glorious views from crappy offices, and surviving another day at sea."

We clinked our mugs together, sealing the unspoken camaraderie that only those who spend their days on a salvage ship could understand.

A sudden call echoed from the upper deck. "All hands, prepare for dive operation!"

"That's our cue," Juan said, putting down his cup and pushing back his chair.

"Let's go earn that shitty paycheck, shall we?" Carlos winked at me, gathering up his gear.

As I followed them out, the laughter and chatter of the crew behind me, I couldn't help but feel a sense of guilt. They were oblivious to what it was we were searching for. To them, it was just another dive, another paycheck as they'd so blatantly put it, but the reality was it was so much more—a weapon to stop an otherwise unstoppable evil.

Behind them, I made my way to the starboard observation deck, the metal stairs clanging under my feet, and found Gavin leaning over the railing, his face pale and beaded with sweat.

"Still not used to the motion, huh?" I asked kindly, rubbing his back.

He shook his head, not lifting his eyes from the churning waves below. "I'm fine," he mumbled but then gulped and leaned further over the side.

I continued gently rubbing his back in circles, mimicking the movements I'd done with Cara on long car rides. "Deep breaths," I reminded him. "Focus on the horizon."

I heard footsteps approaching and looked over to see Jason stepping out on the deck. "How's he doing?" my boyfriend asked, his brow furrowed in concern.

"He'll be okay. He just needs more time to get his sea legs," I replied. Looking at Gavin, I added gently, "Why don't you go lie down in your bunk for a bit? The medication should start helping soon."

Gavin nodded weakly and headed inside.

I turned back to Jason and wrapped my arms around his muscular frame, breathing in his familiar scent. "Poor kid," Jason murmured into my hair.

I nodded against his chest, taking comfort in his sturdy presence amidst the nonstop motion of the ship. We stood entwined together, the cry of gulls and crash of waves filling the comfortable silence.

After a moment, he pulled back to smile down at me, his eyes crinkling. "Back to the hunt soon. You ready?"

I grinned up at him. "Always."

Around me, the deck buzzed with activity. The hiss and clank of the equipment being prepped by the crew echoed across the vast space. I watched as the robotic arms were maneuvered into launch positions, the hydraulic systems pumping with loud whirs. Nearby, two crew members laughed heartily as they coiled thick cables, their voices nearly drowned out by the periodic blasts of the ship's horn.

Jason and I found ourselves overlooking the ocean. The rolling waves reflecting the sunlight painted a scene almost too picturesque to be real. The tension of the days before seemed to dissolve into the salt air, carried away by the breeze. For a moment, I let myself forget about the horrors that were currently wreaking havoc and the unspeakable evil we were up against.

Then, out in the water, a waterspout shot up—once, twice, three times. Whales.

"You see them too?" Jason said softly, his eyes captivated by the spectacle.

"Yeah," I murmured, but my voice sounded hollow even to my ears. "I wonder what kind they are?"

"Not a clue, but still cool to see."

I should've been in awe, lost in the simplicity of the moment, allowing the beauty of it all to sweep me away. But I couldn't. My mind was a battleground, the siren's call of duty and destiny cutting through any semblance of peace.

Asag was rampaging somewhere out there, not just a threat to us but to the world, and for some infuriating reason, stopping it was my burden to bear.

Here I was, staring at one of the Earth's most magnificent displays, and all I could feel was bitterness. A toxic blend of resentment and duty that left me unable to appreciate the very world I was tasked to protect.

"God dammit. I wish I could just enjoy this," I blurted out, unable to keep it in any longer.

Jason looked at me, his eyes searching my face.

"I'm standing here with you, watching something most people only dream of seeing, and all I can think about is how Asag is out there, threatening to undo everything. Everything we know, everyone we love."

The words flowed like a torrent, a release of pent-up frustration that had been building for too long.

"I'm tired, Jason. I'm tired of the duty of being the 'chosen one,' or whatever the hell they want to call me. Sometimes, I just want to be Ella, who can stand on a ship with the guy she cares about and watch whales. Is that too much to ask?"

Jason looked down, his jaw tense. "No, it's not too much to ask. You're allowed to want those things, Elly. You're allowed to be human."

His words were comforting and exactly what I needed to hear, but they couldn't erase the truth. My role as Guardian wasn't just a job; it was a chain, one that yanked me back every time I dared to think about a different life.

Still, for a fleeting moment, I let myself get lost in the blue of his eyes and the serene backdrop that surrounded us.

"It's a cruel irony," I said softly. "Being tasked to save a world, you're not allowed to fully enjoy."

"Yeah," Jason agreed. "But maybe we steal moments like this to remind us why it's worth saving in the first place."

I nodded, staring back at the ocean, its vastness a mirror to my tangled thoughts. I wanted to believe that one day, I could stand here, unburdened.

TWENTY-THREE

An hour later, we all gathered in the ship's navigation room, hovering around a flickering radar screen. Agent Martinez stood, arms folded, scrutinizing the blips and lines that darted across the display. Captain Sylvanas adjusted the read-out while beside him, Jason's eyes locked onto the screen.

"There," Captain Sylvanas pointed at a cluster of long white lines on the sonar display. "That could be it."

"Could be," Martinez reiterated, her voice laced with skepticism. "Or it could be another false alarm. We've had plenty of those."

I felt a knot of hope and apprehension tighten in my stomach.

"We're not going to know for sure until we go down there," Jason said, turning to me. "You ready for this?"

"Born ready," I replied, my voice tinged with excitement yet held steady by a core of fear. I had dreamed of this moment, but the reality was a far more formidable beast. The ocean was no playground. I respected it as much as I was enamored with it.

Captain Sylvanas weighed in, "You should know, people

have gone missing here. Treasure hunters come often and underestimate these waters. The currents have sunk more than just old ships."

A tingle trickled down my spine at the sobering reminder that we were treading on the edge of danger.

"I'm dropping anchor," the captain announced, gripping the lever and lowering it with a mechanical clunk. "We're as stable as we can be in these currents. Prepare the dive team."

Jason started to get up, then looked at me, hesitating. "Elly, maybe you should stay on board for this first dive. Let us confirm it's the San Juan Bautista before you go down."

I felt a flash of indignation. "I'm a part of this team. I should be down there."

He held up his hands defensively. "I know, I know. But we've got to be sure it's the right wreck before we get every-one's hopes up. Besides, if something goes wrong—"

"I can handle myself," I cut him off, my teeth gritted.

"Ella," Agent Martinez broke in, "it's not about your skill level. We need to assess the risk and make sure it's the ship we've been searching for. That way, if it's a false alarm, we don't waste valuable resources."

I looked at their faces, marked by a blend of concern and reason. It stung, but I knew they had a point.

"Fine," I relented, my heart pounding with a mix of relief and disappointment. "But you better let me know the second you find anything."

Jason gave me a grateful look, squeezing my shoulder as he headed for the door. "You'll be the first to know."

I stood there, watching them gather their gear and go through the pre-dive checklist. They rattled off names of tanks, regulators, and buoyancy compensators—some I recognized immediately, others I was as clueless about as when Cara had asked me about tableware colors being either teal or aqua. I'd murmured something about asking another of her bridesmaids while I'd tipped back the complimentary champagne the venue had provided for tasting.

Soon after, the dive team of six geared up, checked and double-checked their equipment, then descended the ladder at the back of the ship one by one into the dark, swirling water. My skin tingled with the anxiety of waiting, the seconds stretching into minutes, the minutes into what felt like an eternity. I hovered near the radio, straining to catch any fragments of underwater communication. I felt a hollow emptiness settle within me. I was here, yet not entirely part of it.

Blood thundered in my ears as I stared at the monitor displaying the diver's head-cam footage. The underwater world was an eerie, almost surreal landscape of muted colors and diffused sunlight. The visibility was good, but the vastness of the ocean floor made it seem like an endless desert.

"I've found the bow! There's a part of a mast here, too!" The diver's voice crackled through the speakers, tinged with excitement.

I leaned in closer, my eyes scanning the murky images for any sign of the artifacts we were after. "Good, keep going. Any sign of the cargo?"

The screen shifted erratically for a moment as the diver adjusted his position. "No, not yet. I'm going to—wait, what was that?"

My heart skipped a beat. "What's wrong? What did you see?"

"Something moved just at the edge of my light. It was fast." The diver sounded genuinely shaken.

On the screen, a dark shadow flitted across the frame for a mere second. A shiver raced down my spine. My eyes widened, and my grip tightened on the edge of the table.

"It's probably just a Thresher. There are some monsters

down there, but they're harmless," said one of the divers leading the crew, who was watching next to me. Still, there was a catch in his voice that I didn't miss.

Just then, the diver looked down, and the camera picked up something else—tiny cracks in the sea floor, from which tendrils of black bubbles wafted upward.

"Uh, Titan, I think we have some sort of volcanic vents here. Were those on the scans?" The diver's tone had gone from scared to alarmed.

"We've been experiencing seismic activity off the coast," another crew member chimed in, pulling up data on another screen. "But it was considered low-risk for your dive."

Low-risk or not, the appearance of those vents and the potential for underwater lava made my stomach churn with anxiety. "Please, hurry," I murmured, more to myself than to anyone else.

Minutes felt like hours as I waited, the tension in the room palpable. Then, finally, the diver's voice broke through the silence again. "I've found something. It's a metal chest, encrusted but intact."

Relief washed over me like a cool breeze.

"Bring it up carefully," the supervising diver said into the radio. "The rest of you do a final sweep for anything else, then get your asses back to the Titan."

As the camera focused on the chest, the diver's gloved hand swept away the sand on the lid. Its corroded surface tinged with green and brown from years under the sea. I couldn't help but think about how close we'd come to not finding it at all—the vastness of the ocean in comparison to something the size of my suitcase.

I breathed in deeply, in awe at the miraculous feat that was technology. If I'd been born fifty years ago, this might have never been possible. Asag would release the other demons, and there would have been no one left to stop him.

But thankfully, *we* had found what we were looking for.

While Jason and Martinez discussed strategies and plans for returning the handle to the base in Florida, there was nothing for me to do but stare at the radar screen, praying that those tiny, flickering dots would soon translate into the discovery we were all waiting for.

The crew prepared a net as I made my way back onto the deck to watch. A splash resounded as the crate broke the surface, and the team hoisted it onto the deck.

Everyone gathered around, eyes wide with excitement and disbelief. One of the crew members, Luiz, stepped forward with a crowbar and cracked the crate open. A pile of Spanish coins glittered in the midday light, seeing the sun for the first time in nearly three hundred years.

My heart leaped into my throat. This was it. It had to be.

"Holy shit, would you look at that?" Marco, one of the deck-hands, blurted out, his eyes as wide as saucers.

"Is this real? *This* can't be real," Juan murmured, his hands clapped over his mouth as if afraid his words would jinx it.

"Madre de Dios," Carlos whispered, almost reverently, crowbar still in hand as if he might need to fend off pirate ghosts.

"I want to pick the actress that plays me in the movie, okay?" Maria demanded.

"The Unearthing of the San Juan Bautista," Carlos said, waving his hand like the title were on a billboard.

At the sight, however, even as excitement reverberated around me, my shoulders sagged. Old gold coins were super cool, and I'm sure historians and researchers would love to examine them, but it wasn't what we were looking for.

Jason motioned to one of the crew members. "You got a phone that can take photos?"

The man nodded.

"Great. Take pictures of this. We're going to empty it." He then gestured to two other crew members, both standing gawking at the treasure. "Get a bucket or tub." Adding when they didn't immediately react to his request, "Now.

Finally snapping out of their stupor, a pair of deckhands scrambled toward a stack of supplies. One of them knocked over a coil of rope in his haste but didn't bother picking it up. The other crewman came up triumphantly with an empty plastic tote, which you'd use to store holiday decorations or old tax forms. Not exactly a worthy vessel for ancient riches, but it would work all the same.

The first crewman held the tote steady as his partner delicately but quickly began to scoop the old coins into it. Each coin landed with a satisfying clink, the sound a stark contrast to the palpable tension in the air. The hands were efficient but cautious as if they were defusing a bomb made of gold and history.

As the tote began to fill, revealing the layers beneath, I saw it. Buried within the pile was a wooden shaft, intricately carved and strangely pristine. My eyes widened at the sight of Mesopotamian designs etched into its surface. A magnetic sensation coursed through me as if the object was calling out, beckoning me to claim it.

Gavin caught my eye, his own locked onto the shaft. "You feel that too, don't you?"

Before I could answer, Captain Sylvanas crossed himself. "This is the work of something unholy." His eyes went to me before landing on Martinez. "We should return to shore at once. I do not know what this is you have brought me and my crew into, but it is done. Our contract is complete."

Martinez smirked. "Our contract is complete once you get us back safely to shore."

The captain harumphed. "Very well." He then looked to his crew and began barking out orders to pull anchor and chart a course back to the marina.

As Jason continued to pull the coins out of the box, my eyes caught on a golden chain fastened to the corner near the base of the crate.

"Wait," I said, kneeling next to him. "There's something—" I reached in before finishing and tugged at the chain. As I pulled it up, freeing it from the tangle of coins, I saw at the end an eight-pointed star about the size of a quarter. My fingers hovered over it as I peered at the pretty jewelry and touched it. The air seemed to grow denser, the atmosphere an oppressing force above me.

Then, without warning, large waves began to slap against the side of the boat, jolting everyone back to reality.

"Secure the crate," Agent Martinez ordered.

Jason looked at me, his eyes dancing with a mixture of exhilaration and concern. "Are you all right?"

I nodded, still entranced by the mysterious wooden shaft and the gold star.

"Yeah, I'm good," I replied, but even to me, my voice sounded feeble and disconnected. My gaze kept drifting back to the crate—specifically to the wooden shaft adorned with engravings. My heart was racing, but not from fear or exhaustion. It was as if the artifact was calling to me, pulling me in.

Jason raised an eyebrow, his expression telling me he didn't buy my act for a second.

As I picked up the necklace, a pulse of energy rippled through it, tingling up my arm and spreading a warmth that seemed to center itself in my chest. What was this thing? It didn't matter; all that mattered was the overwhelming need and *desire* to put it on.

My hands were on autopilot as I clasped the necklace around my neck, and the moment it settled against my skin, the tingle intensified, spreading through my body like wildfire. The instant after, however, my thoughts cleared, and my fatigue seemed to evaporate like a mid-morning sun burning off the fog.

Jason was still watching me, his face now twisted into an open frown.

"What?" I asked, more defensively than I intended.

"You just put on an unknown object from a crate full of potentially dangerous magical artifacts," he said flatly. "Does that seem like a good idea to you?"

Usually, he'd be right to question me. But this felt different. "Jason, it's okay. I'm fine, see?" I held my hands up as if emphasizing my point that the necklace was doing nothing except looking pretty.

"Jason's right," Gavin said, concern pinching the space between his eyebrows as he turned from me to the open ocean. "Maybe we should head back, you know? We can look at everything once we're on shore."

The ocean just didn't agree with this kid. I opened my mouth to offer him more motion sickness medicine, but then the boat rocked more violently, and I had to grab the railing to stay upright. Jason reached out to steady me as I looked up and saw the ocean's surface growing restless. The boat pitched sideways as the waves swelled, slapping against the hull with increasing force.

"Is it just me," Gavin said, holding the metal railing also to keep from slipping. "Or are those waves getting bigger?"

TWENTY-FOUR

"No, those waves definitely are getting bigger," I replied, my eyes scanning the horizon. Dark clouds were gathering in the distance, merging into an ominous wall that seemed to be advancing toward us. A shiver ran down my spine. "Look. Is that a storm?."

Captain Sylvanas squinted at the horizon, his expression hardening. "Indeed. And it's closing in fast. All hands, attend to the bilges and secure the deck."

The crew sprang into action, frantically moving crates of equipment and closing the windows with metal braces. Shouts and commands filled the air, punctuated by the clang of metal and the creaking of ropes. Despite their efficiency, there was an undercurrent of anxiety that even the most seasoned sailors couldn't disguise.

"Get the chest below deck!" Agent Martinez was shouting orders, her voice cutting through the rising wind.

The atmosphere had changed drastically; a palpable sense of urgency replaced the excitement over our discovery. Gavin— who had been fascinated by the wooden shaft and the gold star

—was now feverishly helping other crew members tie down anything that could become airborne in a storm.

Jason grabbed my arm, pulling me away from the salvaged chest. "We need to get inside. Now."

I nodded, my pulse quickening as I allowed him to lead me toward the cabin. As we crossed the deck, a gust of wind whipped through the air, howling like a banshee and sending shivers down my spine. We made it inside just as the first raindrops began to pelt the deck, quickly intensifying into a torrential downpour. Captain Sylvanas disappeared up the narrow staircase to the helm, as we and the other crew that weren't attending to the engines or securing the hoist on the crane, huddled together by the window, gazing out into the oncoming storm.

"This is bad," someone muttered, an older man with a bald spot on his forehead and deep wrinkles around his eyes. "I've seen storms like this turn ugly fast. Sylvanas will have his hands full with this one. We're going to have to ride it out as we hurry back to land."

A crack of thunder echoed through the sky, followed by a brilliant flash of lightning. My heart thudded in my chest like a drum and each beat synced with the rising storm outside.

"Everyone, brace yourselves!" the man said, wrapping a hand around the railing of the stairs that descended below. The vessel tilted sharply, riding a massive wave.

As I clung to the back of a chair that was bolted to the floor, my eyes met Jason's briefly, and seeing the fear reflected from his usually stoic face, the gravity of our situation sank in.

We were so fucked.

The boat violently lurched as if struck by an unseen force, throwing us all off balance, and my back collided with the wall of the lower cabin.

Rain poured like sheets, pelting the glass windows, until the pounding became the only sound. Suddenly, the boat lunged forward, the engines roaring like some enraged beast fighting against the storm. Outside, what I'd first noticed as dark clouds now appeared almost apocalyptic—a swirling, roiling mass of charcoal and ink that blotted out all daylight; it was as if night had descended in the middle of the afternoon.

The Titan pitched and yawed so violently I could hardly stay on my feet, and then I saw it over the bow, a wall of water, a veritable mountain, rising from the depths as though it wished to touch the clouds. My breath caught, eyes widening in disbelief and terror.

"Elly, hold on to something, now!" Jason screamed next to me, but his voice seemed to come from far away.

As my eyes stayed glued to the monstrous tidal wave, lightning flashed, illuminating the scene, and there, in the heart of the storm, was a shadowy form—unmistakable and terrifying.

Asag.

My heart froze.

Its form was massive, at least a hundred feet tall, and just as wide—a dark, ominous figure under the translucent sheen of water.

Before I had a chance to process what it was, the boat shuddered as if hit by a giant fist.

As I braced myself against the ship's railing, the scent of saltwater was overwhelmed by an overpowering smell of diesel fuel and wet metal. The wind howled like a wounded animal, whipping the Venezuelan flag atop the pole on the wheelhouse, creating an almost deafening cacophony. Cold rain lashed my face, each drop an icy needle of water.

"Turn on the bilges! Secure all equipment!" one of the crewmen shouted, his voice barely carrying over the roar of the wind and crashing waves. All around me, crew members scrambled to obey, their rain gear flapping violently in the tempest.

One rushed to the control panel near the wheelhouse, hammering on buttons to activate the bilge pumps. Another wrestled with bungee cords, straining to tie down crates and scientific equipment that had begun to slide ominously across the deck.

I gripped the railing tighter, my knuckles white against the cold metal as the ship lurched. A mountainous wave rose before us, so enormous that, for a moment, it blotted out the stormy sky. I could hear the ship's engine groaning, fighting to power us up the monstrous wall of water. My stomach leaped into my throat as we crested the wave. I experienced the momentary weightlessness as the ship perched atop the apex before plunging down the other side into the awaiting trough. My insides dropped as if I were on a roller coaster, a thin sheen of sweat forming on my brow. I'd never liked roller coasters. Nausea rolled through me, and I feared riding out more of those waves. I couldn't imagine how Gavin was doing if I thought I was going to be sick.

Another crewman appeared, their arms flailing as they tried to get everyone's attention. "Put these on! Now!" she yelled, thrusting the bright orange vests at anyone within reach. My numb fingers clumsily fumbled with the straps and buckles before finally securing the life jacket around me.

The crew's actions were hurried but practiced, a well-choreographed ballet of chaos.

And then, from the stern of the ship in the back, came an earsplitting scream, rising above the din of thundering waves.

Jason and I jumped forward at once, and as he pulled open the cabin door, I was right on his heels, putting up an arm to brace against the howling wind and rain. I squinted toward the back, trying to ascertain who was in trouble. Perhaps someone had fallen and was hurt; whatever it was, we needed to help them.

The sour stench of sulfur drifted toward me, and Jason drew his gun from his hip, holding it up by his ear as we rounded the corner.

Instantly, I was paralyzed by the sight. One of the divers lay sprawled on the deck, his arms twisted back behind him at unnatural angles and his dark hair mercifully obscuring what remained of his face.

Rain pelted my face, blurring my vision as I strained to see. Looming over him was a single person. It was naked, and its skin the texture of jagged stone, its body twisted into grotesque limbs and appendages. A wave of nausea swept over me, but I kept my attention fixed on the thing standing over him.

The sour stench of sulfur had intensified, stinging my nose and bringing tears to my eyes. Jason held his gun up, bracing his shoulders as he leveled it on the creature.

"Hey, jackass," Jason yelled.

It looked up at the sound of Jason's voice, and I froze.

For a split second, I considered that perhaps a crew member had lost their mind, stripped down, and covered themselves in oil, but as the creature turned its face toward us, there was no doubt it was far from human. Its eyes were uneven pools of smoldering lava, glowing ominously in the dim light of the storm. Blood dripped from its boulder-like hands, which lacked fingers, but if the lifeless crew member's face were proof, they were formidable enough.

Without waiting a moment more, Jason fired a round. The bullet struck the creature's shoulder and ricocheted off, flying harmlessly into the stormy sea. It barely flinched, its molten eyes locking onto Jason's as if to say, "Is that all?"

"We need to go. Now!" I shouted, taking a step back. The creature started to move, its limbs grinding like rocks in a landslide, but before we could turn to run, a thump sounded to my right. I glanced over, and adrenaline flooded my veins. Another creature was pulling itself up over the side of the ship, its form just as twisted and horrific as the first.

Panic surged through me like an electric shock as my eyes darted along the railing, counting half a dozen more of these monsters hauling themselves onto the ship. Each was as night-marish as the last. We were outnumbered, outmatched, and, worst of all, we were trapped on a ship in the middle of a raging storm.

There were two very clear options for us to do: Fight or get to the life raft.

Captain Sylvanas appeared beside me, frantically buttoning a yellow raincoat. "The ocean is cold," he said, handing me another one he'd been carrying. "Hypothermia is not to be trifled with." I took it and placed it on, immediately feeling the warmth even under the thin material.

I squinted through the curtain of rain as the deck erupted into motion while Captain Sylvanas shouted orders to crew members running for weapons — rifles, flare guns, harpoon guns — anything that could shoot, stab, or maim.

My fingers— already numb and clumsy from the cold— trembled on the railing, its metal surface slick with rain.

A deckhand cursed in Spanish, and all at once, they rushed to the starboard side of the ship. I followed their gaze into the dark, murky waters. Emerging from the waves like abomina-tions birthed by the sea itself, ten scaly-skinned creatures, maybe more, streaked toward the boat. Their forms, just under the surface, left trails of what looked like iridescent oil sheens behind them. But as the waves crested and fell, I spotted tufts of smoke swirling upward, marking their passage, and then the telltale smell of sulfur reached me.

"Shoot them!" Captain Sylvanas roared, and a hailstorm of bullets, flares, and harpoons erupted toward the intruders. The sounds of gunfire and explosions mingled with the roar of the storm like a soundtrack to a scene from a nightmare. The weapons seemed almost ineffectual against their stone-like skin; bits of rock chipped off, but the creatures kept coming.

Within seconds, they were climbing the hull and throwing themselves over the deck with movements that were oddly fluid and blazingly fast for creatures made seemingly of rock.

I stepped back, looking to arm myself with something, *anything*. My gaze landed on the emergency box on the wall, and I pulled it open. Packages of bandages, ointments, and creams spilled out, but in the center was a flare gun clipped into a holster. I pulled it free and spun, praying it was loaded before firing it at the encroaching creature. A flare whooshed from it, nearly blinding me as it tore through the air. It struck the creature square in the chest, chipping off a chunk of rock but failing to stop its advance. My heart pounded frantically against my rib cage.

I pulled the trigger again, this time aiming for a crack where the grotesque thing's head would be attached to its neck if it were, say, a human. The second flare soared toward it, lodging into the crevice. The creature halted, its long stringy appendages grabbing at it, but it was stuck. The flare sizzled, continuing to burn, and the stench of rotten seafood enveloped me. The creature growled in what I assumed was pain before gnashing its teeth at me and jumping off of the deck. Refusing to wait for it to return, I snatched two more flares from the case and bolted to the stern.

"Rope rigging! Trap them in the rigging!" someone shouted. Crew members sprinted toward the heavy rope netting used for lowering the smaller boats. Fingers worked furiously, untying knots, repositioning the web of ropes to act as snares. I darted over to help, stuffing the flare gun in the coat pocket and grabbing a handful of rope.

Almost the second the rope was positioned, a creature

flopped onto the deck and into our trap, snarling in a voice like grinding stones as the ropes tightened around it. A rifle shot rang out, and it shuddered, immobilized but still menacingly alive.

More followed, drawn by the sound of gunfire and shouts like moths to a flame. Some we managed to catch, their limbs tangling in the ropes, their stone bodies weighing down the netting. Others advanced, undeterred, swiping at crew members with enormous club-like fists. One grabbed a crewman, lifting him off the deck as easily as I would lift a bag of groceries. The man screamed, struggling in vain before another gunshot took the creature down.

My fear turned into a kind of frenetic energy, propelling me from one part of the deck to another. Using the flare gun, I aimed and fired. The creature staggered back, its rocky surface glowing red from the flare lodged in its torso.

"Keep shooting!" Captain Sylvanas had yelled, almost as if trying to convince himself. A volley of bullets hit another creature, causing it to crumble like a statue subjected to years of erosion in mere seconds.

The air was thick with the smell of sulfur, gunpowder, and fear.

Finally, after what seemed like an eternity, the last creature let out a guttural screech, a sound like rocks scraping against each other, and toppled over, caught in a tangle of ropes and bullets.

The four of us, including the captain plus a handful of deckhands, all stood around panting, soaked and shivering, on a deck marred by bullet casings, bits of rock, and the smell of spent gunpowder. As I struggled to catch my breath, a haunting suspicion festered in the back of my mind: What if there are more out there?

With a guttural cry, Gavin materialized from the mayhem

and swung a loose metal pipe, knocking one of the injured creatures back into the water like a baseball player hitting a home run. Yet still more were coming, too many to count. A rock-like fist struck out, hitting Agent Martinez squarely in the chest, and she fell, her body limp and lifeless before she even hit the deck.

My heart screamed a silent 'no,' but there was no time to grieve, no time to do anything but survive.

The boat tilted alarmingly, throwing all of us off balance. Captain Sylvanas was shouting, trying to steer us away from another massive wave, but it was too late. We were capsizing.

"Fucking jump, Elly!" Jason's voice broke through the chaos.

Gavin was already in the air, plunging into the ocean's furious swell. Jason grabbed my hand, and for a split second, our eyes met. No words were needed.

We jumped.

CHAPTER

TWENTY-FIVE

The cold ocean hit me like a wall, stealing the breath from my lungs. Waves crested over me, forcing salt water into my mouth and swallowing me whole before spitting me back out. I kicked hard, arms flailing to keep myself afloat. Somewhere in the distance, I heard the disheartening groan of metal folding in on itself—the boat.

As I bobbed, I caught glimpses of the Titan. Its decks swarmed with the rock demons, and the few remaining crewmen fended them off even as the vessel slowly sank into the tumultuous waters.

"Jason? Gavin?" I yelled over the roar of the tempest, but the storm swallowed my voice. Thunder rolled, punctuating my growing sense of disorientation. I needed to get to land. To the shore, but where was the shore? Each swell lifted me momentarily, granting a panoramic view of nothing but dark, roiling waters. My heart plummeted; I was adrift in an endless expanse.

Salt water stung my eyes, making it even harder to get my bearings. The skies flashed, the jagged teeth of lightning tearing through the clouds. I spun in the water, disoriented, my limbs beginning to feel like lead. Fatigue was setting in, my muscles burning with each stroke. And then, a gust of wind stronger than any before smacked into me, disorienting me further. I tumbled in the water, unsure which way was up.

Sputtering and coughing, I broke the surface once more. Where the hell were they? Desperation clawed at me, each second stretching unbearably long. And then, through the sheets of rain and the haze of my exhaustion, I saw it—a life raft bobbing wildly in the storm-tossed sea.

With the last reserves of my energy, I struck out towards it, each stroke fueled by pure adrenaline. The chill of the ocean bit into my skin, just as the relentless pull of the currents, like invisible hands, tried to drag me under.

My arms felt like they were shredding apart. My lungs screamed for air, but I couldn't stop. Stopping meant giving up when I still had strength.

I was so close.

Just as I reached the edge of the raft, a hand shot out, gripping my arm. Gavin, his face ghostly gray but determined, hauled me out of the churning water and into the raft. I collapsed on my back, hacking up saltwater, my chest heaving. Every inch of me was spent, yet a strange feeling of triumph surged through me as I felt the reassuring presence of the inflated raft. I was alive. Gavin was alive.

"Where's Jason?" I shouted the second my voice had recovered.

Gavin shook his head. "I don't know!" he yelled over the howling wind. "Here, help me paddle, and we can find him."

Gavin thrust a plastic oar in my direction, and together, we began paddling wildly with no clear sense of where we were going. Every now and then he'd stop long enough to summon a bolt of lightning when he spotted something moving on the surface that was definitely not human. However, with the surging of waves blocking his view, he held back more than he called his power for fear of hitting a crew member treading water.

I clung to the tiny rope running the perimeter of the small raft as it pitched sideways, and every time I called for Jason, my words were whisked away by the wind or snuffed out by the roar of thunder from Gavin's lightning. It was useless.

I scanned the dark waters, my heart in my throat. Jason was a powerful swimmer, but in this kind of storm, even he would be tested. I clung to the fading hope that perhaps he'd found another raft and had drifted further from us too far to see.

Gavin must've sensed my concern, his grip tightening around me. "He'll be okay," he said softly, but his voice lacked conviction.

Saltwater splashed against my face as another wave broke over us. Gavin and I were locked in a relentless paddling rhythm, our arms burning with exhaustion. The rubbery slap of oars against water became a monotonous drumbeat, drowning out the churn and crash of the stormy ocean around us.

The floating remnants of the Titan surrounded us—cardboard boxes disintegrating in the water, splintered wooden crates, and the eerie sight of face-down bodies bobbing like gruesome markers. Each one tightened my chest. Was Jason among them? No, I couldn't let my mind go there. Not yet. I had to hold on to the fragile hope that he was somewhere, somehow, alive.

"Look there," Gavin yelled over the wind, pointing toward a group of floating crates. "Might find something useful!"

Heeding his words, we adjusted our course, muscles screaming in protest. When we finally reached the crates, a quick rummage through soggy cardboard and drenched cloth yielded nothing more than a gnawing sense of despair. It was all useless junk.

As another wave rolled under us, my voice cracked as I yelled Jason's name into the howling wind. Nothing came back but the roar of the storm and the haunting echo of my desperation. I was dreading the moment I'd see his body in these merciless waves.

Gavin abruptly held up his hand. "Hold on! What's that?" His finger pointed at a dark shape lurking under the water, far too coordinated in its movement to be a piece of debris.

My heart stopped. It couldn't be—stone-skinned demons. Here, in the ocean. "We've got to move," I said, no room for debate in my voice.

Without a word, we dug our oars into the water, pushing the life raft as fast as we could. I could feel them behind us, their dark forms gaining, an underwater nightmare in pursuit. My heart pounded in my chest like a second drumbeat, each pulse a countdown.

As if answering an unspoken prayer, a bolt of lightning lanced down from the sky, glaringly bright, revealing in its flash a silhouette of a shoreline.

Land. So close and yet impossibly far.

"Go!" I screamed, and we redoubled our efforts. Oars slicing through the water, we propelled ourselves toward salvation with a manic frenzy. As another wave lifted us high before crashing down again, a grim thought settled in the pit of my stomach. A force hit the raft from below, flipping it like a toy in a bathtub, and suddenly, I was underwater.

Disoriented, I opened my eyes, ignoring the shock of cold. All around me, I could see dark shapes rising from the ocean floor - hundreds of them. My lungs burned for air as I kicked hard and searched for the surface. When I finally spotted it, the light streaming down from above looked so far away. I used my arms to right myself, swimming toward it. My lungs burned as I kicked hard, fearing at any second, one of the encroaching demons could latch onto my leg and drag me under.

Just when I thought I couldn't hold on any longer, my head broke the surface, and I gasped in the sweet oxygen.

I spotted the overturned raft. Gavin was already there, clinging to it, the whites of his eyes visible. "Climb on!"

Summoning what felt like the last ounces of my strength, I lunged for the raft, my arms heavy as lead. Another form shot out of the water near me—ash-skinned, eyes glowing. A scream ripped through my throat as I pulled myself up, sprawling onto the raft's rubbery bottom.

Gavin was beside me, and we started paddling with our hands, a desperate doggy paddle toward the shadow of land. Behind us, I heard the splash and surge of our pursuers. They were still coming, and we were running out of ocean.

TWENTY-SIX

The shock of cold water, the burn of salt on my cuts, the desperate fight against the undertow—it all seemed a blur as the emergency raft finally touched the Venezuelan shoreline. I looked over at Gavin as he jumped off, his bright yellow shirt now clinging to him, waterlogged and darkened.

We had somehow survived, by a blessed miracle, were scratched and bruised, but we were *alive*.

I pushed myself up, taking in my surroundings. The early morning sun shimmered golden on the waves, and I stretched the kinks out of my muscles, feeling like I'd slept on a beach all night. Which I, in fact, *had*.

By some miracle, we'd landed on a stretch of beach that appeared isolated, bordered only by thickets of brush and forest. The sand under my feet felt like gritty talcum powder, hot from the sun's lingering touch, a stark contrast to the icy sea that had nearly swallowed us. A humid breeze touched my face, barely enough to offer relief to my parched throat that tasted of salt.

"Are you okay?" Gavin's voice broke through my daze. He was limping, favoring one leg.

"Yeah, you?" I asked, my eyes scanning his form.

"Ankle is banged up," he said, wincing as he tried to put weight on it. "And my power packs are fried." He tore off the leather gloves that held the micro-batteries Eddie had designed and stuffed them in his backpack. "Could be worse, I guess."

My eyes drifted to the beach, trying to get our bearings and a possible clue as to where we'd made shore, and that's when I noticed them. On the sand behind Gavin—the lifeless forms of a few of the crew from the Titan scattered along the shoreline like discarded dolls. My stomach heaved.

I rose to my feet, my knees feeling weak and shaky, and put a hand to shield my eyes. All these people. They'd only been doing their jobs. They had families. Lives. People would miss them.

A thought hit me with the force of a freight train—Jason. A surge of adrenaline coursed through me, making me momentarily forget my exhaustion.

"Jason!" I screamed, my voice tearing through the salty air, mingling with the sound of the crashing waves. "Jason, where are you?"

Gavin looked at me, his eyes widening in realization. "Ella, wait!"

Ignoring him, I bolted down the shoreline, my eyes scanning each crumpled form that lay ahead. My heart felt like it was in a vise, each turn of a lifeless body tightening the screw. Blonde hair, but too long. A build too slight, too heavy. A tattoo on his neck that Jason didn't have. Relief and dread alternated with each discovery.

Gavin caught up to me, his face flushed and twisted in pain. "Ella, we can't—"

"I have to find him, Gavin! I can't—I won't—lose him!" My

voice broke, the weight of unspeakable loss threatening to shatter me.

Gavin grabbed my arm, steadying me. "We'll find him."

I knew he was right, but logic was the farthest thing from my mind. Fear was corrosive, and each second we didn't find, Jason ate away at my resolve. We started checking the bodies together, lifting heads gently, looking for the face that had become my anchor in a world where I was so often adrift.

Gavin limped beside me, looking back at the dying light and then at the treacherous sea that had spat us out. "Let's keep going."

My eyes darted back to the churning ocean. Unless the coast guard magically appeared through the waves to rescue us, hiking inland was the right choice.

Gavin looked up, his eyes meeting mine, glossed over with an emotion I couldn't quite place. "Ella, I have to tell you something."

His voice was barely above a whisper, the words coming out like a confession. "I told Asag everything. About the shaft, the handle, where we were going, everything."

I felt my stomach drop, the betrayal cutting through me like a razor. "Are you serious? When? How?" I demanded.

Gavin collapsed, and his knees dug into the wet sand. His shoulders hunched forward, looking broken and defeated.

"After you touched me at the pawn shop, you blacked out," he stammered. "Asag approached me. I didn't have a choice, Ella. He was going to kill me—and you. So I made a deal with him."

"How could you?" My voice trembled, barely able to contain my anger and confusion. "*You're* the reason Asag attacked us on the boat?" I jabbed a finger at the ocean. "Holy shit, Gavin. I can't believe I'm hearing this."

He looked away, shame flushing his face, and it only fueled

my rage that he wouldn't face me. "People died," I shouted. "Martinez. The Captain. The crew. Innocent people. Good people, all because of you? You made a deal with it. What the hell were you thinking?"

"My grandparents," he choked out, keeping his eyes down. "Asag removed the curse from them. They're better now because of the deal. Because they're all I have." His voice broke at the end, and he buried his face in his hands.

The wind swirled around us, kicking up sand just as my mind raced.

All this time, Asag had known. All those moments we'd spent researching, planning, fighting, he'd known. The silence stretched between us, tense and uncomfortable as I processed all that this meant. All the signs were there: Gavin's vague recalling about how he'd survived when I'd been unconscious at the pawn shop. Why he'd been so eager to leave only hours after his grandparents had gotten better?

"I'm sorry, Ella," Gavin said finally, his voice frayed with desperation. "Please, I didn't think he'd hurt anyone else. He'd promised he'd only take the weapon."

"And you believed him?" I snarled.

Gavin flinched as if I'd slapped him. "It was stupid. I know that now, but you have to believe me. I didn't know they would do this."

I folded my arms and spun, not able to face him anymore, and stepped back, putting physical distance between us as if it would help me understand the emotional chasm that had just opened. My thoughts were a storm, as tumultuous as the ocean behind me. Anger, disappointment, confusion—they all swirled inside me, each demanding me to do something, say something.

His head dropped, his eyes fixed on the wet sand beneath him. "I know I screwed up. I'm supposed to be a champion of

Ninurta, a fighter, and I chose to put my personal needs before my duty, and now we're here. Washed up on a shore somewhere. No one even knows we're here. If you never speak to me again, I'd understand."

"What you did was so wrong, Gavin, I can't even…" I ran a hand over my face and sighed. "Look, I can't deal with this, right now. Right now, we need to see if there are more survivors and if there's a way to get in touch with Division 12. Asag is still out there, and the only advantage we *had* is now gone. But we're not through with this yet. Not by a long shot."

He nodded, slowly getting to his feet, his eyes never leaving the ground. "I know. And I'll do whatever it takes to make it right. If it's even possible to make it right."

"If?" I shook my head. "We don't have the luxury of 'if,' Gavin. We only have 'must.' We must fix this. *You* must fix this. Whatever it takes."

He looked up, his eyes meeting mine again. Resolve steeled his gaze and set his jaw, reminding me all too much of Jason.

"I will," he said, his voice stronger now. "Whatever it takes. I promise."

A promise. These days, those felt like currency in a world I no longer understood, a fragile offering at the altar of trust and friendship. Should I believe him? Could I? For now, we had more immediate problems to deal with.

Minutes felt like hours, and growing panic tightened its grip as my eyes searched desperately for any sign of him. My arms trembled with each body we checked, my soul cracking a little more each time the face wasn't Jason's. The sun continued its descent, oblivious to our despair, casting long shadows that danced with the incoming tide.

Then I heard it—a faint moan, almost too soft and nearly drowned out by the roaring ocean.

TWENTY-SEVEN

My head snapped toward the sound. "Did you hear that?" I said.

Gavin nodded, urgency replacing the pain in his eyes, and together, we moved toward the sound, calling out for Jason as we scrambled over rocks and debris. Finally, we found him—Jason, lying half-buried in the sand. Fear propelled me forward, my shoes sinking into the wet sand, making every step feel like a chore with my sore muscles. By the time I reached him, my breaths came in shallow gasps.

"Jason!" I fell to my knees beside him, my hands shaking as I touched his face, reassuring myself that he was real.

I hesitated for a moment, not sure I was ready to confront what I'd find. His skin, when I touched it was cold, and he was eerily still. Tears stung my eyes, blurring my vision.

"Jason, you can't leave me like this," I pleaded, choking back a sob. "Please, no."

And then, unexpectedly, a familiar chill touched my fingers. My Inanna necklace. Almost forgotten in the chaos, it now felt different—like a dormant pulse awakening. In that heartbeat of a moment, I wondered: had my own emotions, my internal clamor for normality, drowned out the magic all along?

Drawing a deep breath, I felt a calm stillness within, and it was in this quiet that I found it—a gentle yet insistent tug of magic. As it flowed, I realized I'd been blocking my power, mistaking its subtle presence for absence.

I placed my hands on Jason's chest, willing him to come back to me. I had nothing to compare to the sensation—I didn't just touch him. I felt him. The rhythmic beat I willed his heart into, the water I pushed out of his lungs, all with a certainty that was calm yet commanding.

His body seemed to respond to me, the faintest quiver beneath my palms. I felt something pass between us, something tangible, something alive, and I knew that I could bring him back to me. I closed my eyes, and the power coursed through me as if an invisible force connected us.

And then suddenly, his eyes fluttered open. His chest heaved as he gasped for air. When his eyes locked with mine, a wave of relief washed over me.

"Elly," he rasped, his voice tinged with disbelief and relief.

I exhaled. He was alive. He was with me.

For a moment, nothing else mattered. The dead crewmen, the looming threats, my role as Guardian—it all faded away, leaving only the overwhelming relief that flooded my senses. I wrapped my arms around him, pulling him close despite his groans of pain, feeling the tension bleed out of me for the first time since we'd hit the water.

I laughed, a wet, messy sound of sheer relief, and rocked back on my heels. "Jason Stanley Price. Don't you *ever* do that again?"

He gave a tired smile, and a warmth bloomed across my chest. "No guarantees, but I'll try."

"Dope trick," Gavin said, standing a little ways off. "Hopefully, *you* won't have to do it again."

Do it again? I hadn't even known how I'd managed it the first time. My thoughts buzzed. My power had returned.

But how? Because Jason had been dead. Or at least close to death.

They'd come back to me when I needed them most, when I'd had my world crushed beyond belief. Despair had reached into me and torn them from wherever they'd been hiding.

I flexed my hands, staring at them in disbelief, and a laugh bubbled up from me. I dug my fingers into the warm sand and felt the rumble of power rise in my chest. The sand was full of organic material: billions of crushed shells.

I buried my hands into the sand and cupped them together. I closed my eyes, focusing. No statues, no scars, no elaborate gestures, just the purity of my intent. When I opened my eyes and opened my fist, I held a radiant seashell sculpture in my hands. The delicate ridges of its curves were like lace, smooth and strong as bone, shimmering with radiance like the surface of a bubble-filled pond at dawn, colored like a rainbow.

For a second, I was too stunned to speak, to react. Then, the joy exploded inside me like the finale of a fireworks display. "It's back!" I yelled. "My magic is back!"

I leaped to my feet, holding out the shell. It glowed faintly in my palm, and I willed it to change again. Instantly, it transformed into a different shape, this one more elongated with speckles of blue and yellow. I danced right there on the sand, spinning and whooping like I'd won the lottery. Sand flew everywhere, and Gavin and Jason shielded their eyes as my feet accidentally sprayed them, but I didn't care. My magic had come back. I was whole again, complete in a way I'd almost forgotten.

"Hell yeah," Gavin said, his hazel eyes wide and his grin wider.

Jason, however, was not smiling. "Are you sure, Elly? How do we know this isn't something to do with Asag?"

His words stopped me mid-twirl, but the bubble of my happiness didn't burst—it just hovered, waiting. Dammit. Was he right? Could Asag somehow be the cause my magic had returned? I had no idea the extent of his powers. However, summoning demons from the earth and causing hurricanes and tidal waves was no small feat, so could he have somehow triggered my magic to awaken? But why? Wouldn't that be the exact opposite of what he wanted?

No. I refused to believe that horrible creature was somehow connected to this.

This was on me. Something I had done had brought it back. I studied Jason's gaze and furrowed brow. And then it hit me, a truth so simple and so profound I couldn't believe I hadn't seen it earlier. My magic had returned because I'd needed to save Jason.

Because I undoubtedly, with every molecule of my being, loved him.

I closed the gap between us in three quick strides, and before he could say another word, I blurted out, "Because of you. It's back because of you. Because I needed it to save you."

Jason's blue eyes widened. The shock was there, a flicker like a skipped heartbeat, and then something deeper started to swirl in his gaze. Surprise gave way to understanding, and understanding deepened into a raw, almost vulnerable emotion that made my heart somersault.

As if on autopilot, my hand reached up to touch his face. When my fingers brushed his skin, I felt a jolt, a tiny electric charge that wasn't just my newly returned magic but something purer, more primal.

His eyes searched mine as if looking for something he was afraid yet hopeful to find. What he saw must have satisfied him because the corners of his mouth turned up in a hesitant but genuine smile.

"Then I guess we both got something back today," he finally said, his voice soft but laden with a gravity that anchored me to the spot. He leaned down and kissed me, and my magic surged, excited by the emotions that fluttered through me.

Gavin coughed forcefully, pulling us from our trance.

Jason rubbed his chest. It hadn't been real CPR, yet I was sure his heart muscles and lungs were sore from me forcing them to contract with my power.

Gavin's eyes roved over the white sand and encroaching jungle. "So, now you've got your power back. What are we supposed to do now?"

Jason's arm draped over my shoulder for support, and the weight of our reality settled back in. "We need to notify Division 12. Then, we should scour the beach for survivors and supplies," Jason said. "Carry them away from the ocean to the tree line before the tide gets any higher." He felt around in his pants pocket and pulled out a satellite phone.

"It's soaked. Is that still going to work?" Gavin asked.

"Let's hope so." Jason clicked on a power button, and it chimed in response. "Guess that's a yes?"

Gavin's eyes widened, impressed. "iPhone could never."

I watched Jason pull out our lifeline, a satellite phone built like a tank. He dials, shoots me a look, and turns away. He dialed a number and asked for Director Ferguson a few seconds later.

"Director Ferguson, it's Price," Jason said, not mincing words.

I tuned into the waves crashing on the shore, but their relentless ebb and flow was soothing, like white noise.

"We were attacked on the boat, and the Titan is at the bottom of the ocean. Agent Martinez is dead. We need medics and possible evac," Jason rattled off, military-precise.

Ferguson's pissed-off voice floated over to me.

"This was a recovery mission. What the hell happened, Price? And the ship sank?" she snapped. "God damn, this is going to be a fucking PR nightmare."

Jason's jaw clenched. "With all due respect—"

"Enough, Price. Got any good news?"

Jason's eyes found mine, and it was like we were on the same miserable wavelength. Then he reached into his pocket and pulled out the wood rod. "We have the shaft, ma'am."

My pulse skipped a beat, and a mischievous grin appeared on his face.

I mouthed the words, "You are amazing!"

He shrugged like it was no big deal, which it totally fucking was, and held it out to me. I relished the comforting weight of the piece of the mace before gently stuffing it into my shoulder bag I'd found washed ashore.

"Secure it," I heard the director say after a momentary pause. "Division 12 will be there in an hour. Don't disappoint me."

Jason hung up. "They're coming," he said.

While we waited for the Division 12 cavalry, the three of us combed the beach, looking for any of the Titan's crew. Two women who had been divers were face down in the sand, their hair tangled with seaweed. At first glance, I assumed they were both deceased, but then one moaned. I called for Gavin to help me, and carefully, we carried her over the sharp rocks and up the beach. Her face was pale, and her pants were torn, revealing a bloody wound, but apart from that, she appeared unharmed, cold, and shivering but alive.

When we'd walked the length of the shore, we'd found six

crewmen deceased and four injured, including the woman diver. I swallowed down the guilt that there had been twenty-two aboard the Titan, which meant twelve families would have to bury empty caskets. My throat clenched further, including Agent Martinez.

I shot a glare in Gavin's direction, seeing him slowly drag a dead body up the dunes into the dry grass. It had been because of him. Their blood was on his hands. How could I ever trust him again? We were both chosen by the gods, destined to be a team and work side by side to stop this evil, and he had betrayed that duty. Betrayed me.

However, together, we were the only ones that seemed to have any power against Asag. And as much as I wanted to keep hating him, he'd admitted his mistake. And from the looks of it, he was seeking his penance.

Which meant I needed to move forward from what he'd done. Not forgive, not yet, but continue onward, or the Titan's crew's deaths would have been in vain. Countless others would die if I let my resentment stop me and wedged a divide between me and him.

The distinct thumping of helicopter blades reverberated through the air, drawing me from my thoughts. They grew louder as it approached, and I looked up, shielding my eyes from the setting sun, as a sleek, black helicopter emblazoned with the insignia for Division 12 touched down on the sand, sending a spray of grains into the air.

Eight agents— clad in combat gear and carrying an assortment of high-tech gear— jumped out as the helicopter's blades slowed. Their faces were hard and focused, scanning the area as if expecting an ambush at any moment. One of them, a woman with a stern face and close-cropped hair, approached Jason.

"Agent Price," she said, nodding at Jason, "We've been briefed on the situation. What's the plan?"

Jason gestured toward us. "First things first, we need to make sure everyone is stable. We've got survivors—"

The agents sprang into action, their movements coordinated and precise. Two of them spread out along the shore, scouting for additional survivors, while others unpacked crates from the helicopter. Within minutes, Venezuelan coast guards were contacted, initiating a comprehensive search for any survivors still in the water.

Another agent handed out dry clothes and MREs. I grabbed one of the vacuum-sealed packs, the physical hunger suddenly breaking through the fog of emotional exhaustion.

Weapons were next. The agent presented a compact assortment—handguns, stun guns, and even what looked like small energy weapons designed to disrupt magical fields. My fingers closed around the grip of a handgun. It was cold and impersonal, but in a world with an evil entity with the power to summon rock monsters, a little conventional firepower, along with my own magic, felt reassuring.

Gavin hesitated, looking from the weapons to me, his face twisted in a cocktail of emotions—guilt, uncertainty, maybe even a little fear. He shook his head and backed away. "No. I can't," he said quietly.

The agent looked puzzled but didn't press the matter. Instead, he nodded at Jason. "What's our next move, sir?"

Jason glanced at me as if I had a plan, which I totally did not. I shrugged, my hand going to the necklace.

"We follow the coordinates Eddie sent us," Jason finally said, breaking eye contact. "But we stay alert. Expect anything and everything to come our way."

The agent nodded, then turned to address her team. "You heard Agent Price. Let's get ready to move out."

As the agents bustled about, prepping for departure, my eyes landed on Gavin. He was physically present but emotionally miles away, lost in whatever labyrinth of guilt and regret he'd constructed for himself.

Even as we moved away from the shoreline, my thoughts kept pulling me back to Gavin's confession. He had risked everything for his family—what would I have done in his shoes?

I reached for the pendant hanging around my neck. The power within it was subdued, but the familiar pulse of energy still tingled through my fingertips. A momentary distraction but one I needed.

Gavin, sensing my unease, fumbled with a waterproof bag he'd managed to save before the ship sank. "Here," he said, handing me the shaft we had recovered. It was heavier than I remembered, the weight not just physical but emotional too.

I sat down in the sand and took out the leather-wrapped handle I'd safely stowed in my backpack and had managed to make it to shore with.

I felt the weight of Jason and Gavin's eyes on me as I inspected both pieces, turning them this way and that. They were supposed to fit together, a seamless combination of ancient craftsmanship and magical potential. But nothing seemed to work. The pieces repelled each other as if I were putting the same sides of a magnet together.

Jason peered over my shoulder. "Want me to try?"

Frustration bubbled up in me. "It's not just 'snapping' together like it should.

"Maybe it needs superglue or something?" Gavin supplied.

"I don't think they had superglue back then," I said, my tone harsher than I'd intended.

"We're obviously missing something," Jason said.

My fingers still toying with the pieces, I felt a sudden pull from my necklace, a magnetic sensation urging me inward, away from the shore.

Just as I was about to comment, Jason's phone buzzed. "It's Eddie," he said, answering the call.

While Jason talked, his face growing more serious with each passing second, I kept feeling that magnetic pull from my necklace. It was like a compass in my gut, directing me to something —somewhere—important.

Jason hung up and turned to us. "Eddie and Kat have been doing some research. The shaft was originally intended for an explorer in the 1700s—some rich guy roaming around Venezuela. His journals mention a hidden temple, a door to the underworld that locals warned him to avoid."

"That can't be a coincidence," Gavin said, his eyes widening. "That's got to be where the head of Sharur is."

Door to the Underworld. Nope. Not ominous at all. "Where is it?" I asked, already getting flashbacks of descending tunnels into cities buried underground.

Jason swiped through his phone and showed us photos of aged, handwritten journal entries. "Eddie sent these over. Our last clue is here. Coordinates. Or at least, the 18th-century version of them."

We pored over the images, trying to make sense of the archaic handwriting and vague descriptions. Finally, an incoming email notification popped up. It was Eddie again, sending us a modern translation of the coordinates.

I met Gavin's eyes, then Jason's. Despite the emotional turbulence, despite the betrayal and secrets, we had a mission. And maybe, just maybe, completing it could mend the rifts between us.

"We've got a location," Jason confirmed, pocketing his phone.

"And we've got a direction," I said, feeling the pull from my necklace more strongly now. It was as though the universe was condensing, focusing all its energy on this one quest.

Gavin clenched his fists, summoning his resolve. "Then, let's not waste any more time."

Jason broke the silence. "We'll need to get a team and supplies together."

With that thought that I wouldn't have to face this alone this time and would have Division 12's aid backing me, steadying my racing heart, I looked at Gavin and Jason, already anticipating the dangers that awaited us, both natural and supernatural. Sure, demons were dangerous, but so was malaria, poisonous plants, and snakes that fell from trees. "Let's do this," I said, "let's go find the missing piece."

TWENTY-EIGHT

"Last call for weapons," the stern-faced agent announced. I looked at Gavin one more time, hoping he'd change his mind, pick up a weapon— anything to show he was with us, that he was prepared to fight, but he only met my gaze with a sorrowful look, shook his head, and turned away.

So be it.

My boots crunched on the gritty sand as I followed Jason to meet the Division 12 agents. They stood next to a jeep, looking like characters from a Jason Bourne novel, all in black tactical gear.

"You must be Agent Price," one said, extending a gloved hand to Jason. "I'm Agent Reynolds. This is Agent Clark."

Jason shook the hand firmly and then nodded at me. "This is Eleanora Dawson."

"Just Ella is fine," I said, shaking their hands and not missing the little thrill I got from Jason calling me by full name.

"We've got the guides who will take you to the coordinates," Agent Clark said, pointing at two men approaching.

The men walked over, both in their mid-forties, sun-tanned with backpacks.

"I'm Rico, and this is my brother, Tomas," the taller one with a worn baseball cap said. "We guide biologists, researchers, and the like."

"We are owners of a jungle tour company here in Venezuela," Tomas added.

Rico pulled out a tablet and showed us a digital map. "You gave us these coordinates," he said, pointing. "It's near a pair of Tepui close to Sarisariñama."

"Tepui?" Gavin asked.

Rico nodded. "It means 'House of the Gods'. It's in the Gran Sabana region in Venezuela. It is formed by water erosion over a billion years, which makes them have vertical cliffs that rise dramatically, almost out of nowhere. You see, they are remnants of a much larger sandstone plateau that once covered the granite basement complex between the north border of the Amazon."

Rico zoomed in on the tablet's map, tracing the outlines of the plateaus with his finger. "What makes them so special is that they are ecological islands, separated from the ground forest by their cliffs. This isolation has led to unique ecosystems —completely different kinds of flora and fauna. We're talking about plants and animals that you can't find anywhere else."

I raised an eyebrow. Man, Kat would be loving this. "Like an ecological time capsule?"

"Exacto. You've got it," Rico beamed. "Because of their isolation, they serve as a window into the past. For example, atop some Tepuis, you can find black, acidic soil, which is perfect for acid-loving plants. Carnivorous plants like the sundew and the pitcher plant."

"And not just plants," Tomas continued, "Some Tepuis have big sinkholes and caves. Sarisariñama, for example, has sinkholes that are 350 meters deep. These are not just holes in the ground; they're like isolated ecosystems of their own, a world within a world."

"House of the gods, indeed," Jason muttered, clearly impressed.

Rico grinned. "There's more. Indigenous Pemon people believe that Tepuis are the home of 'Mawari' spirits and consider them sacred. Many of the Tepuis have never been summited because they are so difficult to climb. The vertical cliffs and the near-constant rainfall make them a formidable challenge even for experienced climbers. And that's not to mention the fact that the ecosystems are so fragile, human activity could easily disrupt them."

"So, we're dealing with something that's not just geologically unique but also culturally and ecologically significant," Gavin summarized.

"Yes," Rico affirmed. "This is why we need to move carefully, respecting both the land and its history."

With that, he flipped the tablet around, and Jason and I leaned in as he showed our current location, a blue dot on the coastline, then another along the border of Southern Venezuela.

"That's over 300 miles from here," Jason noted.

"Correct," Tomas said. "You'll need a helicopter."

I did some quick math. "So we're 100 miles east from the port and another 300 miles to go?"

Rico confirmed it, zooming out on the map.

"Great," I muttered. "The Titan sank a hundred miles off, and now we're chasing coordinates 300 miles away?"

"Seems so," Jason said, his eyes still on the map.

"When do we leave?" Gavin asked.

"Helicopter's ready when you are," Agent Reynolds said. "Supply list?" he asked, turning to Tomas.

"Rico will get it to you," he said, and the three of them

wandered back to where a laptop was set beside the ammo and gun crate, leaving Gavin and I to stare at each other, wondering what it was we were going to find at the 'House of the gods.'

❧

AN HOUR LATER, the helicopter blades whirred overhead, a mechanical contrast to the wild expanse of green unfolding below us. I watched as the Venezuelan jungle stretched out like an unending carpet of foliage. The noise made conversation difficult, so we were given headsets that allowed Tomas to continue the discussion of the plan.

"I told the pilot about the landing zone," Tomas yelled over the rotor's clamor. "There's only one spot clear enough for the helicopter. After that, we're on foot."

Rico pointed to a tablet displaying a map. "We've taken biologists through this route before. The jungle's thick, full of ravines and thick brush. You're not going to enjoy it if you're claustrophobic or scared of bugs."

"Once we land, what's the next step?" Jason asked.

"We'll have to hike for about two miles to get to the Tapui ridge," Tomas explained. "After that, we rappel down."

"Rappel?" I asked, exchanging a glance with Jason.

"Yep," Rico said, grinning. "There are no ladders or stairs."

"And once we're down there?" Gavin added, his voice crackling through the headset.

"That's where the fun begins," Tomas said, a mysterious undertone lacing his words. "There are many ravines between the Tapuis. Most are unexplored. We've been down in several before and have never found anything out of the ordinary except the biologist we were with went wild over the frogs. However, the locals have their stories."

"What kind of stories?" I leaned forward, interested despite myself.

Rico laughed dryly. "The tribal natives say the caves are haunted. They talk about ghosts that wander the dark corridors, luring victims into the abyss."

I glanced at Jason, whose expression was unreadable. Then I looked at Gavin, who was doing a poor job hiding his skepticism.

Tomas caught my eye and added, "In fact, some locals call it 'La Entrada al Inframundo.' The entrance to the underworld."

I felt a chill. The name carried with it an eerie resonance that settled in the pit of my stomach. "Well, isn't that lovely," I said, not hiding the sarcasm in my voice.

Jason raised an eyebrow but said nothing. It seemed we were all contemplating the same thing: what exactly were we getting ourselves into?

"Look, whatever's down there, we're not leaving without what we came for," Jason finally broke the silence. "We've got a mission, and we're going to complete it."

Gavin nodded, all jokes aside now. "Agreed. Haunted or not, we're going down there."

"We'll make sure you're equipped and prepared," Rico assured us. "The terrain's harsh, and if you're not careful, you could easily get lost or worse."

I turned my gaze back to the window, watching as the jungle zoomed by below us. The shadows between the trees seemed to deepen as we flew as if the earth itself were swallowing the light. And yet, amid the nerves and the unanswered questions, a part of me thrived on the uncertainty, the adventure. It's what I'd trained for, after all.

The helicopter started its descent, and I felt that familiar rush of adrenaline. We were moments away from stepping into an unknown world, armed with little more than our wits and a set of mysterious coordinates. But whatever awaited us in the depths of the Venezuelan jungle, one thing was clear: there was no turning back now.

As the helicopter touched down and the rotors slowed, I took a deep breath. Jason looked at me, his eyes meeting mine in a moment of unspoken understanding. Tomas and Rico began unbuckling their seat belts, preparing to disembark.

"Ready?" Jason asked, his voice tinged with that soldier-like resolve I'd come to rely on.

"Let's do this," I said, my grip tightening around the straps of my backpack. "After all, how bad could the entrance to the underworld be?"

Jason laughed. "Famous last words, Elly."

As the helicopter blades came to a complete stop and the din of the rotors faded into the background, Tomas, Rico, and two other agents started unloading the gear. "My cousin used to work for a logging company not far from here," he said, his tone somber. "Four months ago, a mudslide took out nearly everyone on his crew. He was the only survivor."

My ears perked up at that. "Four months ago, you say?"

"Yeah," Tomas continued, "It was a mess. We had to shut down operations. This area can be treacherous, unpredictable."

A thought flickered in my mind, connecting dots I hadn't even known were there. Four months ago, I'd stopped the Bridge of Vela from completely opening. There couldn't possibly be a connection. Could there?

As if responding to my inner turmoil, the necklace grew warm against the sensitive skin on my chest, its pull increasing the whole time we were in the helicopter.

Gavin, sitting a few feet away, seemed restless, like a dog sensing an impending storm. I couldn't shake the feeling that he, too, was drawn to where we were going.

"Is everything all right?" Jason's voice broke through my thoughts, pulling me back to the present.

I glanced at Tomas and Rico, who were engrossed in a discussion about the rappelling equipment. Then my eyes shifted back to Gavin, who seemed lost in his thoughts, a far-off look in his eyes.

I hesitated before answering, debating whether to share my burgeoning theory. "I'm not sure," I finally said. "But the timing Tomas mentioned—about the mudslide four months ago—it coincides with something else. Something potentially significant."

Jason's eyes met mine, and I saw a glint of understanding there. "The Bridge of Vela," he murmured.

I nodded.

"Well, let's keep our eyes open," Jason said. "Something tells me that the more pieces we put together, the clearer the bigger picture will become."

TWENTY-NINE

The first step into the jungle felt like crossing an invisible line between two worlds—the familiar, safe, and unknown everything flora or fauna could kill you. The air was thicker here, ladened with the scent of damp earth and decaying foliage. A cacophony of sounds filled the air: birds cawing, insects buzzing, the distant echo of a howler monkey's call. The sunlight filtering through the canopy of leaves and branches dappled the ground in shifting patterns of light and shadow.

Tomas led the way, machete in hand, cutting through vines and overgrown bushes with practiced ease. Rico was right behind him, holding a GPS device that mapped our path. The six Division 12 agents followed, their eyes scanning the terrain, fingers near the triggers of their guns.

"Watch your step," Tomas called over his shoulder. "There's a type of venomous snake around here, fer-de-lance, and they're worse than rattlesnakes because they don't give you any warning."

My eyes darted to the ground, suddenly aware of every rustle of the leaves. The jungle itself was teeming with colors, sounds, and smells. Orchids bloomed in surreal hues of violet and crimson, tangled with ferns and creeping vines. Birds of every imaginable shade flitted through the branches: toucans with their oversized beaks, parrots squawking in discordant harmony, and tiny hummingbirds hovering like winged jewels. Every now and then, a larger animal would make its presence known—a rustling in the bushes, the distant grunt of a peccary, or the brief flash of a jaguar's eyes before it disappeared into the brush.

As we trudged further, the terrain began to slope downwards, and my boots sank into the mud, making each step an effort. We were getting close to the crevice between the Tepuis that Tomas had told us about.

"Listen up, everyone!" Rico bellowed while beside him, Tomas began unrolling ropes and carabiners.

Rico cleared his throat. "Descending between these plateaus will not be easy. With slick rock walls on either side, it will be extremely dangerous to those without experience rappelling," he pointed to the narrow opening between the towering cliff faces, "so I need to know—anyone here done this before?"

Jason and another agent raised their hands. I smiled inwardly. Of course, Jason had. I was positive they had some plaque or award for him at the rock-climbing gym he frequented, and I was moderately sure the agency had required him to rappel into buildings for reasons.

"Excellent," Rico smiled. "Next, then, what's the number one rule of rappelling?"

Jason was quick. "Never rappel alone," he said, and the other agent murmured in agreement.

"Exacto," Rico said. "The buddy system is non-negotiable. If you go down, you need someone to either rescue your sorry ass or tell the tale of how bravely you fell. Tomas?"

His brother clapped his hands together, redirecting our attention. "I need you all to watch very closely." With deft fingers, he tied a figure-eight knot and looped it through his harness. "This knot is your lifeline; make sure it's secure."

We all tried mimicking the knot, some more successfully than others.

"Now for descending," Tomas continued, "You want to keep your weight balanced. Use your legs, not just your arms. Your arms will give out long before your legs will."

Jason grinned at me. "Guess your tagging along with me to the gym will come in handy after all."

I punched his arm lightly. "You know I went so Cara would have a workout accountability partner while she made her pre-wedding fitness journey to fit into her dress."

"Fine. But who dragged you out of bed on the second week when you wanted to sleep in and skip?"

I rolled my eyes, then checked my harness, making sure everything was secure. I noticed Jason's eyes on me. He had that furrowed brow, I'm-concerned look that I'd come to recognize.

"I'm fine," I said. "Just double-checking."

He grinned, but I could tell he was still worried as he stepped closer, his fingers lightly touching my harness. "Mind if I...?"

"Be my guest." I grinned and raised my arms as if surrendering. Who was I to deny Jason's hands all over me?

Jason's hands moved over the straps and buckles, adjusting here, tightening there. His touch was deliberate and gentle. I could feel his fingers against the small of my back, the pressure light but firm. It was a small thing, this simple act of making sure I was safe, but in that moment, it felt like so much more.

"There," he said, looking up. "That should do it."

"Thanks," I replied, my voice breathier than I'd intended.

Our eyes locked, and for a moment, I thought he might say

something more, but he didn't. Instead, he stepped back, his face all business again. "Ready?"

"Ready," I confirmed.

Rico walked around and inspected our knots while Tomas held up and explained the parts of the harness attachment.

"Control your descent with the brake hand." He pointed to the clip at the back of his harness. "It's your best friend on this descent, and remember, keep it behind you."

"Also," Rico added, "Stay alert for loose rocks and always keep three points of contact."

"Like a cat," Gavin quipped, and a few agents chuckled.

Tomas nodded. "Si, like a cat."

"We all good?" Rico interjected. "Great. Tomas will go first, and I will stay up top until everyone is down. Straighten your ropes, double-check your knots, and let's go."

One by one, we hooked up and began the descent into the crevice. Jason, Rico, and Tomas looked like Spider-Man, lowering themselves down the narrow opening with ease while I focused on my technique, taking the guides' advice to heart, feeling the slick rock under my fingers and the pull of my muscles.

It was exhilarating once I got over the fact that a rope was all that was keeping me from plummeting a hundred feet to my death. To keep my mind from spiraling, I imagined I was at the gym back in New York, and the rock wall was one meant to be climbed, so it allowed me to find better hand and toe holds more accessible. This fantasy also allowed me to pretend that the ground was a mere ten feet below me.

Halfway down, a scuffle broke out below me, and a handful of rocks rained down upon my head and shoulders. I peered down. One of the agents had lost his grip, slipping a few feet before his rope caught him. My heart raced as Tomas leaned over and pulled the slack from the agent's rope, then muttered something in Spanish about going slower.

"Remember the rules!" Rico shouted from the plateau ledge just above me. "Take your time."

I'd made it down another ten feet or so when I heard a crunching sound, like grinding teeth but amplified a thousand times. More rocks and dust landed on my shoulder, and I raised my gaze, assuming another agent had slipped, but when I looked up, the entire crevice seemed to shudder. The bits of moss and brown rock vibrated as if going in and out of focus. I tightened my grip just as pieces of sandstone sloughed off like dead skin, and a heartbeat later, the entire opening felt like a bucking bronco trying to throw me off.

"Earthquake!" Tomas' voice cut through the rumbling.

My eyes darted downward past my dangling feet. The trees below were swaying violently, and I caught sight of a dark shadow disappearing into the jungle below.

Asag.

We'd traveled by helicopter to get here. I'd felt so sure that we'd left it far behind and given us a hefty head start. Apparently, I'd been wrong.

My adrenaline spiked again, and I reached for the next handhold. Somehow, *somehow*, it had not only found us but caught up with us from hundreds of miles away. As my fingers strained, trying to find purchase on the all-but-smooth surface of the rock walls, memories flashed of Asag when he'd impersonated Jason. Fuck. Asag could assume the shape of anyone and appear like anyone. A Division agent, a police officer, hell, an army general who needed to hire a helicopter to get him somewhere fast without a pilot asking too many questions.

How could I have been so stupid? There was no way we'd ever outrun him, outmaneuver him.

"¡Apúrense! ¡Bajen rápido!" Rico and Tomas both were shouting from below, their faces taut with urgency.

Still, I had to try. I hauled myself down another foot just as I heard more shouting and chanced another look upward. A massive boulder had broken away from the crevice wall and was now plummeting straight toward me.

With a surge of adrenaline-boosted reflexes, I flattened myself against the rock face and prayed it was enough. The boulder whizzed past, missing me by inches, and the disruption of the air wafted hair over my face. My breathing seized in my chest as I realized the agent below me wasn't so lucky. They hadn't had time to react, and the boulder collided with him, knocking him off the crevice wall. As the rock crashed onto the ground far below, the agent's unconscious or possibly dead body dangled from his rope, swinging like a grim pendulum.

"Ella," Gavin called out, and I tore my eyes from the agent and looked to Gavin off to my right.

The whites of his eyes shone as he stared at the rope in front of him. The boulder must have scraped it as it went by because the fibers around it were frayed, nearly cut through.

"Stay there," I yelled and began crab-crawling sideways across the slippery rocks, closing the space to him.

"Hurry," he said, his voice trembling.

"Don't move!" I said, "I'm coming."

Harnessing every ounce of strength I had reserved—which was rapidly dwindling— I managed to reach Gavin. My fingers gripped his harness, and I urgently clipped him onto mine. For a second, we both dangled there, connected by my harness, swaying perilously as the earth below us rumbled and the crevice walls around us disintegrated.

"Okay!" I yelled, my voice raw and breathing ragged. "We're going to have to go down together."

Gavin clung to me, his face ashen, but gave a determined

nod. My arms and legs were on fire, my muscles screaming in agony, but I refused to let go. Refused to give up. The pull of the necklace and Gavin's determined gaze instilled in me an unwavering desire to keep pushing on.

Fuck Asag.

Foot by painstaking foot, we lowered ourselves downwards, clinging to the rocks when another earthquake rumbled through it, then continuing.

"¡Ahora! ¡Ya casi estamos!" Rico was almost hysterical, urging us down the last few treacherous feet. I dug deep, pushing off from the cliff face with my legs, letting us fall a dozen feet before breaking and swinging us back in. It took a few attempts before Gavin and I were finally in sync, a gravity-defying waltz.

In, push out, swing back in.

Tomas and Rico reached up, hauling us down into the crevice, just as another aftershock trembled through the crevice, sending a fresh shower of rocks plummeting to the ground below. At the bottom, sweat was dripping from my forehead and clinging to my back as Rico untethered us, and the harness dropped to my feet. I collapsed onto the ground, dotted with bushes and small trees, gasping and trembling. Gavin moved further away and bent over to catch his breath.

Tomas quickly began assessing the team, checking for injuries and ensuring everyone's safety, but my eyes sought Jason. He stood beside Rico, helping him lower the dangling agent to the ground. When they finally got him to the ground, Rico pulled off the agent's helmet and peered into his eyes. Jason hovered above him with his hands on his hips. When Rico looked up, his eyes darkened, and he shook his head slowly. Jason cursed, sending a handful of small birds resting in the neighboring tree to take flight.

Rico reached down and gently closed the agent's eyes.

. . .

THEN JASON CONVEYED some instruction to him, and his eyes, wide with a mixture of relief and terror, finally lifted to meet mine.

He stalked over. "You okay?" he asked, his gaze sweeping over my body for injuries.

"I'm fine," I managed to say, despite the dryness in my throat. "I'm sorry about..." I hesitated. "Him," gesturing to the dead agent. "Was he a friend?"

Jason's jaw clenched, and he frowned. "No, but I still knew him. He was a good agent. He'll be missed."

"I'm sorry," I said. "If there's anything I can do."

Jason's eyes sharpened. "Kill that fucking demon, Elly. Destroy it. Make it suffer for all it's done."

My tongue swept the back of my molars, and the conviction in his words made the power inside me shimmer with eagerness. I flexed my hands, anxious to let it out. Unleash it upon the trees, igniting them in an attempt to flush out Asag. *Dodge that, asshole.*

However, my better sense stopped me, and instead, I leaned over and hugged Jason. He pulled me close in a fierce embrace as if he could shield me from all the dangers in this treacherous world. I resisted the temptation to lean in, press my face against his shoulder, and cry. I couldn't let myself break. Not now.

OUR MOMENT WAS SHATTERED by Jason's radio crackling to life. "Price, do you copy? This is Wendler."

Reluctantly, Jason stepped back and took the radio. "Go ahead."

"We've picked up movement from the Asag, two clicks to your east."

No shit, I thought.

"We'll set up a perimeter, try and buy you time, but you need to proceed with caution."

"We're in the crevasse. We need evac for Norton."

The radio crackled confirmation.

"The coordinates are not too far from here," Rico said, eyes scanning the jungle-infused horizon as he pointed. "If everyone is ready, it's just to the other side, less than half a mile."

I caressed the necklace at my throat, the tug forward stronger than before, and caught Gavin watching me.

"I feel it too," he said, keeping his voice low as we started walking single file through the brush. "It's like we've been here before. I don't get it."

I nodded, knowing what he meant. It was the worst case of Deja vu I'd ever felt. Every tree, every rock, every bird, felt familiar, and as we moved deeper into the trees, I found I was no longer looking to our guides to point out the best pathway because my instincts had taken over, and each step onward felt more certain than the last.

THIRTY

The jungle at the bottom of the ravine's air felt like a wet blanket against my skin, sticking to every pore as I weaved through the maze of vines and leaves. My pulse pounded in my ears, drowning out even the nocturnal sounds of the wilderness. Somewhere in this tangled mess was a creature out of a nightmare, and every minute drew him closer to us.

I stole a glance back at Jason, who moved agilely even among the tangled undergrowth of the jungle. His eyes were hard; his jaw clenched as he treaded through the vines and knotted roots. He was infinitely more trained in combat than I was, but still, fear for him twisted in my gut.

Suddenly, a roar shattered the air, and my heart nearly hopped out of my chest. The monster wasn't just near; it was closing in. Trees splintered, and boulders crashed as it rampaged toward us.

"Positions, now!" Jason barked. The agents dispersed, taking cover behind whatever the jungle offered. Gavin's tattoos lit up, humming with arcane energy, and he held his hands in a ready position like he was waiting for a pass on the court, only with crackling energy dancing between them instead of a ball.

The atmosphere seemed to suck inward as the creature burst into view, a living black hole that seemed to devour the light itself. My skin tingled with the static of its magic—old, malevolent, and famished. Every fiber of my being screamed 'run,' but my feet were anchored.

The demon bellowed, wrenching stone from the ground and turning it into another monstrosity. The rapid-fire sound of Jason and the other agent's guns punctuated the air.

"Fall back!" Jason roared. We dashed into the thicket, hacking through obstructing vines. My lungs felt like they were on fire, but there was no stopping.

I risked a glance back, only to find that our pursuers had grown in number with every second we delayed its advance. They hurled trees aside like toothpicks and created massive crater-like trenches that appeared wherever they touched the ground.

They were getting closer by the second –and despite my ragged breathing and burning legs, I pushed onward until I finally spotted a faint glimmer of hope on the horizon: a clearing in the jungle canopy far ahead of us.

Gavin sprinted for it first, his tattoos blazing brighter than ever as he began channeling his magic. He was faster than me and was the first one to make it, and he beckoned to me frantically as I sprinted towards him, narrowly escaping a giant branch crashing down where I'd just been a second before. Breathing hard, we stood in the clearing, surrounded by a wall of trees, as flashes of dark movement darted amongst the twisted trunks.

I sucked in a breath, drawing from the untapped well of magic deep within me. I was the only thing standing between this horror and the people I cared about. No way in hell I was backing down now.

Jason, Gavin, and I, along with two other agents, ran, sliding down a grassy knoll. With the slight cover, the agents and Jason reloaded their guns while Gavin and I caught our breath. Above us, the fight continued. The cracking of wood and gunfire punctuated the air.

Gavin unleashed a flourish of lightning bolts that stopped the demon in its tracks. Seizing the moment, I channeled my energy through shards of bark, hurling them like deadly projectiles and trying to penetrate the cracks in their skin.

The creature's screams filled the air as it sagged to the ground, glowing holes peppering its form.

My hands shook as I extended them, focusing on the ground beneath the demons. I didn't need to touch anything anymore, a development that had transpired when I reawakened my powers that still startled me. I willed the carbon in the soil to transform, and sharp spikes of graphite erupted under the demons' feet, but there were too many, and I was getting tired. Magic waning, the spikes crumbled to dust.

My mind zeroed in on the carbon atoms in the trees around me, and with a clench of my fist, I pulled the carbon fibers together, forming a hardened but elastic rope, and wrapped them around a sturdy tree trunk. I yanked myself forward, sling-shotting through the underbrush. *First hurdle crossed*, I thought. *Now, where the hell is—*

Something massive lunged from the darkness, and a rocky arm smashed into my shoulder. I found myself face-down in the mud. Quickly, I rolled over, spitting out a mouthful of dirt, just in time to see another agent get lifted and hurled against a tree by a second rock demon. He crumpled, face down, unmoving.

Shit. Agents were getting swatted like flies, and here I was, eating mud. I forced myself to my feet, feeling the magic dance at my command.

Another demon blurred into view, darting among the tree trunks. Shards of wood and bark splintered in all directions. My arms shot out, unleashing a torrent of graphite spikes that found their mark, drilling into the demon's rocky skin, and it let out a satisfying, however loud, guttural screech.

More demons emerged, filling the air with a nauseating mix of sulfur and rot. This is bad, I thought. Really bad.

My eyes darted around. Then I spotted it—a fallen tree, ancient and carbon-rich. I focused, tugging and breaking apart the carbon bonds. The tree erupted into a cloud of pure carbon, needle-like shards hanging in the air. With a final cry, I unleashed them. They buried themselves into the demons, who crumbled and disintegrated.

My ears rang from the gunfire and explosions that had been our last line of defense. Now, it was just Jason, Gavin, and me. We stood back-to-back, surrounded by an ever-tightening circle of shadowy demons. Their skin resembled cracked cement, and more bullets ricocheted than penetrated, but still, they *did* damage them.

Jason fired off another round. "Elly, can you do anything?"

"I'm trying," I choked out, my voice barely a whisper. I stretched out my trembling hands once more, praying for the magic to obey my will. I focused on a demon closing in, its eyes glowing a vicious red. My heart pounded in my chest as I pulled from the last dregs of my energy and envisioned its carbon-based structure imploding. For a moment, the demon shuddered and let out a screech—then lunged forward, unfazed. My magic was a flickering candle in a storm, and the wind was winning.

Jason let out a guttural sound, somewhere between a growl

and a scream, as he emptied his clip into another demon. It barely flinched. "We can't keep this up. There are too many."

"I know," I admitted, the words like shards of glass in my throat. A part of me wanted to crumble right then and there. But I couldn't, not when Jason and Gavin and so many more were counting on me. "Do you have any more grenades?"

"Last one," Jason responded grimly, pulling the pin and lobbing it into the throng. The explosion took out a handful, but others quickly replaced them.

At that moment, looking at Jason, his face slick with sweat and coated with dirt, I was hit by a wave of raw, crushing despair. We couldn't save everyone. And the way he was looking at me as if committing my face to memory told me he was thinking the same thing. Still, he was Jason, and I was me. Both stubbornly determined to die as martyrs.

Another demon lunged, partially blocking my view of Jason; it howled a deep sound and fell back, a knife protruding from its eye. But Jason had only enraged it, and it reached up, pulling the knife free, and turned its attention to Jason once more. Bile rose in my throat as the stony skin pulled together, its eye socket already starting to repair itself.

"Jason, look out!" I screamed.

He pivoted just in time to avoid its gnarled hand, and I took advantage of the opening, firing point-blank with shards of hardened graphite spears into its gaping maw. It staggered back, then disintegrated into a cloud of dark mist.

Gavin dashed into the clearing, his face streaked with dirt. "We're not going to make it," he said, panting. "Are we?"

CHAPTER

THIRTY-ONE

My breath came in ragged gasps as I flung shard after shard of stone at the advancing horde of Asag demons, trying desperately to drive them back. Sweat dripped down my brow, my limbs growing heavier with each attack. I didn't know how much longer I could keep this up.

Maintaining that constant focus was draining, like flexing a muscle nonstop, and my body ached from the effort.

Sweat trickled down my forehead as I took another staggering step back. The Asag demons came at us like a tidal wave of darkness and malice, and no matter how many the Division agents took down with a flurry of bullets, they just kept coming. Jason unloaded his clip beside me, his face tense with the strain of our quickly losing battle.

It took at least twenty well-aimed bullets to take one down, and while my math was terrible, even off the battlefield, the twelve agents remaining alive with us were calling out that they were on their last clip. A cry to my left drew my gaze. An agent was pinned beneath a fallen tree, a rock demon looming over him, ready to strike. With the last dregs of my energy, I transformed the tree to ash. It disintegrated, coating the agent in soot, but he scrambled to his feet, coughing.

My vision swam, and I stumbled backward. I braced myself as the nearest demon stalked toward me, its craggy maw split into a hideous grin. All I could do was await the inevitable end.

I extended my hands toward the spongy soil beneath the demons, concentrating on the carbon elements mixed in the jungle floor. Graphite spikes erupted from the ground, piercing through their dark forms and twisting around their legs, but for each demon that fell, two more took its place as if they were spawning from the very shadows of the trees. My energy was waning; I could feel the drag in my bones, the pull at the corners of my mind. If I'd thought I was tired before, I had been wrong.

This was exhaustion. The unrelenting slog of defend, attack, defend. Gone were the first and second bursts of energy. I was running on pure adrenaline, anger, and fear.

Jason threw me a glance. Sweat beaded his brow, and it furrowed with concern. "You and Gavin can't keep this up. We have to fall back."

He was right. But what choice did we have?

With a bolt of cobalt lighting, two especially large earth-molded demons collapsed to my left, revealing a panting and dirt-streaked Gavin. His hazel eyes sparkled with light, glowing especially green in the shade of the jungle from his unfettered use of his powers.

"We have to retreat!" I shouted.

Gavin shook his head. "They're just going to chase us down. We can't."

"But if we stay here, we'll die," My voice sounded as strained as I felt, pulled taught and seconds away from snapping.

"We can regroup. Make a new plan."

"It's no use," I pleaded. "I can't keep fighting them."

Gavin lifted his eyebrows as he used the batteries on his wrists to charge another ball of electricity. "You're right. You're not a fighter, Ella," he shouted over the din of firing guns, agents cursing, and the rush of wind through the trees.

"Thanks?"

He threw the ball of crackling energy, and it streaked through trees, colliding into the side of a demon charging a downed agent. "Think like a Guardian. Be a Guardian!"

His words pierced through my fog of exhaustion.

Guard. The word struck me like Gavin had shocked me with a bolt of his lightning, traveling down my spine and igniting something deep within. A reservoir of untapped magic, a latent force I didn't know I had. Called for my desire to guard those around me, those I cared about. It surged through me, filling me with an indescribable sensation of power and clarity.

I wasn't here to kill; I was here to protect.

The fire in my veins reignited as understanding settled over me, and my skin began to itch and pull. I flexed my hands, feeling the tautness in my fingers and knuckles. The feeling was strange but oddly soothing, like each cell was crystallizing into a new, impenetrable form. I looked at my dirty hands. They sparkled with a lustrous sheen as if I was turning into a diamond, a manifestation of my Guardian essence. Carbon in its purest, most resilient form.

With renewed confidence, I extended my arms not to strike but to shield. The oncoming pair of stone demons faltered in their approach, stone claws hesitating inches from my face. I glared back at its soulless, luminous eyes.

"You will not touch them," I said through gritted teeth.

The demons attacked. But against my glittering armor, their claws and fists glanced off harmlessly, allowing me to summon jagged spikes of graphite up through the soil and pierce the cracks. They howled in pain, shrieking in frustration at the non-existent damage their assault did to me.

My diamond skin shimmered just as a wall of the same material erupted from the ground before us, forming a nearly invisible protective barrier spanning out for hundreds of feet against the encroaching demons. They slammed into it and recoiled, their shrieks filled with confusion and rage. They couldn't penetrate it, and their dagger-like claws barely marred its surface.

An excited yelp escaped my throat. I felt invincible.

I was a Guardian. *This* was my duty, my role in this shit show of a war of good versus evil. But it was more than just a role; it was my identity, my destiny. For the first time since Enheduanna had spoken to me, I truly understood what it meant to be a Guardian.

The demons were confused, angry, and far from done. Within seconds, they'd regrouped to ten at least, maybe more, all uttering growls that filled the air, and I felt a shiver of unease; they were preparing for another assault. Still, they could rage and claw futilely all they wanted. As long as I stood, the shield would not fall. I used the brief reprieve to wipe the sweat from my eyes and catch my breath, formulating what to do next. I couldn't stand here indefinitely.

Jason looked at me, his eyes wide with awe and something more profound that sent a flurry of butterflies into my belly. His hand brushed the back of mine, and the touch was electrifying, even through my diamond skin. "I like the look," he whispered, his gaze roaming over my face, which I could only assume was covered in glittering diamonds as well. *Edward Cullen, eat your heart out.*

I smiled, feeling the tightness in my cheeks as I tore my gaze from him, refocusing on the leering horde of demons. Drawing on Gavin and Jason's presence beside me, I felt the nearly infinite reserve of energy flow through me. Time to get rid of these assholes *for good*.

I closed my eyes, channeling my focus. I wasn't just wielding my power; I was embodying it, becoming one with the elemental force that coursed through me.

When I opened my eyes, my diamond shield had transformed, pulsing with a brilliant light, pure and blinding, casting the demons' gnarled stone faces into sharp relief. They cowered, shielding what glowing voids passed for their eyes, and whatever dark magic had constructed them dissipated under the onslaught of radiant energy.

With a final, guttural cry, they disintegrated. Not just defeated but utterly destroyed, reduced to nothing more than wisp-like tendrils of smoke that the wind quickly scattered.

Vanished as if they'd never been.

As the last traces of the demons disappeared, my shield shrank back, its luminous glow fading to the simple, unadorned sheen of diamond. My skin followed suit, the diamond receding to normal skin. The transformation had drained me, but in its wake, I felt a sense of serenity, of completeness. I was who I was meant to be.

Jason wrapped his arms around me, pulling me close. "Elly, you never cease to surprise me. I knew you could do it," he murmured into my ear.

I looked up at him, my heart swelling with a love and gratitude that words could never capture. "I couldn't have done it without you," I said softly. "You reminded me of who I am, of what I'm here to do."

"And what's that?" he asked, his eyes searching mine.

"Love," I said, not missing the tremble in my voice. "To protect those I love. That's what's important."

As he kissed me, I realized that I'd found my place in this world, not just as a Guardian, but as Ella. Darkness, ancient and hungry, had awakened, and if it ever hoped to devour the world or touch Jason, it would have to get through me first.

My pulse was still thumping in my ears from the earlier skirmish, adrenaline mingling with the heady scent of damp earth and foliage. Water trickled down from the towering tepui plateau above, a serene counterpoint to the staccato rhythm of my heart.

Mist hung in the air, shrouding the space in an ethereal veil. The quiet was almost disorienting, a profound stillness that contrasted sharply with the gunfire and chaos we'd just left behind.

Gavin stood next to me, his breath as shallow and hurried as my own. His eyes met mine, filled with questions I couldn't answer.

There it was—the temple door, almost camouflaged among the overgrown vines and moss, as if nature itself tried to claim it back. Old, ancient, like it had known a thousand years of solitude and was thirsty for the touch of the present.

"I can't believe we found it. I can't believe we're *here*," Gavin muttered.

My feet drawing me forward, I said, "You and me both."

"I'm going with you," Jason insisted, as I knew he would.

I shook my head, putting a hand on his chest. "No. You can't."

"The fuck I can't. I'm not letting you in there alone."

"I won't be," I said, motioning to Gavin. "Please. You have to wait here."

"Why?"

"I don't know. It's just a feeling. Something about this place. It's like the feeling I had before the bridge opened. A *wrongness*. Like we're trespassing or something."

"She's right, bro," Gavin added. "Definitely creeping me out."

Jason's eyes sharpened. "I trust you, Elly. I do, but you have no idea what you're walking into in there."

"I know, but this feels like Guardian-only territory. I swear if anything so much as looks funny, I'll come back out, agreed?"

He rested his hands on my shoulders. "I hate everything about this." He kissed my forehead. "But fine. Twenty minutes, and if you're not back out, I'm coming in."

I flashed him a reassuring smile. "Thank you."

I stepped up the rocky incline to the giant stone door with Gavin flanking me. Already, my fingers tingled with anticipation, the magic hovering just below the surface at attention should anything attack us. A shiver of energy crawled up my spine, and a mist formed around us as if the temple sensed our presence, our intent.

Remembering the city under the Syrian desert that had acid sand, I braced myself for hidden traps set to deter intruders. Still, before my fingers could make contact with the door, it creaked open on its own as if the temple had been waiting for us.

THIRTY-TWO

Dust and age enveloped my senses, feeling like a tomb that had been sealed for centuries. But this was no tomb; it was a palace of reflection and mortality, a statement in stark contrast to the world above. Mirrors covered the walls, their glass smudged and clouded. I saw the reflections of hundreds of human faces. A chill seeped into my bones.

In the center of it all was the throne made entirely of bones. Both beautiful and grotesque, an artful assembly of femurs, skulls, and spines that looked as if it could've been the skeletal remains of various creatures, each bone masterfully carved and interlocked with the next, as if in a grim dance of death.

And there, on that macabre seat, sat a woman with long hair as black as the night sky when I'd lived in Syria. A dress of woven gold and gray netting draped her slender frame. Her eyes, glowing gold, were as unreadable as they were unnerving, and atop her head sat a copper crown, patinated with age to mottled green skeletal hands intertwined.

"Greetings," she said as Gavin and I entered. "Come

forward, Guardian of Inanna and Champion of Ninurta. No harm will come to you."

"Wait, how do you know us? Who are you?" Gavin asked.

She tapped on her chest. "I am Ereshkigal. Queen of the Underworld."

Around us, the glass-covered walls portrayed reflections of every different kind of human. Young. Old. Men. Women. All in clothes and styles from different times, all strolling about like they had business to attend to, places to go.

They were the souls of the dead. They had to be.

"Mistress," I said, totally guessing as to how to address her, and took the shaft and handle from my backpack. "You know us. So, then, you must know why we're here. Asag is wreaking destruction. We're here to try and stop him. Do you know where the head of Sharur is?"

Ereshkigal leaned back on her throne, her dress barely skimming her bare feet. "It is true, then. I had heard Asag had returned to this world." She paused, leaning forward slightly and pinning me in her two golden pupils. "Tell me, Guardian, why should I help *you?* After all, you were the one that released Asag in the first place."

My gut twisted like it was trying to strangle itself as Ereshkigal's words confirmed the fear that had been gnawing at me for days. The harsh truth tightened around my thoughts like a noose. *I should've been faster.* If only I had stopped Derek Kane sooner before he had the chance to open that accursed bridge. The sensation of failure settled in my bones, heavy as lead.

It wasn't just an abstract sense of dread anymore; it was real. Ereshkigal had brought my worst fear into the light. I could almost feel the comatose breaths of every victim Asag touched and hear the distant rumble of each earthquake that tore the world apart. Every catastrophe that had unfurled in the wake of Asag's escape was a haunting echo in my conscience, a tally mark scored against my soul. And why? Because I hadn't moved fast enough. Because I'd been stupid to think I could make a deal with Kane by trading him the statue, and he'd double-crossed me, imprisoning me, and still Taamir had ended up dead.

My eyes slid to where Gavin stood beside me. It must be the Guardian's curse to think we could trust the evil in this world. Believe they've morals like us and can still be bargained with.

"I promise, until my dying breath, I will amend my error." I finally said, answering her questions. "With Sharur, we will stop him."

Ereshkigal arched an eyebrow and scratched the side of her face with a long nail. "And you?" She said, fixing Gavin with her gaze.

"I will do the same. I fight alongside Ella as the champion of Ninurta."

The goddess leaned back and rested her hands on the arms of the throne. "I supposed I should tell you that I don't desire the release of my demons any more than you do. And as Asag is intent on breaking the gates of my domain, I wish for him to be halted. He has broken all but the last of the seals. Asag only needs to accomplish one final task, and I'll no longer have control over the demons. The servants of the underworld, the foul creatures my sister and uncle imprisoned after my grandfather, Enlil, released them thousands of years ago, will be freed yet again."

"What is the final seal?" I breathed the question.

Ereshkigal smirked her perfect lips. "He'll spread the disease until it reaches every corner of the land," she said, defying an answer. "A thousand souls then must perish in a single breath. The final seal will shatter. Those currently afflicted are doomed to awaken as vessels of *hul*, of evil." She waved her hand dismissively. "After that, there will be nothing my family, the other gods, and goddesses, not even me, can do."

My throat tightened, threatening to cut off my breathing.

A thousand. How many were in comas now? Seventy? Eighty? And those had been in less than a week. Quick math meant if Asag kept up that current rate, we had less than three months. That was if we didn't have a cure by then to wake them, which I still was clinging to that hope.

"So," I said. "We can stop it. It doesn't have to happen. We're on the same side. Can't you see that? Give us the final piece of Sharur?"

Her eyes narrowed, and she laughed, the sound echoing off the stone walls of the chamber. "I cannot simply give it to you, Guardian. Even I must abide by the laws of the divine. No one leaves my domain without a proper replacement, a tribute. A soul for a soul. That's the price."

"A soul?" my stomach twisted. "What are you talking about, a *soul?*"

She tossed her hair over her shoulder as if that answered my question. I glanced at Gavin, who seemed as irritated as I was, but then recognition flickered in his gaze, and a heartbeat later, I, too, realized what she meant. Gavin steeled his eyes and took a step forward.

Oh, no, you don't.

"Fine," I said before he could move another inch and tilted my chin. "You want *my* soul, my life as a trade, is that it?"

She shook her head slowly as her unsettling eyes drifted past us to something behind me. "No, there's someone you love even more than yourself."

My heart ceased beating in my chest, and I knew before I turned what I'd see, *who* I'd see.

Finally, I surrendered and looked over my shoulder. Jason stood at the doorway. He'd followed us in even after promising to wait outside. His eyes met mine, and in them, a realization, an understanding so profound it ached just to look at him.

"Until Asag is defeated," Ereshkigal said. "He'll remain here, in the Underworld. With me, unharmed, of course."

Jason stalked forward, his face resolute. "If it means stopping Asag. I'll do it."

I looked from him to Ereshkigal, feeling as though I was splitting in half. No. He couldn't do this. I refused to let him go. The air in the room grew heavier, like I was being crushed from all sides, and it was becoming harder and harder to breathe.

"No!" I shouted. "Please, there has to be another way. Anything. Just tell me, and I'll do it!"

"Don't worry, Guardian. I'll take good care of him," Ereshkigal grinned as if she'd just won a twisted game. "Complete your task, call my name, and you can have him back."

I stared at Jason as he approached her throne, my heart pounding so hard I thought it would burst from my chest. God, I felt so helpless. "There has to be another way," I demanded.

Ereshkigal laughed again, a sound devoid of warmth. "Time is ticking, Guardian. Make your choice. The weapon or the man you love."

My mouth went dry, and my knees threatened to buckle, but I forced myself to look into Jason's eyes. Swirling in the blue of his irises, I saw his silent plea begging me to agree. It was as if the world had narrowed to this single, unbearable moment. He was sacrificing himself for the world, for me. Did I actually believe he *wouldn't?* This was Jason. He'd do anything to protect me—even this.

"Okay," I choked out the word, my voice barely audible. "We have a deal."

A predatory smile spread across Ereshkigal's face. "Very well. Destroy Asag and return the mace, and you will have your love back."

I nodded, swallowing hard.

"Say your goodbyes," she said. "Quickly, I have other matters to attend to."

I gritted my teeth, wanting to lash out and tell her to screw her other matters. How could anything be more important than this?

As Jason stepped toward me, his eyes were distant, as if he'd already departed, and my ribcage felt like a vice around my heart. "You'll stop that bastard. I know you will."

The desperation in his voice was a knife to my gut. "I swear it. I love you," was all I could muster.

"I love you too, Elly," he said, his words thick with emotion. Then he leaned in to kiss me, a bittersweet collision of lips and words unspoken. "One more thing." He slipped his hand into mine, and I felt the outline of a small box. My body convulsed as if my heart had been torn from my chest. "I wish I'd had more time to do this right, but I don't. You hang on to this, okay?"

"No," I breathed the word, tears cascading down my cheeks.

Jason laughed, a weak sound. "I don't want an answer. I just want you to have it." Without waiting for me to argue further, he shoved the small box into the pocket of his jacket, took it off, and draped it over my shoulders.

"Jason, I—" I started to say, but then he was gone, pulled into the shadows by Ereshkigal with a wave of her hand and was swallowed by the Underworld.

I was suspended. Frozen. Time was meanliness. A vast expanse of nothingness as deep as the pit of grief that I never would be able to fill. Sobs rocked me, and tears streamed down my face. Finally, I gave into the sorrow, falling to my knees.

Silently, Gavin had come to stand next to me, and he rested a hand on my shoulder.

"He's gone," he said, his voice hollow. "I promise we'll get him back, but we have to go."

"No," I murmured, "I can't leave him." A hundred thoughts pummeled my skull. I was the Guardian. It was supposed to be me who protected, not him. It wasn't supposed to end like this. We were supposed to finish this together.

Gavin made a pained sound. "You have to. He gave himself so we could keep going."

I hated this. Hated *her,* but I understood. He was right. Taking a deep, shuddering breath, I stood, willing my legs to keep me upright.

"Sharur, as promised," Ereshkigal said, gesturing toward a pretty blonde woman seeming to drift out of the shadows.

My mind hummed with a thousand burning questions. Sharur was a *woman?* How had we not known this? Further, why was she in the underworld? Had she been human but died? Even as these questions burned inside me, I couldn't ignore the pain of the loss that still haunted me. I'd traded Jason for *her.* This woman looked like she'd fallen out of an ethereal Instagram filter. Long blonde hair framed her face, and she had large round eyes of a violet hue that you couldn't find in any human DNA. She stepped forward, dressed in something nearly as sheer as a soap bubble, her sandals whispering against the dark ground.

Gavin nervously shifted his weight beside me, no doubt captivated by this girl's beauty. Sharur gazed at her surroundings as if she'd just woken up in a dream before her eyes landed on me, or more specifically, the pieces of the mace still gripped in my hands. A wide smile appeared on her face, and she swiftly stepped up to me, soft whispers trailing as if her dress were made of cobwebs.

When she reached me, without hesitation, she went for the handle and the shaft and joined them together. As soon as her fingertips brushed the wood and leather, a chill ran through my arms and into the weapon. Then, with a flash, she was gone.

I raised my eyes back to Ereshkigal, ready to demand some answers, only to find her throne empty. Vanished.

"Ella," Gavin said, "Look."

Anger still flaring inside me that we'd been tricked, I glanced down at the mace in my hands, realizing it was heavier than before.

The handle and hilt were affixed as if one piece, and on the end was a softball-sized sphere of bronze covered in two-inch long spikes that glinted off the torch light.

The oxygen evaporated from my lungs. It was whole. Sharur was complete.

THIRTY-THREE

The way back was a blur. Jason's face haunted every step I took, our last words, his kiss.

The cost of this task wasn't just a soul; it was a part of me, something far more intimate and irreplaceable. And yet, with every fiber of my being, I knew I had to succeed. The alternative was too grim to consider: a world in ruins, an Underworld unleashed, and a love lost forever to the depths of damnation.

As I began the walk back to where we'd rappelled down, Sharur was heavy in my bag, and my soul even heavier in my chest.

My feet moved as if of their own volition, barely registering my sore muscles, the smell of damp earth, and the chill of the night air. I tried to find comfort in the darkness. But with each step, however, it felt as though I was leaving Jason behind. Abandoning him. All of this was wrong.

Gavin was silent beside me and only spoke enough to help me attach myself to the harness and rappel upward in the dark. My body was on autopilot as I climbed the slippery rocks, and at several moments, the thought crossed my mind to let go.

Unclasp myself and just let go, but Gavin's harsh words drew me from my dark thoughts.

"Don't," he'd said as if reading my mind. "Don't you dare!" His stern gaze, laced with fear, had broken the hold the grim ideas had on me, and we'd ascended to the top of the ridge.

While I sat on the ground, Gavin used the sat phone he'd found off a dead agent and contacted the agency.

I found one of the odd-shaped rocks and sat. Exhaustion tugged at the edges of my consciousness, and I gave in, leaning my head back and closing my eyes.

A kink in my neck roused me sometime later, and the first hints of morning light were appearing on the horizon. Gavin dozed beside me, his head pressed against a folded jacket.

The distant sounds of helicopter blades signaled our rescue, and I nudged him gently awake. He almost looked relieved to see me, and I plastered a smile on my face just for him and stood.

My necklace felt warm against my skin as I drew Sharur from my bag that I'd kept close to me all night. My eyes focused on the distant speck of approaching helicopters. While I was set on the path ahead, my heart was forever anchored in the shadows behind me.

So, I thought, let the shadows come. I was ready to send them screaming back to whatever hell they crawled out of.

With the mace gripped in one hand and my magic hovering, waiting for me to instruct it, I stared at the jungled valley before me. The mace vibrated lightly in my hands.

"Finally," a woman's voice chimed inside my head. "I've been starving for thousands of years, and I am so very *hungry*."

The End

COMING SOON FROM
AMELIA COLE

A thrilling new dystopian romance fantasy series set in a shattered world where lost legends aren't forgotten but reborn, and romance blazes as bright as the stars.

Druadan Legacy Book One

March 2024

ACKNOWLEDGMENTS

I want to thank you so much for continuing this journey with me, Ella, and the rest of the Vela crew. The sweet comments I've received through email and DMs have been tremendous. This book was one of the hardest things I've ever written, primarily because I wasn't sure where I wanted to push Ella, and whether or wish I could make sure to tell her tale right.

Lots of late nights combing through Mesopotamian lore, searching Reddit boards, watching history shows on YouTube, and playing Civ 6 with my brother Isaac and his wife, Morgan.

Big shout out to my beta readers, Kate Valent, JoAnna Illingworth, and Brianna Schlegel.

My editor Roxana for her laser-sharp eye. You're amazing!

My llamasquad writing group for all their never-ending support and encouragement.

And last but not least, my husband and two kids for letting me brainstorm ideas on long car rides or over froyo.

ABOUT THE AUTHOR

Amelia Cole is an adult contemporary fantasy writer. She has won various awards for short stories and has been featured in an anthology. She lives in the Pacific Northwest with her husband and two children, on a small farm. You can find her on Instagram, TikTok, and Facebook @ameliacolebooks

www.ameliacolebooks.com